Early praise for *Food Fight*

"Erin Brockovich with chocolate. A heart-warming and very funny voyage to the dark soul of the food industry."
Angelique Chrisafis, *The Guardian*

"This addictive novel is closer to real life in Washington DC than we'd like to think. Fun yet insightful about the lobbying and politicking in the American capital, this take-down of a fictional American food giant is irresistible. Dollars to donuts, it will be the sleeper hit of the year."
David Usborne, *The Independent*

"Bite into this crisp and bitter-sweet novel. Enjoy the exact flavour of life as we now live it. Savour the odyssey of an able young woman through its heartaches and delights."
Godfrey Smith, novelist

"Lightly told, this timely and provocative novel is a dark tale that will interest anyone who has ever wondered what happens when the pleasures of the palate intersect with the politics of Big Food."
Meg Bortin, author of *The Everyday French Chef* blog

FOOD FIGHT

A novel

ANNE PENKETH

for Johanna
with love from
Anne

GARSTANG PRESS

Published by Garstang Press 2015

This novel is a work of fiction. With the exception of historical events, all characters and organisations are the products of the author's imagination and any resemblance to actual persons, living or dead, is entirely coincidental.

A CIP catalogue record for this book is available from the British Library

ISBN-13 978-0993215605
ISBN-10 0993215602

Cover illustration and design by JD Smith Design

For my parents

Chapter 1

THE LAST TIME Susan saw her daughter it didn't end well.

"I don't like American comedies," Mimi had announced outside the cinema in Leicester Square.

"Oh. Do you want to see something else?"

"Don't bother."

Then came Mimi's assessment of the "rip-off" blockbuster merchandising on the way in. That was followed by Oscar-worthy throat clearing and a phone call during the trailers which had the people behind "shushing" while Susan cringed.

"Well, that was side-splitting," Mimi said afterwards. "God, I hate the West End." It was pointless asking her if she wanted to go for a Chinese. Mimi was already heading towards her bus stop without saying goodbye, stranding Susan with her mouth open like a goldfish.

That was five months ago. But now Mimi had been persuaded to come round for dinner.

Susan rushed out of the tube to help Serge with the shopping. They hugged outside the supermarket but she was so anxious she could barely look at him. She couldn't express her misgivings – Serge had been the one to reach out to Mimi in the first place.

He tried to steer her towards the meat counter. She tugged his sleeve. "We don't want to provoke her unnecessarily. Not again. Just pretend you're a vegan for the night."

They stocked up on lettuce, carrots and beetroot. It would have to be salad. Serge was sent in search of chickpeas and returned with two sirloin steaks which he dropped into the trolley. "For tomorrow, *chérie*."

On the way past the dairy section, she paused in front of

the ice cream freezers.

"Your empire," said Serge with pride, placing his arm round his wife's shoulder. She nodded towards the biscuits and cereals aisle.

"Not only mine, it's the DeKripps' empire." Even after a year as Marketing Director for the London branch of DeKripps Foods Inc., she still had to pinch herself.

It was dark and chilly. They adjusted their scarves and set off for home in Serge's car. He had some marking to do before Mimi arrived.

"What, on a Saturday?"

"Look who's talking, Madame workaholic."

The Christmas lights along Essex Road on their way back to Hackney reminded her that soon they'd be needing a tree. Serge loved the English rituals.

"Don't forget fire crackers for the table," he said.

"*Christmas* crackers." He banged his hand on the steering wheel in mock frustration. Despite more than a decade in London his attempts to master the English language never failed to amuse her.

Serge parked and went straight upstairs to his study, while she tidied the living room and banked up the fire. She lit a couple of nightlights on the coffee table.

Mimi had a key but refused to use it. When the doorbell rang, Susan started and glanced nervously at Serge, who dropped his half-smoked cigarette in the garden and closed the French windows.

"You're the one who invited her," she said.

"Seasoning of goodwill," he smiled. "Be nice. She's come all the way from Wandsworth."

Mimi had moved across town to be as far from her mother as possible, after dropping out of a media studies course.

"You know she's hated me and everything I stand for

since I joined DeKripps," said Susan. "But she also forgets that Big Food is paying her rent on that flat. It wasn't all that long ago that she had the comfort of this four-bedroom home."

Serge's parted lips revealed his gap-toothed smile as he went to open the door. Mimi had always got on better with him than with her mother, even though he'd only come on the scene when she was a headstrong five year old. Mimi used to say she'd been "abandoned" to child minders while Susan was on the road organising focus groups.

She heard her hanging up her coat in the cloakroom and the clunk of vegan Doc Martens on the parquet floor.

Her daughter appeared in the kitchen, holding out a bottle of wine like a weapon.

"Hi Ma," she said. Susan examined her matted strawberry blonde hair, her elfin face upstaged by a metallic stud poking through her left nostril.

"I think I preferred it when you called me Mum," she said. They didn't kiss. Susan busied herself setting the kitchen table for supper, salad bowl at the centre.

They chewed in silence for a while. Serge opened the wine and began pouring, but Mimi stuck with tap water.

"How's work?"

She only knew that Mimi was an activist with a non-governmental organisation where she was supposed to be doing 'consciousness raising'.

"Fine." Mimi turned to Serge. "What about school? The youth of Camden enjoying their Molière?"

"Less and less. They prefer to do car maintenance at A level, not French. Soon, I will have no job." Mimi smiled at his joke. The two of them began discussing *L'Avare,* which had been one of her set texts at school. Susan noticed the eye contact, and felt an inexplicable stab of jealousy.

Serge ensured that conversational reefs were avoided for

the rest of the meal. He announced that he'd agreed to sacrifice his usual cheese course. Susan got up and came back to the table with a packet of DeKripps biscuits.

"Biccy? They're new."

"Your mother invented the name," said Serge. "Crumblies."

"Congratulations." Mimi grabbed the packet and began to read the list of ingredients out loud, swinging back in her chair.

"Look at all the sugars. Are you trying to kill us all? I can't believe you're selling this junk."

"Not selling, Mimi. Marketing. Creative stuff. And excuse me" – she couldn't help herself – "people actually like the *junk* as you call it."

"You've sold out to Big Food, that's what you've done," said Mimi, her face reddening.

Serge stretched out his hand as though to quieten her, but she flicked it away, glowering at Susan from across the pine table.

A moment later she looked at the enormous watch on her delicate wrist, and stood up.

"Better go," she said, and disappeared down the hall without a backward glance. A ladder snaked up the back of her black tights.

Susan waited for the sound of the front door before throwing the biscuit packet at the kitchen wall. A stream of crumbs dropped to the floor.

"Why do we bother? Honestly, why do we bother? I've done my best for her and this is what I get in return!"

Serge embraced her in silence.

"It'll take time. She's changed. She's had a political awakening that's all. It happens to everyone," he said.

"Does it? I don't remember treating my mother like this for years on end. I'm sorry, but it just gets to me."

In bed, later that evening, Serge said: "It's painful for me too, you know."

She snuggled up to him. She would always be grateful to him for treating Mimi like his own. She thought of their first cramped flat in Kentish Town, and how he'd agreed to try teaching in London so they could be together.

The day they met, she was on a flight to Paris for a meeting with French dairy reps and found him sitting in her seat.

He stood up straight away, brushing his dark fringe from his eyes, and apologized in broken English. As he smiled, she noticed his slightly chipped front tooth, a childhood fall from a bicycle, she would discover.

She guessed he was a few years older, couldn't quite put her finger on why she found him so attractive. He wasn't handsome in the classical sense – was it the way he looked at her, his head tilted, his deep voice enveloping her like dark chocolate? They'd chatted about nothing in particular as the Airbus idled at the stand. There seemed to be some sort of problem and their flight was running late.

Then Serge turned to her and said in English, "I want damage!"

"What?"

He tapped his watch and said again, "I want damage."

"Oh, *damages.* Yes, from Air France."

She'd asked in schoolgirl French why he'd been in London. He'd been at an international conference on Albert Camus, the writer.

He was a French teacher in Paris, he said, though he was hoping for a transfer to his native Brittany.

Didn't Camus write *The Outsider*? That's right, he said. *L'Etranger*. Any man who doesn't cry at his mother's funeral will eventually be sentenced to death. Camus is saying that's what happens if you don't play the game. It's a little masterpiece. Written half a century ago and more relevant every day.

As the plane surged forward, engines screeching like missiles, Susan's heart raced. At that terrifying moment after takeoff when the plane dips slightly, she was convinced they were going to plunge back to earth.

Without asking, she'd grabbed Serge's hand. He'd held onto hers for the rest of the flight.

Susan slid away from Serge to look at his face. He was tense. "Don't let Mimi get to you too. I shouldn't have flown off the handle," she said, raising a hand to ruffle his hair. She pretended to do a double take.

"Is that a grey hair I see?"

"If you don't want to see it, you can switch out the light, *chérie* ."

"Night." She turned over to switch off the bedside lamp, before giving him a kiss. He pulled her close. The next day, he was dead.

Chapter 2

"SERGE THAT'S THE door," she called out. He'd taken the car to pick up the Sunday paper while she lingered in bed with the radio, and she presumed he was lazing downstairs. Neither of them had slept well.

"Can you get that?" She shouted when the bell rang again. The house was silent. She grabbed her dressing gown and ran downstairs. Two policemen were at the door. She knew what they were going to say as soon as she saw the expression on their faces, but couldn't take it in.

They said he'd been driving on the wrong side of the road and had crashed head-on with a Subaru estate, whose driver was unhurt. But Serge was dead. There was an investigation to find out what had happened. The car may have skidded on black ice. Mortuary, post-mortem, coroner, would you like to sit down, Miss, it was all swirling around her head and making her dizzy. She was digging her fingernails into the door as she tried to steady herself.

They left after promising she could view the body later.

Her first reaction was to run back upstairs to the bedroom and burrow under the duvet where his smell lingered. When she eventually forced herself downstairs, still wearing her dressing gown, she half expected to see him unlacing his shoes and grumbling about the price of the newspaper. She wandered into the kitchen, her slippers knocking on the floorboards of the empty room. She breathed in the aroma of his morning coffee.

She stood at the sink, stirring tea with a trembling hand and staring out of the window. With a sigh, she switched on the tap and let swirls of cold water gurgle down the plug-hole. Holding the tap for support, she ran the other hand under until it began to ache and whiten and her freckles began to fade, just like she'd done as a child. Then she pressed it against her burning face.

She opened the fridge, where the two steaks mocked her solitude. She grabbed them and pushed them into the freezer, out of sight.

Walking into the living room, she collapsed onto the sofa with the phone.

She noticed the invitation cards to Christmas parties on the mantelpiece addressed to Serge and Susie, Susie and Serge. Another slap in the face.

She rang Mimi, who hung up immediately, and found herself howling into the empty phone. She dialled the number again. Engaged. She tried again. "Answer, will you?" she said. Her palm dampened on the receiver. Her next call was to her mother.

Pick up, pick up. "Oh, it's you, dear. I was half way through Your Money." What, she's spending my inheritance? Then she remembered her mother's obsession with the stock market since the big crash a couple of months earlier. She must be checking the paper. There was a long silence, then a sigh. She imagined her mother wiping away tears. Finally, she heard:

"Are you alright, darling?"

"Of course not." Her throat tightened and hot tears dripped onto her lap.

"I know what you're going through." Susan's own father had been killed in a motorway pileup only months after her parents divorced. "Tell me exactly what happened."

Then she had to find the strength to call Serge's younger brother in Brittany.

A frantic search produced Serge's address book on the phone table in the hall. He and Jean-Louis weren't close, particularly after his marriage to Marie-Christine, an upwardly mobile blonde with a taste for designer scarves.

She dreaded having to make the call in French, but mercifully, Jean-Louis, and not his wife, answered the phone. Speaking through a dense fog she heard herself agreeing to organise the transport of Serge's body to Brittany for the funeral.

After trying Mimi again, she rang her assistant, Martin, and summoned enough composure to tell him she wouldn't be back at work for a few days. "Take all the time you need," he said. "I'll let Frank know. That's such a shock, I can only imagine how you must feel. Let me know about the funeral arrangements, and if there's anything we can do."

She knew he was sincere. But how could he imagine how she felt? And how could she ask DeKripps for help, when she didn't know herself what she needed?

Her closest friend from university days, Lily, showed up within hours, carrying her battered flute case. She provided a comforting mix of compassion and firmness. She made sure Susan got up in the mornings, that she ate at mealtimes. And they talked, endlessly, about Serge.

Susan just wanted to know that he hadn't suffered. Her doctor went through the post-mortem results with her and reassured her that he'd been killed instantly.

"Look, here it says that there was no evidence that he braked" – she gasped inwardly –"and with those kinds of injuries death would have been instantaneous. The fact that he wasn't wearing a safety belt, I'm afraid, was a contributory factor to the gravity of the injuries."

"Oh God, not again," she said. He looked at her quizzically over his reading glasses but said nothing.

"So no black ice?"

"No black ice." With the timing of years of experience, he pushed a box of paper tissues across the desk just as she began to sob. He handed her a leaflet on bereavement as she left the surgery.

"What do you mean, he wasn't wearing a safety belt?" Lily said when she got home. The two friends were curled up on the sofa holding mugs of tea with the television on mute.

"He didn't like wearing them. It was part of his Gallic charm. He used to say rules are for fools. Stupid, stupid." Susan shook her head.

"But why was he on the wrong side of the road?"

"He did that sometimes. But usually in an unfamiliar place. He'd just set off on the right on auto pilot."

"So maybe he had something on his mind, and wasn't thinking properly."

Susan didn't dare mention the unspeakable: The row with Mimi the night before he died.

"But do you know the worst thing? I never said goodbye. I never told him I loved him. He just walked out of the house and never came back."

There was so much to do before the funeral. Lily offered help in notifying people as the condolences began dropping through the letterbox. One was from a colleague in Washington offering to help if she needed a change of scene.

"Thanks, but I'll do it," she said with a sigh. "I'm going to have to get used to it. From now on, I'm on my own."

Chapter 3

FRANK CALLED HER into his office on her first day back at work.

"Hey, Susie. How you doin'?" He'd insisted after the funeral that she shouldn't come back to work until well into the New Year.

"Sure you're okay?" He arranged his pudgy features into an expression of genuine concern. "Take more time if you need it."

"What else am I going to do? I can't stay cooped up in the house while his things are still there. I need something else to think about."

"How was the funeral?"

"Grim, of course. It didn't stop raining. And it was pretty hardcore. I'd forgotten how religious they are in Brittany."

"And how's Mimosa?"

"You know what Mimi's like. She went AWOL before the funeral. She took the phone off the hook for two days. And you should have seen her outfit. She described it as *distressed*. Why does she need so much attention?"

"What a girl," he said. "How old is she now?"

"Twenty." Frank couldn't conceal his surprise.

"I know. A bit old for that kind of statement. You can imagine how it went down in Dingy. They're very conventional over there." Serge's home village was called Dingé but Susan's family and friends called it Dingy.

"I know what you mean."

Did he? As far as she knew, all Frank knew of France was their frustrating resistance to all things DeKripps. At the moment he was battling with the company's Paris office which had given up trying to push a new flavoured yoghurt into French supermarkets.

"Too much sugar for the French palate," he'd complained. "Surrender monkeys, of course. Back in the States, we could sue them for insubordination. Raising the white flag before we get a chance to tailor the recipe."

Thanks to her contacts in the French dairy industry, not to mention unhelpful comments from Serge about the invasion of "American junk food", she knew there was little hope of changing their minds.

She'd worked for Frank in DeKripps' marketing department for years. They'd watched company profits soar the more added sugars went into their products. Her work with focus groups bore it out. In the '90s, the added sugars compensated for low fat, providing necessary bulk and taste, and now they were king. DeKripps just rode with the market, as did the rest of the industry. "Who are we to argue with our customers?" Frank would say. "If they didn't like it, they wouldn't buy it."

He wasn't known for holding his tongue, but that morning, she was grateful he kept his counsel about the French. Her colleagues offered condolences but Susan could see they didn't know how to deal with her new status as widow.

Was it embarrassment? Most of them seemed to think it best not to mention her loss, which suited her. It was so intensely private, and yet so public at the same time.

She kept forgetting what she was supposed to be doing at work, and covering up was stressful too. "I'm sorry, I've lost the plot," she finally confessed to Martin. He made an expression of shared suffering she'd seen him use when their secretary's cat passed away. "Don't worry. It's not a problem."

"It must be the lack of sleep."

She didn't mention she could barely wake up in the mornings after crying herself to sleep.

"You coming down the pub for a quick one?" Martin, who concealed his ambition under unthreatening cordiality, would always include her. A month ago, she would have joined her team willingly for a drink on the way home. But now, she looked up from her desk with a regretful smile.

"That's really sweet of you. But I can't tonight," she would say, gesturing to her computer. Then she'd kick herself for saying no. After all, she had nowhere else to go. She'd stopped accepting invitations altogether, particularly from couples.

But she wanted desperately to talk about Serge, so she sought solace with Lily. At least she could raise a laugh with her imitations of his mangled English, which Lily called "Serge-speak". And she took it in her stride when Susan burst into unprompted tears.

One morning, she was sitting at her computer holding her face in her hands, forcing herself to concentrate on a graph, when Frank walked in. He threw the wrapper from a bar of DeKripps chocolate into her waste paper, looking surprised at his own dexterity and licking the chocolate from his fingers.

"Good timing," she said. "Take a look at this spike."

Frank stood behind her, puffing out his cheeks, studying her screen as she turned her chair round to face him.

"It certainly confirms our hunch," Frank said. "Given what we know about HFCS in the US. This could be great news for DeKripps here."

The graph showed results from a focus group on Delight, DeKripps's vanilla ice cream sweetened with High Fructose Corn Syrup.

HFCS was the miracle ingredient, cheaper and sweeter than sugar, and revolutionising the industry. As far as they knew, there was only one similar ice cream product on the market, distributed by a competitor.

The group had been given a month's supply of Delight and another DeKripps ice cream containing sucrose. There was no room for doubt in the results.

"Irresistible" was scribbled over Delight's report cards. Given a list of words to choose from, the final study group had picked "more, please".

"I'll pass it to advertising," Susan said. "Look, this is interesting too."

She pointed again to the questions on her screen.

How important is it for you to know the ingredients of your ice cream? Very important.

Do you read the ingredients? No.

"That's lucky."

"Let's not get carried away," she said. "This could be group-think. They're unanimous, so could they have fallen behind a leader? I've seen people trying to outdo each other before. It's like they think the most fanatical will get a bonus payment."

"You're the focus guru," Frank said. "Who was the DeKripps rep in there?"

She skimmed through the report on her screen.

"Someone Martin sent along. I'll have a word with them. I'll also contact the researcher."

Frank stopped at the door. "You know, our people in the US are beginning to take the defensive about added sugars."

"I'm not surprised. Plenty of journals suggest a link to obesity. Mimi seems to think I'm to blame for diabetes."

Frank rolled his eyes and made off. She sat back. The industry research showed that while diabetes and obesity were on the rise, sugar consumption had actually gone down in the UK in recent years. So she was safe on that score. Correlation isn't cause, Frank would say. There's no proof of a connection between illness and added sugar.

Her mind wandered again. She picked up a biro and stuck the pointed end into the palm of her hand, which did the trick. For some reason, the letter of condolence she'd received from Ellen, the company Brand Manager in Washington, came into her mind. Maybe Ellen was right, maybe she did need a change of scene.

She got up to stretch and looked out onto the street below, office workers in their shirt sleeves heading for sandwich stores.

Her grumbling stomach told her it was time to do the same. But instead of going downstairs, she found herself following Frank along the corridor.

The words came tumbling out. Would he support her if she asked for a temporary transfer to Washington? He blinked warily at her. Why would anyone want to leave behind their family, friends and routine so soon after their husband had died?

He opened the top drawer of his desk, took out a large checked-cotton hanky, and swiveled away from her to blow his nose. He turned round and mopped his brow, then returned the hanky to his drawer. Placing his hands together as though in prayer, he spoke gently, like a hospital consultant to a patient, and asked her to take time and reconsider. He obviously felt she was acting irrationally and must be half-crazed with grief.

But she knew already that her mind was made up. It just feels like the right thing to do, she told him, before walking out in search of a salmon sandwich.

What Frank wants, Frank gets. Susan had sometimes felt her boss was coasting in London, but the speed with which he arranged her transfer was impressive.

First, he lined up a job for her in the marketing department, reporting in Washington to Barney McManus, described by Frank as "next to God" in the DeKripps company structure. Then he hired an immigration lawyer who secured a visa for her in a matter of weeks, despite it being subject to a quota system. By the end of August, she had rented her house through an estate agent, sold her car and was ready to go.

All that remained were goodbyes.

She took Mimi for a last supper at her favourite vegan place on the South Bank. She couldn't tell her how long she'd be in Washington because she didn't know.

"I hope you'll visit," she said. "Obama's Washington. It should be interesting. Exciting. The hopey, changey thing, you know."

Her voice trailed off as Mimi shrugged. Susan wasn't expecting promises, she knew her better than that.

"So maybe not this year, unless you want to come for Christmas. But think about coming for the cherry blossom in March?"

"Christmas?" Mimi usually found an excuse to avoid the call of ceremony. "I'll let you know. And you've got to settle in first."

Susan looked at her. The nose stud was back in place, but she could tell from the way she flicked her head slightly too defiantly that the self-confidence was a veneer. "Look, you would tell me wouldn't you, if you need me to stay?"

The vulnerability was gone again. Her daughter met her gaze. "I'm fine."

"You're sure? You only took a couple of days off work after..." She stopped to take a breath and Mimi interrupted: "Mum, I just told you. I'm fine."

She spared her a lecture about how everyone at her little NGO was indispensable, compared to the cogs in the giant DeKripps machine.

Susan tried one last time. "Are you really sure you don't

mind me going?"

But she knew the answer. Mimi had her own life, her own job and she'd be fine. She wanted to hug her tight, so tight, before leaving the restaurant, but she knew how Mimi would react. In the end, she was allowed to deposit a discreet peck on the cheek after paying the bill.

Susan's mother didn't throw up any obstacles either. Had she wanted her to? Living so far from home would be such a big change, and the consequences of her decision were only beginning to sink in. Her mother also refused to commit herself to a visit. "I'm very pleased for you, darling. I'm sure it'll do you the world of good to be in New York," she told her on the phone.

She hardly paused for breath when Susan reminded her the destination was Washington. "Anyway. Do try to come down to Lymington whenever you can."

Her mother had chosen the Dorset coast to recover from divorce with her third husband, a golf professional called John.

Susan had never understood her mother's taste in men. Although she could hardly remember her father who'd died when she was a toddler, her mother's relationships had always ended in disaster. Still, after each divorce she hit the jackpot. Over the years, she had collected property across the south of England as though skipping along a Monopoly board.

This time, Susan reflected, the housing crash had brought an end to her mother's dreams of a sea view near the Royal Lymington yacht club. She'd had to settle for a
house up the hill but conveniently close to the shops.

Frank invited her for dinner on her last day in the office.

"Come as you are. We'll have a kitchen supper while the kids finish their homework."

She looked forward to the chance to quiz him about the

way things worked in Washington. She also wanted to know their strategy for dealing with growing media criticism of the food giants.

She'd been aware of the company bosses starting to hit back, as she put the finishing touches to a DeKripps Buried Treasure ad before she left.

"You'll see, Barney spends half his life on the Hill lobbying for a bit of slack from our elected representatives," said Frank, his frame swaying as they headed for Waterloo to catch their train. "He'll be relying on you to keep things on track in the office. The big picture stuff."

Home for Frank and June was a thatched cottage only a short walk from the high street of Cobham, the picture-perfect Surrey village. The front door was framed by a rambling red rose, its outstretched branches always reminding Susan of the arms of a flamenco dancer, but that night she didn't linger, and followed Frank inside.

"What's cooking, honey?" he called into the low-ceilinged living room. It amused her that oversized Frank had picked such a twee little place for his wife and two children, who were nowhere to be seen. Muffled sounds could be heard from the floor above. June emerged from the kitchen in an apron and gave her a kiss.

"Hey, Susie. Good to see you."

"You too, June. You look great. Smells good."

"Oh, it's nothing special," June smiled. "How are you, anyway after everything that's happened?"

"Oh, you know, okay under the circs," Susan said, trying not to let her voice give her away. "Can I give you a hand?"

Susan knew that June, who'd never been known to taste the processed food available from her husband's company, would have spent considerable time rustling up the supper.

Frank wolfed his in a matter of minutes, and had seconds. He reached for a toothpick and cupped his hands over his mouth, probing his molars with a frown. Susan and June lingered over their *vichyssoise*, monkfish *à l'armoricaine* and cheesecake. The children were upstairs with cheese on toast.

June made herself scarce after dinner, "filling the dishwasher", and Frank led Susan to the living room for a glass of claret.

"So you're sure you're ready for this?" He stretched out his legs and lit a cigar, his face slightly flushed.

"Actually, I'm looking forward to it. You know, new challenges, things like that."

"Great, Susie. It's just what we need right now." He relit his cigar. "You know better than I that things are going to get difficult from here on."

She nodded. They both knew that on each side of the Atlantic, the number of exposés and probes into the food giants and the so-called health dangers of HFCS were on the rise. She didn't mention her daughter and her NGO. Frank leaned back in his armchair and dispatched a pungent cloud of smoke in her direction.

"You know this could be our 9/11," he said. "Of course we've done nothing *wrong*, we give the consumer what they want. But it could be our turn for a walloping. It's happening to the banks, telecoms have gone through it, newspapers have gone to the dogs. Look at Big Tobacco. Every industry has its turn and it may be ours next."

"Well in some cases, like the banks, it's completely justified," she said. "It surprised me that no-one went to jail over the toxic loans."

Frank lowered his voice a little. "The reason nobody's gone to jail is that they didn't break the law," he said.

"They were passing a parcel and the music stopped on someone else's turn."

"You mean it's only wrong if you get caught?"

"I mean everyone was doing it. You have to look at the

context. There was a bubble and everybody benefitted. Nobody expected it to pop when it did."

He leaned back again as another cloud of smoke swirled around him. "Anyway, I just wanted to say, we've got your back."

"Do you mean watch my back?" she said.

"No. That's what we say in America when we mean we'll watch out for you." His white teeth glinted in the lamplight.

It was one of her last evenings in London. Lily had come to Hackney for a few days to help her clear up and they were tucking into a microwaved lasagne at the kitchen table. The French windows were thrown open onto the warm evening air, but Susan sighed at the view and pushed her plate away.

"Susie, you OK? I've got whatever you need in my bag, courtesy Doctor Handsome-but-Married."

She shook her head. "I've tried to avoid taking anything, even sleeping pills, actually." She added sharply, "What have you got there, anyway? Uppers or downers?"

"Both. Need to keep things under control. There's nothing worse than a tremolo when it's not in the score."

Lily had given up a promising career as a soloist after suffering from stage fright, which paralysed her at unpredictable moments. Now she eked out a modest living, performing with a woodwind ensemble and giving private flute lessons.

"You should be careful," Susan said, but Lily pretended she hadn't heard.

"Want to play Name that Tune?" Lily stretched a blue-veined alabaster hand across the table. They had their own version of the old TV show where one guessed the song being drummed silently on the other's arm. Amazingly, nine times out of ten, they would both recognise the mystery tune together, high-fiving their rhythmic brilliance.

Susan shook her head. "I was just thinking this is the second time I've lost someone. You know my father died after their divorce. Not to mention the break-ups, and the bastard who left me two months before Mimi was born. It's so bloody unfair."

"Yes, it is. But you know Rod was never really going to leave his wife. He wouldn't have been a good father for Mimi. Not like Serge." Lily let her fingers run along the table as though tapping on her flute. "Besides, you were probably too young to get married."

Susan had become pregnant in her final term at university and suffered morning sickness during exams. She knew with hindsight she'd been lucky not to get pregnant the previous year, when she'd just met Rod and was completely in love.

"I was wrong to try to trap him with a baby. I just thought he'd come round in the end. How wrong I was. Maybe I'm just a bad judge of people."

"No you're not. Look at Serge. And talking of inappropriate men, what about my track record?"

"Inappropriate maybe, but they were all dishy."

"Yours always had the best chat-up lines," said Lily. "I want *damage*!" she said, imitating Serge's accent. "Brilliant!"

They smiled at each other. Their differences were probably exactly what had glued them together for more than twenty years. They'd never been in competition, professionally or romantically, since the day they met at Sussex and became flatmates.

Lily tucked her empty plate beneath hers. It had always amazed Susan how she could eat as much as she liked without gaining an ounce.

"Right," Lily said, looking at her watch. "I'm going to bed. You okay?"

"Sure. I've got to finish packing before having a bath."

"Need any help?"

Susan shook her head.

She went upstairs to the bedroom, where three piles of clothes sat neatly folded on the floor. Yes, No and Maybe were ready for the suitcase, charity store or the loft.

She opened the wardrobe.

What could she do with all this stuff? It would have to wait until tomorrow. But she was running out of time. She walked up one more flight of stairs to Mimi's old room, under the gable, where she now slept in the single bed. It didn't help—she found herself reaching out for Serge's warmth automatically in the night, only to find him gone, peering into the darkness in shock.

She stretched out on the bed, making a mental note to pull down the giant poster of Siouxsie and the Banshees above her head. She'd have to get rid of the empty fishbowl on the chest of drawers. There were wonky nails in the door, and something else caught her notice: Was that Blu-Tack or discarded chewing gum on the wall?

She curled up and closed her eyes as she began to fret about the move to Washington. When the phone alarm sounded next morning, she sat up with a start. The Victorian lattice window cast a shadow over the bed. She'd forgotten to close the curtains.

She was fully clothed, with the imprint of a dangling earring on her left cheek, a knot in her stomach, and an uneasy feeling that she hadn't a clue where her passport was.

Ready or not, her new life was about to begin.

Chapter 4

THE GLASS DOORS at DeKripps Foods Inc. slid open. The clock in the lobby said 8.30 a.m. Dressed smartly in a navy blue trouser suit, she felt dwarfed by the soaring marble hall.

"Susan Perkins, DeKripps marketing," she said to the security guard, and signed in before she picked the first in a bank of lifts to the sixth floor.

Barney, a towering perma-tanned figure in steely grey, was leaning over the receptionist at her desk. The bearded face of the founder of DeKripps looked down on them from the wall like an avuncular Van Gogh. Two small sofas made a corner, where TV news was on mute with subtitles. A coffee table, dominated by a vase of exotic flowers, displayed the latest trade magazines in a perfect arc.

Susan hoped Barney wouldn't catch sight of her wiping the nervous moisture from her hand before she greeted him.

"Hi, Susie. Welcome to DC."

He shook her hand with an iron grip and walked her along a beige carpet to his office.

"You know the drill. Ellen will show you around, and we'll expect you at our video conference with LA in a couple of hours."

"Great, fine. And thanks, Barney, for arranging this. It's much appreciated."

"You're very welcome. I'm sorry for your loss." She noticed the dazzling shine on his shoes as he stopped outside his door. His trouser creases were knife sharp.

The receptionist led Susan to her new office. The blinds were down, so she switched on the light which revealed a bare and functional space.

The furniture was designer, minimalist: A black ergonomic chair behind a pale desk, on which a computer and a phone were perched, and two black leather chairs for guests.

An empty bookcase stood in a corner, with a single ornament: A gold bar of DeKripps chocolate. On her desk she noticed a picture frame with a stock-photo of a couple and two kids, huddled and smiling giddily in black-and-white.

She pressed a button to raise the blinds, and was peering at the street below when she became aware of someone in the doorway.

"How are you settling in?"

It was Ellen, whom she'd met and liked during conferences and drinks in London. "Did you sleep okay?"

"I did until Martin rang at four in the morning. Apparently he didn't realise I'd left the country already."

"Oh dear. You don't look jet-lagged, if that's any consolation."

"Thanks, Ellen. And the office is fine, by the way." She noticed a garish painting on the wall beside her door. It was a scene of swaying cornfields, presumably in the Midwest, the DeKripps heartland. It would have to do.

"It's not a corner, I'm afraid, but you have a window." A corner office was to a DeKripps executive what castles were to medieval kings.

"Cool. And the view's much bigger than Covent Garden." Susan gestured towards the National Mall. She could just see the point of the Washington Monument if she craned her neck.

"I've arranged baby-sitting tonight, so let me know when you're done, and we can have dinner together."

After work the two women strolled from the DeKripps offices to Jaleo for tapas.

"So how are you coping, really?" Ellen asked as they ordered drinks. "I think it's extremely brave of you to move so far away."

"I hadn't thought of it like that. I knew I had to reinvent myself after what happened. In fact it was your letter that spurred me on, in a way."

"I wanted to say how sorry I was. I didn't know Serge very well, obviously, but you could tell he was a really special guy. He had that *je ne sais quoi*, you know, but what impressed me in particular was how much he respected you." Susan put down the menu and swallowed hard.

Did she want to burden Ellen with her troubles? She liked and trusted her, even saw her as a younger, more determined version of herself.

But she hesitated. The violence of her grief had surprised her. Sometimes she'd felt waterboarded, submerged to the point of drowning, then spluttering and gasping for air, only to be forced down again.

"It's tough." She pretended to scrutinise the menu, glancing sideways at Ellen who was searching for her phone.

"In case the twins are rioting." She placed her mobile on the table. "How long were you married?"

"Eleven years."

"Eleven," Ellen said, shaking her head. "And how's your daughter?"

"Mimi? Taking it hard, probably harder than she admits to me. But it's difficult to tell with her. She seems to blame me for what happened, as though sending him out for a newspaper was, I don't know, selfish. She hasn't said anything, but it's there."

"Poor you," Ellen said. "I'm so sorry."

"I feel guilty enough as it is." Susan sensed she wanted to ask her something.

"Was she a problem child?"

"No, not really," Susan said, defensively. "Mimi was always going to be a handful for anyone. I'm afraid she was born screaming and hasn't stopped since. It wasn't easy bringing up a baby on my own, on a tight budget, rushing round the country before I joined DeKripps."

She couldn't help envying Ellen and her supportive husband who could afford all the domestic help they needed. They'd met at Yale, the corporate ladder seeming to stretch directly from their freshman dormitory window.

"Maybe there's something more to it," Ellen said, breaking into Susan's reverie. "It strikes me she's always been pretty aggressive. Have you considered anger management?"

She said nothing. Mimi had been a full-on teenager turned rebellious adult, that was all. Susan was the one with a psychology degree – she knew her daughter didn't need therapy, and neither did she for that matter.

The waiter was standing beside them, pen in hand. Susan chose patatas bravas, squid in ink and beans with sausage. "Anyway, enough about my worries," she said. "Tell me about you? How are you coping with the twins?"

Ellen was finding motherhood rather exhausting, as she was breast-feeding both of her baby boys and had a long commute from Chevy Chase.

"I bet your hormones are still berserk."

"How did you guess?" Ellen said. "I sure had baby brain after the birth. But I figure it's under control now. Of course it's not something I'd even mention at work." Then she asked, "How do you feel about working with Barney?"

"Nervous. I've got so used to Frank that a two-toed sloth would seem dynamic. But it was a little dangerous, in its way. Possibly too comfortable. Mimi used to call Frank my partner in crime."

"I'm starting to like this girl," Ellen said. She took out a shiny powder case and pursed her bee-sting lips in the mirror, freshening up with a dash of scarlet.

"As you're probably aware, Barney doesn't take any prisoners, by the way."

Then she frowned as though she'd said too much, and added: "I'm sure you don't need to worry."

Susan's new home was a DeKripps apartment a short walk from work. It reminded her of her office, with all the charisma of an airport lounge, furnished entirely in beige, reproduction Modiglianis on the wall.

Standing in the gleaming white-tiled shower, she missed her daily soak in the bath in London, and Marmite on toast. At this time of year, the sun would have been streaming through her French windows, a posy of fresh flowers from the garden on her kitchen table. She'd brought family photographs with her but already regretted leaving her favourite glass ornaments packed away in the attic.

Everything about Penn Quarter was grey. Its anonymous blocks of uniform height cast a dark shadow over the streets and towered over characterless bars, expensive restaurants and cut-price basement stores. It turned out to be the dead heart of Washington, its streets deserted after office hours. And that meant after 6 p.m.

In the mornings, she'd amuse herself by opening the bedroom curtains with a theatrical swish by remote control, then close, then open. The bleakness of Washington was at her feet. People were already dressed and heading to their desks and screens.

They were streaming out of the Metro heads down, thumbing their phones, carrying coffee. This was a city that took work seriously.

Everyone seemed to be dragging a suitcase, even if it only contained a laptop.

On the few occasions she had a social engagement with a new acquaintance who inevitably turned out to be a lawyer, lobbyist or Congressional aide, they would always suggest a bar or restaurant in trendy Adams Morgan or Eastern Market, rather than downtown where she lived.

Her main hobby was killing time. If she wasn't trying to find an English accent on PBS to remind her of home, she'd be on the phone to her mother or Lily. Sometimes she'd drag her self-pity to the E Street Cinema, where she could sniffle in the darkness surrounded by the sweet smell of popcorn and images of Judi Dench or Hugh Grant.

She missed her colleagues in London, and yearned for that British kind of teasing that was frowned upon, possibly outlawed, in politically correct DC.

At the office, she got used to the little transatlantic miscommunications. Once, she asked a colleague where she'd got her suntan. "Saint Tropez," came the reply. "France?" she said, intrigued. "No, L Street." It took her a while to realise that when people said "Fax" they meant Fox News on TV.

She confessed to Frank on one of their regular calls that she was finding it hard to adjust to the monumental perfection of Washington after the anarchic sprawl of London. He wasn't surprised. He was originally from Chicago and had never liked DC, which he described as a "phoney" town with equally artificial inhabitants.

"What about friends?" he asked. "Making any?"

She admitted that Ellen was practically the only person she saw outside work. "But I plan to get out more," she said. "What are you working on?"

He told her a colleague had just dropped a report on his desk about children's eating habits, how at different times of day they would crave either salted or sweet food.

"That's an angle," she said. "Let me think about it. You should get one of your pet doctors on the case too."

"You know perfectly well that every single one is of the

highest integrity and independence."

As usual, he'd risen to the bait. She could never resist teasing him.

She'd long suspected the doctors on the DeKripps payroll, who sat on government food advisory boards and wrote for medical journals, were anything but independent.

Little by little, her anxiety about working for Barney subsided. Before Washington, she'd only met him on a couple of occasions when he had breezed into the London office.

She'd always sensed an awkwardness between him and Frank, and it had been fascinating to watch the interaction between them; Frank seemed to shrink physically beside Barney who radiated animal masculinity.

Susan knew she had no reason to be insecure. She'd given Crunchaloosa cereals their slogan: "DeKripps, caring for you and your family".

The words had everything DeKripps wanted to say about nurturing through the generations. Needless to say, her accolades provoked a hurtful remark from Mimi: "What on earth do you know about caring for a family?"

She was praised for the Buried Treasure cartoon she'd developed in London.

It featured a rabbit, a mole and a badger digging for buried treasure – a chocolate bar containing nuggets of glittering golden honeycomb.

"Kids will love this ad," said Barney, who decided to give it a TV spot in the US, a rare transatlantic transfer for a corporation that had to be so careful about British commercials and children.

As Frank had predicted, Barney was rarely in the office. Michelle Obama had launched an anti-obesity drive and the food companies were feeling the heat.

Barney was quietly informing Congressional staffers, and

sometimes their bosses, about DeKripps' "bold" decision to – slightly - cut the sugar content in its flavoured milk. He came to rely on Susan to chair video conferences with the American staff and the rest of the DeKripps empire.

"Got to keep them on message, Susie," he would say, before heading out to a meeting on the Hill. "People need to realise we weren't waiting to be told what to do. We got there before them, as any responsible company should."

At the end of her first month in DC, Barney invited her to join a select group in the DeKripps box at baseball.

It would mean missing her first Pilates class, something she'd forced herself to join, but such professional invitations were loaded with obligation.

"I should warn you that I've never been to a baseball match before," she told him. "I hope I won't let you down."

"You just did, Susie. It's not a *match*. It's a *game*. Don't worry, you'll be fine. You might even enjoy it."

She doubted it. All she knew was that it was the end of the season and the Washington Nationals had been on a winning streak despite languishing at the bottom of their division.

They followed a sea of red into the stadium in the balmy September heat. Everyone seemed to be wearing bright red with white numbers on their backs.

"See that number 11 shirt? Zimmerman?" said Barney. "That's Ryan Zimmerman, the third baseman. The face of the franchise."

Barney had covered his shock of grey hair with a red baseball cap with a curly W on the front, and wore a pair of aviator sunglasses.

Susan wondered whether she should have changed out of her suit into something less formal.

Just as she was beginning to feel out of place in her heels, they reached the box overlooking home base and found a small number of chairs had been set out.

"Congressman Wilde, thank you for coming," Barney said, holding out his hand to a corpulent man with bad breath and dark greasy hair.

"How do you do, Congressman," said Susie as she greeted the Representative from Iowa.

"Congressman, this is Susie Perkins from DeKripps London. She's strategising with us, but only she knows what that means."

"We're expanding the brand," said Susan. "Top secret, of course."

"You from England? I just love that accent," said the Congressman. He grabbed and pumped her hand while his eyebrows leapt with enthusiasm. She glanced at Barney for help, but he'd already moved on to another guest.

She smiled. "Yes, I've been working with Frank in London."

She could almost touch the fetid air from his mouth, as though dredged from the Anacostia river, and struggled not to turn away.

Why did she mention Frank? Nobody would know him here. She added, "I do cereals. And ice cream."

"Great," the Congressman said, leaning forward. "I've got a pack of Buried Treasure in the office."

She smiled again, reaching for a strand of hair and twiddled it under her nose to avoid the stale blasts.

"So you're from London?"

"No. Not really. I've moved around a bit. Southern England really. University in Brighton, if you know it?"

"Naw." A bucket of chicken wings appeared, and he helped himself to two. Susan declined, thinking she didn't want her hands to go where his greasy fingers had been. Then abruptly, he turned his back on her, and began calling to a new arrival.

The box was filling up.

There was room for about a dozen people, and Susan was introduced to a couple of young Congressional staffers and a woman from the federal regulator.

She'd done her share of corporate hospitality with Frank, and had always enjoyed schmoozing clients, but tonight she was unsure of herself.

It was nothing like the banter over champagne and strawberries at Wimbledon. She understood the guidelines on lobbying in Washington were strictly defined.

Behind them was a bar, and most of the guests were drinking beer. They set their glasses down and placed hands on hearts as a soloist began The Star-Spangled Banner.

The game was interminable.

The batsman – or hitter, she heard someone say – stood there avoiding the ball.

Susan was afraid of making a fool of herself, and didn't ask anyone the rules. For long periods, nothing happened. Sometimes when the batsman missed the ball, the crowd applauded.

She suppressed a yawn, taking an occasional swig of light beer. From time to time, one or two of them would join the chant of "Let's Go *Nats.*"

The lack of action on field meant plenty of time to chat. Susan found herself discussing sales of salted crisps with one of the House Agriculture Committee staffers while he devoured a hotdog that oozed bright yellow mustard.

She tried to ignore his eyes darting behind her as he sought more high-powered company. She caught sight of Barney deep in conversation with Congressman Wilde. Barney intercepted her gaze and winked.

She noticed that Wilde was on first name terms with most of the people in their box. DC is a revolving door of lawmakers and lobbyists, she recalled Frank saying.

It was time for the Presidents' Race. Barney had explained on the way that the Teddy Roosevelt mascot had never yet won against the other former presidents.

Susan felt stupid yelling "Come on, Teddy!" but all the grown men in their box were doing it.

They jumped to their feet when the giant mascots burst onto the outfield. She recognised George Washington with his long white hair drawn back in a ponytail, then came Abe Lincoln. The mascot with a white moustache, who jostled Lincoln on the way onto the field, must be William Taft. But where was Teddy?

Shouts pierced the air when the figure with the dark moustache appeared, bringing up the rear on a tricycle.

"He's gonna do it this time," she heard her neighbour say. "Come on, Teddy!" The mascot, pedalling furiously, reached the others at the corner. The cheers grew as he began to overtake them, raising his fist. "Come on, Teddy!"

But suddenly there was chaos. Teddy toppled over as he cycled into the lead. Jefferson fell on top of him. Susan heard muttered disappointment in the box as a cry went out from the crowd.

Then Teddy scrambled up and began hurling T-shirts into the audience, to delighted screams from children in Nats headgear, who jumped and shouted, "Over here, Teddy!"

Susan looked round the DeKripps box as they sat again. They must have expected Teddy to lose. "Hey, that was exciting," she heard someone say.

She turned round to see whether the woman from the Federal Drug Administration might share her awkwardness, but she was flirting with one of the staffers. She could hear her tinkling laughter from behind her.

A hush fell as the waiters brought more trays of hot dogs, nachos and buckets of chicken. Then the chatter resumed after a pause. Somehow they'd found the time to change seats, like a corporate musical chairs.

Someone at DeKripps had ensured that not a moment of precious networking time had been wasted.

The cheerful organ began again, prompting more calls of "Let's Go Nats!" or "Let's Go Zimmerman!"

Once again, spectators stood in unison, this time for the seventh inning stretch. They stood up, stretched their arms and legs and sang "Take me out to the ball game!" at the top of their voices, prompted by words on the giant screen.

What fun they all seemed to be having. She was relieved when she overheard someone remark there were only two more innings to go.

They left the stadium with a surge of pumped-up fans after the home team subjugated the New York Mets. Barney raised an imperious arm to hail her a cab, hardly pausing for breath to say goodbye as he continued a rapid fire exchange with a lobbyist in a red baseball cap.

Instead of taking the highway, the driver headed past the illuminated dome of Congress before cutting across the green swathe of the National Mall.

To her left was the gleaming white obelisk whose pointed summit was blinking red. The nation's capital, in the stillness of a late summer evening, was a stunning sight. But she felt like the baseball: Tossed coolly, mostly invisible.

As she shrank into the upholstery in the taxi air conditioning, she suppressed a shiver.

Chapter 5

A GROUP OF ten DeKripps executives was summoned to a strategy meeting in Barney's office.

Susan had never seen him so agitated. He kicked the door closed with his foot as he strode to the end of the table and swung his jacket over the back of his seat. He rolled up his sleeves as though readying for a fist-fight.

"Do we have the hook-up with LA?" he said. It was barely 8 a.m. in Los Angeles.

"Hi, Barney. Luke here," said the surf-bleached blonde on the video. Like 3D portraits of Dorian Grey, the company managers were getting younger every day.

"Let's start from the beginning. Luke, what are those motherfuckers in California trying to do to us?"

"Well, Kramer and his team are publishing another book. It'll likely add to the stink about HFCS. There's a whole chapter about DeKripps."

Susan knew all about Bill Kramer, the child obesity specialist who'd likened sugar to cocaine in front of every journalist who would listen.

Now, his ideas about High Fructose Corn Syrup seemed to be gaining traction with mainstream media, not just "the granola set" as Frank called them. America's obesity epidemic was visible to all, with one child in three overweight.

The question is, who's to blame? Frank had seen it coming, she realised, remembering their conversation in Cobham. It was only a matter of time before Kramer put all his bile into a blockbuster and hurled it at DeKripps.

"Let's unpack this. Randy, what's the legal position?" He barked at his legal counsel. "I mean, can we throw the book at Kramer?"

Randy cleared his throat, studying his bitten fingernails as he played for time. "I'd have to examine the chapter in detail," he began.

"I want a report on my desk by tonight. What else can we do?"

Barney now sat on a corner of the table, hunched into a pile of muscle like Rodin's Thinker as all eyes fell on him.

He looked around the table and sat up.

"We do two things. We make a gesture to the consumer who will see that we are a responsible company with their interests at heart.

"We make an announcement. Get Kramer and those fuckers on the back foot."

Susan caught Ellen's gaze from across the table. What could he have in mind?

"Second, we find another bad guy. We know it ain't sugar. The link between obesity and HFCS isn't there. It is *not* proven. Sugar does *not* cause diabetes. Get me any expert and have them tell the world. The customer has a choice. If they want to buy a banana, they can buy a banana.

"But the fact is they would rather buy DeKripps cookies because they're delicious. What is important here is that the consumer chooses what to buy. If they want to find out what they're eating, we have taken the trouble to tell them on the pack. It's on the pack!"

Susan had heard this speech so many times at DeKripps, and delivered it herself at focus groups and in arguments with her daughter, that she no longer needed convincing.

But who was the other culprit Barney was about to finger?

As though answering her question, after pausing for breath, he punched the air. "It's not the sugar, it's the lack of fibre."

He looked at them, expecting nods of approval which

never came.

"Look, DeKripps recommends a balanced and healthy diet. We know that. We're going to put less sugar into our soft drinks. Then we'll make the cans and bottles a *tiny* bit bigger. After that, we fund research. Fibre deficiency as a possible cause of obesity and diabetes. *We're* the good guys!"

"What about bread?" Ellen asked. "If we're taking the bull by the horns, we could reduce the added sugar in DeKripps loaves."

Susan agreed with her: She too had never understood why her company added so much sugar to bread in America.

"Ellen," Barney said, with a stare that said *get with the programme,* "today's conversation is about soda and juice. I'll be talking to Susie about whether we need a new name to go with the improved flavour, or whether Angeljuice is as heavenly as it sounds to me. Give us our daily bread some other day. Let's keep our powder dry."

Ellen pretended not to notice that everyone's gaze had fallen on her, and returned to her doodle.

"Barney," Randy said, "you're aware of the FDA warnings about misbranding."

"Which one? You mean *Nutrition Facts,* evaporated cane juice in yoghurt? Of course. But number one, I would point out that letter was non-binding. Number two, I would point out again that we are talking about soda. And number three, our compliance people were onto that and we no longer list it on any of our *lite* products.

"Not like some of the competition, I might add. I think these assholes down the street are heading for a fall with their alleged *no sugar added* yoghurt. It's got evaporated cane juice on the pack! Once again, folks, we do not want our soda guzzling customers to believe for a second that we're concealing sugar."

"Just checking," Randy said. Like the rest of them, he was intimidated by Barney's aggression.

Ellen and Susan exchanged another surreptitious glance. They both knew the Food and Drug Administration monitored compliance by them and their competitors like a sniffer dog.

"Judy," Barney snapped at his head of comms, who stopped scribbling and looked up. "Get me some talking points. We need a press release and some cameras."

"Fine. But I'd suggest you call a journalist with an exclusive," she said. "You could talk to Barbara Miles from the New York Scrutineer. It's pointless asking her out to lunch, she won't go. But she'll drink a cocktail if we let her know you want to take shots at Kramer. She'll get to thrash out the issues. She loves a fight."

"You're right. That way we don't have to get into a shouting match with any of these hairy vegetarian bloggers in their PJs. Get Miles on the phone. One more thing," he told her. "We put together a fact sheet on myths and reality about the so-called danger of added sugars. Think about it. Questions?"

No one spoke. "Team, that's it. We've got our ducks lined up in a row. Now go out there and make some money. We're the good guys, remember. Oh, and Luke, see you next week in LA."

The screen went dark and the little group filed out. Barney gave everyone a high five as they left. Susan was the last to reach the door.

"Good job, Barney," she said.

"There's another thing," he said, lowering his voice. "I wasn't going to say so publicly. We are going to shut that motherfucker down. Kramer needs to go to school. I'm going to have people eating his trash. Remember Yudkin?"

"Of course." Susan nodded. The late John Yudkin was a

British medical scholar whose health warnings about sugar had been rubbished by the food industry in the 1970s.

"Kramer ain't seen nothing yet. He'll wish he was Yudkin."

He leaned against the table and took a breath.

"I mean, what are we supposed to do? Stick of celery in every box of cereal? Slap on a warning? Consult a doctor if your erection lasts more than four hours?"

Susan looked at her feet.

"The bottom line," he said, "is that people are responsible for what they put in their mouths, right? Goddamned nanny state."

He grabbed his jacket and strode out.

Chapter 6

THE FIRST ANNIVERSARY of Serge's death drifted into Susan's mind like a waking dream. Her thoughts strayed constantly across the ocean, into their home, into the bedroom as they lay together, or the kitchen as they cooked, a silhouette world of still-sharp memories.

Although she struggled to concentrate, she sensed Barney was pleased with the new product development. It was so sensitive that it was referred to only as Project Candy by the few in the know.

"What we're looking at is a new ingredient with a totally new flavour," Barney said.

"I'm a marketer, not one of your R and D scientists," she said. "Get me the ingredient and I'll promote it for you."

"We're on it, I assure you. And, you can bet your last cent that the scientists at Chewers are praying to the food gods at this very moment. By the way," he placed his tanned forefinger against his lips. "The guys in compliance don't need to know about this. And the same goes for regulatory affairs."

DeKripps, like all the multinationals, had entire departments devoted to feeding the ravenous appetite of the Food and Drug Administration to ensure everything was above board.

"The best thing we can do is target higher incomes."

"I thought we like caretakers?" He sounded doubtful. DeKripps had built its fortune on the mass market.

"And car mechanics. Yes, of course. It would be a departure. And I'm advising that DeKripps keep a low profile for now. One product can contaminate another. But we can still move upmarket."

Later that day, Ellen asked her for a favour. "I've a

consumer research evening tonight. Daiquiris and demographics. Would you stand in for me? It might take your mind off things."

She explained that a friend did contract work for a cosmetics company, and Susan had often gone to similar evenings in London.

It was usually fun, with decent nibbles and sometimes a token payment.

"My friend lives in Chevy Chase, though. I hope you don't mind."

"That's fine. But who am I supposed to be?"

"It doesn't matter. You could be a housewife if you like. Tiffany is testing a new foundation for people with freckles, so I figured it might interest you."

As night fell, Susan pushed through the hordes of Caps fans in red wigs spilling out of her local Metro. Ice hockey season had arrived, the supporters congregating at the Green Turtle bar before surging into the stadium next door.

She rode the Metro to Friendship Heights where she hailed a cab in the rain, waiting beside a little pile of discarded umbrellas.

Extreme weather was one of the features of Washington life, particularly the mortaring downpours with gusting winds that turned umbrellas inside out.

Occasionally the city would be flicked by the tail of a hurricane as it exhausted itself barrelling up the east coast. The violence reminded her of the Great Storm that uprooted so many of the ancient trees at Sussex, strewing them across the university campus.

The taxi took her up a driveway and delivered her to the door of a white clapboard house where the porch light was swinging dangerously.

Tiffany opened the door, haloed in light, straight from the pages of the Washington Gazette Style section, blue Jackie cardigan over pinched-in dress, shoulder length blonde hair tidy and sleek, the discreet self-confidence of understated wealth.

"You must be Ellen's friend. I hope you're not too wet."

Five or six young women were draped decoratively on the floral armchairs and a sofa arranged in a semi-circle around a marble fireplace. The first thing Susan noticed was that they all had freckles, from tasteful sprinklings about the nose to a neck-and-shoulder shower or the full Monty like herself.

"I guess we're all here for the same reason," she said.

She headed for the only empty seat and introduced herself to her neighbour, another ginger-haired woman with a bob whose name was Linda.

"This could be a big night."

"You mean for the magic cream?"

"I've been waiting a long time for this moment," Linda said, reaching for the first unmarked jar of foundation.

"Me too."

Linda and Susan rubbed a sample on the backs of their hands, which they held out to examine. Then they smeared more onto their cheeks. They had to score each cream on appearance, texture, skin-feel, and finally freckle concealment. Each sheet of scorepaper had room for comments.

"Something tells me we'll have to wait a little longer," said Susan, as she held up a small mirror to her face with a squint. "But then, it's all about packaging."

"How disappointing. What line are you in?"

"Marketing. Sorry."

She picked up another jar and went through the motions. Linda had fallen silent. Surely nobody believed that one of these creams could really cover freckles? The other women were doing the tests with gusto, smearing the stuff over their arms and necks, anywhere the dark flecks lurked. Tiffany was providing wipes as required, checking with her waiter that everyone had a drink and a mini Red Velvet cupcake.

After a while, Susan wandered off to find the loo. As she crept upstairs, she could feel that invisible hand stretching out to shove her head back underwater again. She pushed open a door into the biggest bathroom she had ever seen, sat down heavily on a side of the free-standing bath, gripped the sides and waited to be overcome.

She began to weep. She stood up and looked at her trembling face in the mirror. It was shiny from tears, makeup and wipes, and distorted by her sobbing. As she paused for a deep breath before letting out another sob, she heard footsteps coming along the corridor, followed by a gentle knock.

"Susie, are you OK?" It was Tiffany. She must have been missed downstairs.

"Coming."

She grabbed a towel to wipe her face, unlocked the door and came out, blinking at Tiffany.

"I just can't do this tonight. I'm not in the mood. Maybe too many people. I don't go out much these days. I don't know if Ellen told you about how I lost my husband. It's the anniversary of his death coming up. I thought it'd take my mind off things, but I feel so lonely. And just now I was obsessing about my freckles. It's stupid, isn't it? I never know what's going to set me off."

"You've had a terrible shock," Tiffany said. "It'll take time to get over it. Have you considered a widows' group?"

Susan was sure she meant well. But she wasn't ready for the American way of grief, sharing her bereavement with strangers. She'd already said too much. "I'm not sure it's for me," she said. "But thanks. I'm sorry to be such a wet blanket. I'd better get going."

Grabbing her raincoat, she turned down Tiffany's offer to call a cab, and allowed the waiter to open the front door. The downpour was now a steady drizzle.

Turning to wave while walking down the drive beside a gentle rivulet of rain, and even as fresh drops mingled with her tears, she thought: These people are the ideal target group for Project Candy.

Chapter 7

SHE'D BEEN IN Washington for about three months before she was able to assure herself of Barney's trust. He invited her one morning to accompany him to a meeting with one of the two Senators from Kansas, a Corn Belt state and home to DeKripps headquarters.

"Wanna walk?"

It was a twenty minute hike from DeKripps to Capitol Hill, less at the speed with which Barney powered along Pennsylvania Avenue. She practically had to run to keep up.

"Just leave it to me, Susie," he instructed as they marched along. Was this his way of shutting her up or just casual sexism? "We'll only have 15 minutes with the Senator, so I'll brief him on how we're staying ahead of the competition."

Susan had noticed that for Barney, everything came down to competition, and he was determined to win.

"What sports did you play at college?" she asked.

"Football." She could imagine him helmeted and shoulders padded as he elbowed and pummelled his way to the touchline. He emptied his pockets onto the security belt at the entrance to the Russell building, where two Capitol police officers stood chatting. Susan picked up her handbag at the other side and headed for the lift.

"So is this just a hand-holding exercise?"

"Keeping them happy. Congressmen like to feel they're in the loop."

Two young interns followed them into the lift, unaware that Barney's eyes were burning shamelessly through their dresses. "And I'm like *yeah,*" one of them said, "and he's like *well,*" while the other nodded.

More long-legged, long-haired creatures slunk by in the marble hallway, each in full makeup and formal attire in line with the Congressional dress code.

They reached Senator Dailey's third floor office and stopped at the receptionist who blocked their way.

"Good morning, Mr McManus, Ms Perkins. The Senator's expecting you," she said.

They were ushered into a wood-panelled office where a large man in a white shirt was leaning back in his chair opposite two aides. A third excused himself and left the room as they entered.

"Ah, Barney, good to see you," he said, standing to shake hands. Susan was introduced to the chief of staff and a press officer.

"We've had some bad news this morning," said the Senator. "Hey, Jerry, bring some chairs for our guests would you?"

"What's up Senator?"

"It's this damned Tea Party. It's the end of politics as we know it. Any dumbass now thinks he can run for Congress by saying they want to claw back government. And now it's happening to me!"

Dailey explained he would now face a primary challenge from a Tea Party candidate in next year's midterm elections. The problem with American politics, Susan had discovered in DC, was that there was always an election to win. How did they ever have time to think about anything else but fundraising?

She looked at Barney. He'd got the message.

"Well, Senator, is there anything we at DeKripps can do to help? You know we have cash for red states, you know we have cash for moderate Republicans."

The Senator acknowledged the offer with the blink of an eye, loosening his striped tie beneath a double chin and rolling his sleeves to the elbows.

"What they don't realise, these assholes, is that their

policies will destroy government," he said. "Maybe that's what they want. Hell, why don't they just throw a grenade into Congress? But after two terms as Senator, I'm not going to roll over for a Tea Party guy. Right, Richard?" he said to the young press officer.

"Right, Senator, that's what we're going to tell them."

"I mean, none of us want Obamacare. Can you imagine what socialised medicine will do to your life expectancy? I won't be voting for that. I was against the auto bailout too. But these people are insurrectionists. They're anti everything! And now the Tea Party wingnuts are polluting the minds of Kansas voters. *My* voters."

He'd picked up a pen and slammed it down on the desk. His collection of family photos jumped with the impact. "But Barney, that's not what you came to hear. What can I do for you?"

Their time was almost up. Barney gave his pitch about how DeKripps was taking its responsibility to the nation's health seriously by easing up on added sugars and taking a stand on fibre.

"We remain America's most trusted brand and we intend to keep that trust," he said. "All we're doing is changing the conversation, just a tad."

The Congressman nodded at the mention of High Fructose Corn Syrup. Not only did he come from the Corn Belt where HFCS was produced, but he sat on the Senate Agriculture, Nutrition and Forestry Committee where he was a champion of American corn growers and processors.

"That's terrific, Barney. Thanks a lot for stopping by."

Barney stood at the signal and motioned to Susan.

"Senator, always a pleasure," he said, stretching out his hand and pumping Dailey's firmly as they power-eyeballed each other.

"DeKripps is right behind you," he said meaningfully, as

he pressed the Senator's stubby paw. "Give my best to Shirley."

"I will. Goodbye, Ma'am," said the Senator, shaking Susan's hand. His press officer whispered something into his ear, and they all stepped outside together. The glare of a TV camera caught them leaving Dailey's office.

Susan heard the Senator saying, "I look forward to debating with Mr Burdock," as she and Barney set off down the hall.

"How do you think that went?" he asked.

"Not quite as I'd expected, I must say."

"Let's have a coffee." He took her downstairs to the basement, through a brick tunnel labyrinth which eventually led to a coffee bar.

"Welcome to the only privately owned coffee bar in Congress," Barney said. He showed her into the little café with a hot and cold self-service buffet at one end. A couple of Congressmen, vaguely familiar to Susan, were seated at a table. Staffers waited in line for coffee to go. Susan and Barney took theirs into the next room.

"This is obviously not my area, but should we be taking this Tea Party thing seriously?"

"DeKripps? We are, don't worry. Dailey's probably safe, but I can think of a few others in Congress who should be worried. I'm from Philadelphia, and right next door there's this crazy woman who wants to run for Biden's seat next year. She's Tea Party and she's a witch! I mean, a *real* witch. Can you imagine it? A witch on the Senate foreign relations committee? We'd be the laughing stock of the whole world."

"There's a real revolutionary streak in America, isn't there? It reminds me of France. I think the French and the Americans have more in common than we realise."

The comparison seemed to leave Barney cold. He sipped from his coffee and winced.

"What I'm saying is, it's dangerous, Susie. Dangerous for the Republicans. And everything that's happening is good news for Democrats, although God knows they've got enough problems. Look at how Obama's screwed up healthcare. He's been in office for almost a year and Congress is still jammed with this goddamned thing."

"From what I read, the gridlock in Congress isn't just on healthcare. There's warfare on any reform that comes to the floor. It might even affect us with HFCS."

"True, I've never seen it this bad. Never. But foodwise, it'd be dangerous if people start seeing nutrition as a political issue, not a health issue." He narrowed his eyes. "We're not there yet, though."

Susan thought of Mimi. For her daughter, food was already political. After giving up media studies, the subject *du jour*, she'd ended up in her NGO, which had completed her political education. She knew that Mimi did communications, although her latest job seemed to consist of holding childish protests, dressing up in public places to shout about policy reform. Or awareness raising, as Mimi called it.

Barney began jiggling his knee with caffeinated impatience. When she'd finished her latte, instead of heading the way they came, he took her past the sprawling Senate cafeteria, its food stations spread out in the basement. This was the place where French fries had been rebaptised Freedom Fries during the Iraq war.

Serge, a Bush-hater, had been apoplectic, and hadn't seen the joke.

A little further along the corridor, Barney showed her the little subway train that ran to the Capitol.

Beside it was a well-stocked Senate gift shop. It would be the perfect place to pick up some Christmas presents, stamped with the Senate seal.

They walked in silence along Pennsylvania Avenue, then as they neared the office she asked, "How's Project Posh?"

"Project Candy? It's dandy."

He obviously intended to leave it at that. But then he added, "You'll be impressed. We've got one scientist in particular who deserves a Nobel Prize."

"The peace prize? Let them eat Candy?"

He laughed. "The prize for chemistry. Or biology. One of those. You've not mentioned Project Candy to anyone, right?"

"Of course not."

"You know loose lips sink ships," he said, pulling an invisible fastener across his mouth. "Zip 'em Susie."

Chapter 8

AS CHRISTMAS APPROACHED, a blizzard dumped a record sixteen inches of snow at Dulles on the night of Susan's scheduled flight to London, disrupting her travel plans.

Ellen invited her home for Sunday brunch on December 13th, the anniversary of Serge's death. Her husband Jed, a K Street lobbyist for one of the banks, was in charge of the kitchen that morning.

"Looking forward to Christmas?" Jed asked, chewing gum and handing her a cup of coffee. He was preparing a pile of blueberry pancakes, spooning the mixture onto the stove from a mixing bowl. Ellen was taking care of the twins, holding one with each hand as they trotted unsteadily round the kitchen like string puppets. Susan perched on a stool by the counter.

"Sort of. Not really. It's a bit of a schlepp to my mother's on the coast, and my daughter's doing her own thing," she said. "And as Ellen probably told you, there's a cloud hanging over the family. So it won't exactly be festive."

"Sure," Jed said. "So you're going to France as well?"

"I kind of feel obliged to see Serge's family. His brother lives in Rennes, he's a chemist."

"What, chemistry?"

"No, drugstore. Problem is I think he helps himself to a few too many of his drugs."

"You mean he's an addict?"

"More a hypochondriac. There's always something the matter with him, so he self-medicates."

"Oh, man. And are you done with all the paperwork now?"

"I'm not sure. That's another reason I need to travel to France, their family notary was handling all that, but it should be pretty straightforward. It just takes time."

She turned to Ellen. "So which of these lovely boys is Darren, and which is David? They both look so much like you, by the way."

"Jed says they've got my nose, poor things," said Ellen. "This one in blue dungarees is Darren. And this little fellow is David."

"They've got Jed's chin though," Susan said. Jed, stroking his square jaw, grinned from behind the kitchen counter. "They're a year old now, right?"

"Fifteen months exactly."

Susan got down on her knees to play. "They're such fun at this age," she said. "I remember when Mimi learned to walk. Oh for the days when she couldn't answer back!"

"Don't you believe it," Ellen said. "Once one of them starts emptying his lungs, the other follows suit straight away."

Jed gave her a lift back to the Metro after brunch, and she asked how his firm was doing after the banking collapse last year.

"Let's just say it was bad," he said in a Texan drawl, lingering on *bayed* as he checked the rearview. "It's tough right now. Customers hate us, and blame the banks for the recession."

"I guess that's where DeKripps is recession proof," said Susan. "Even in a crisis, people love sweets. And of course the worse people feel, the more they eat."

"Did you prove that in focus groups?"

"No, but others have."

"Seriously, do you mind if I ask you something? It's about Ellen. Do you think she's working too hard?"

"Why?"

"She's listless. Distracted when she gets home. She's usually as focused as a laser beam."

"Did she say anything about Barney?"

"Of course," he said.

"Do you think she's under too much pressure from him?"

"Could be. It's this new product, right?"

"It's in development stage right now. Our department is going to be under a lot more pressure once it launches. We're the ones who have to sell it. But I'll make sure Ellen's okay. She's got my back too."

"Thanks. Appreciate it." But she could see he was hoping for more.

Susan was restless on the flight to London.

She clicked through the movies on offer but couldn't make up her mind. When the flight attendant brought drinks, she picked up her can of tomato juice and examined the Nutrition Facts on the side, squinting at the print size which seemed to be even tinier than usual. The "one hundred percent" tomato juice contained nine grams of sugar. Well, if Chewers think they can get away with it, good for them.

She caught the train to Lymington, where a yapping Yorkshire terrier named Nellie greeted her at her mother's front door. "Why didn't you tell me? And why did you give it such an old-fashioned name? It's as bad as Susan."

She'd always hated her name. She could never decide as a child which she hated more, being ginger, being freckled, or being Susan.

Over the next few days, braving the misty chill, she pottered around the shops, their Christmas lights sparkling on the cobbled streets in the lower town.

She would raise her head from time to time to look towards the Solent and the Isle of Wight's dark hulk.

Christmas Day meant capon, sprouts and roast potatoes, shared with the dog which only seemed to stop barking when it was eating.

They didn't bother to buy crackers. Her mother's attempt to lighten her mood, by inviting her to lunch at Sticklers on the high street, collapsed as soon as the subject of Mimi was raised.

"Do you think I'm a bad mother?" Susan asked as she tackled a generous helping of cod and chips.

"What do you mean, dear?"

"Well, I must be to blame for Mimi turning into the daughter from hell."

"You did your best. It's nature as well as nurture, isn't it? And who knows what genes the girl inherited from her father." Her mother had never approved of her married boyfriend, despite having broken up a marriage or two herself.

"I wouldn't worry about it if I were you." That sounded like the final word. Her mother had never been one for introspection.

"But I do worry. I worry I should have done things differently. And is it a coincidence that she's a vegan as well? All this unconscious attention-seeking. Maybe I didn't give her enough attention when she was young."

"She'll grow out of it."

"Do you really think so? I'd be surprised. It's not a diet, you know, it's a belief system." Susan pushed away the remainder of her chips. "Do you think Nellie wants one?"

"She doesn't eat junk food." The little dog was sitting at her mother's feet, had been quiet for most of their lunch. Susan was amazed she'd been allowed into the restaurant.

"I don't understand why Mimi has to be so aggressive about it," Susan said. "All this nonsense about bee's vomit. I'm not sure she's getting proper nutrition, but she'll never listen to me."

"The other day she told me I shouldn't sprinkle sugar on

my oatmeal because it's refined with cattle bones. I do hope that you're not responsible for that."

"Of course not, mother."

She'd always found it difficult to confide in her mother who remained a private person, averse to raking over feelings and motivations.

Susan scrutinized her face as her manicured hand searched her handbag for a wallet and powder puff. She was still beautiful at 72, dignified, lipstick intact. She'd always seemed slightly distracted but few outside the family noticed that now she was increasingly deaf. She dabbed her cheeks with powder. The words remained unspoken. If Susan had been a bad mother, what about her own? Had she unconsciously followed the same pattern of benign neglect with Mimi?

Then her mother said something that surprised her. "Do you know, when I look at Mimi, I see you," she said. "You want to be different too. That's why you married a Frenchman, don't you think?"

Before she had a chance to reply, her mother put on her reading glasses to look at the bill, and feigned shock. "If it gets any worse, I'm going to have to go out to work," she said. Susan wasn't aware that her mother had ever had a job.

"Come off it. You've got your investments."

"What do you mean? For two years now that income has been more than cut in half." She pulled on her woolly poncho which gave off just a hint of mothballs, scooped up Nellie, and sailed out of the restaurant, Susan following behind.

The fish restaurant in the old town of Rennes had an open air seafood counter where a young man in an apron and gloves was shucking oysters in the freezing cold.

"I've booked a table for three in the name of Pairkeens."

She Frenchified her last name for the benefit of the *maître d'*.

"Ah oui, Madame Pairkeens, suivez-moi," he said. He gathered together the menus and a wine list. Susan glanced back and saw Marie-Christine extinguishing her cigarette on the pavement, then heard the clicking of her stilettos.

It was the first time they'd seen each other since the funeral. The ritual kissing greeting was perfunctory. Susan watched her perma-frown deepen as she surreptitiously scanned her outfit while they took off their coats. As usual, she was made to feel that her fashion sense wasn't up to scratch.

Jean-Louis, his polo shirt collar turned up in the French way, was seated on Susan's right, and his wife opposite them. They'd left the children, François-Xavier and Lucie-Anne, at home with a babysitter. She'd always thought there were too many hyphens in that family.

Minutes later, the table was piled high with an imposing *plateau de fruits de mer* of crab, oysters, *langoustines,* prawn and whelks.

"Well, *bon appétit,*" she said. She picked up a mini-spear and wondered whether she had the stomach for a slimy grey-green whelk.

"*Alors,* Suzanne," said Marie-Christine - Susan had long given up correcting to *Soo-san* - "tell us about America."

Her sister-in-law had made no secret of her lack of interest in her move to Washington. As a Frenchwoman who'd once said she had no need of a passport, she was convinced that her native land was paradise.

"I bet you don't have seafood restaurants like this in Washington DC," stressing the *dee see.*

She was obviously expected to reply in the negative.

"It depends where you go," she said in as neutral a voice as she could muster, determined not to be goaded. "The food's okay, actually."

"But how can it be? Americans are so fat," said Marie-Christine, pouting in disapproval. "Obese. Everybody knows the Americans eat nothing but fast food, genetically modified." She added a dismissive *pff*!

Susan felt targeted. "Well, would you believe that every bottle of tomato sauce in the world comes from genetically modified tomatoes? You can't even escape it in Brittany."

Her sister-in-law raised a carefully plucked eyebrow and returned in silence to her dish. Jean-Louis didn't say anything either. He knew when it was best to keep quiet.

Susan noticed he wasn't serving himself with the expensive Pouilly-Fuissé she'd ordered. He explained that he'd woken with a tummy upset, and kept on disappearing to the loo.

But Marie-Christine had put Susan on the defensive. As she looked around the restaurant, she noticed that nobody was fat. How did the French do it? They simply had a different attitude towards food.

She watched as the family at the table next to theirs was ordering. None of them was asking the waiter to "hold" this or that, like they did in DC.

Her sister-in-law was sounding off again. "All those GM crops in America, Frankenstein food," she said. "At least we have Bové here to protect us from the *malbouffe*."

"I have colleagues at DeKripps Europe," Susan said, reaching for her water, "who consider José Bové MEP to be the symbol of European over-regulation."

"*Notre héros*," Jean-Louis said, gripping his stomach and heading again for the loo.

"And who else is on our side? Who else is fighting GM food?"

My daughter for one, Susan thought. But she said: "I think we've been through this before. You defend Bové, but why don't you consider for a change what intensive farming brought to Brittany. It's called progress."

She was struggling to find her words, it had been a while since she'd had to hold down a conversation in French.

"Those Breton villages you love so much have been yanked out of the dark ages. It's thanks to progress that farmers have been able to do up their properties, and drive around in expensive 4x4s."

She came to an abrupt halt with a shrug. Marie-Christine's self-satisfied smirk was unchanged. She could almost hear Serge saying "José Bové is right."

Not long after she joined DeKripps, they had a testy exchange in which he defended the trashing of a French McDonalds. Susan might have agreed with them standing outside and shouting at customers, but she couldn't justify Bové breaking the law. She'd been vindicated when he was eventually sentenced to a jail spell.

Now, of course, more McDonalds burgers were sold in France than anywhere else outside America.

Marie-Christine had cupped a hand in front of her mouth and was muttering something to Jean-Louis, who was leaning back in his chair stroking his tummy. Susan heard *"les Anglo-Saxons."*

She was back on her hobby horse about the American multinationals, and their supposed quest for world domination. Susan knew that Jean-Louis agreed that globalisation was a threat, not an opportunity.

What's the point of having this argument again? They were just going round in circles. As for Bové, he's Frank's problem now. Poor Frank virtually had apoplexy every time he saw the "French poser" with his droopy Gallic moustache on the news.

Marie-Christine was twisting the head off a prawn and sucking its contents before adding it to the pile of translucent shells on her plate.

Susan finished tearing apart her crab and asked, "Dessert, anyone?" just as Jean-Louis began lining up his pills neatly on the tablecloth.

It was only after she left the restaurant that Susan realised her in-laws hadn't asked her about Mimi, and that she hadn't enquired after their children either.

As usual, nobody had asked about her job. For Serge's family, the notion of a career woman was beyond the pale. His late mother had made it plain from the start that she disapproved of foreigners, particularly one with a child out of wedlock. Marie-Christine had simply carried on the family tradition of closing ranks against the outsider.

They said polite goodbyes with the minimum two kisses on the cheeks on the pavement outside.

The in-laws didn't offer to accompany her to Dingé to visit Serge's grave. Had she expected them to? So, the next day she drove to the village alone.

Standing graveside brought back memories of the funeral which struck Susan so forcefully she found herself leaning on the granite cross for support.

She looked back towards the church, and mentally retraced their muddled procession down the hill to the tomb in the rain.

he remembered Camus and *The Outsider*, who hadn't cried at his mother's funeral. She'd been too numb to cry. But now there was no denying it: Here was Serge in the family plot. He was never coming back.

His name was spelled in full, Serge André Victor Gautier, and the dates of his birth and death – March 22nd 1962 – December 13th 2008 – carved into granite.

There had been no question of an inscription like "Beloved Husband of Susan", because, as Marie-Christine had told her during the preparations, "That's how we do things here".

The in-laws had also insisted there be no hymns, nor readings by friends. Her tentative suggestion that Lily might play at the service had been ruled out as *"trop..."*, as they raised their hands and eyebrows in surprise, but trop what had never been explained.

Why had she given in so easily? There was no point in fighting back. Serge had always wanted to be buried in his home village where his relatives made it plain she had no rights.

As she contemplated the grave, bare apart from a pot of white chrysanthemums, she couldn't decide whether the Gautier family's hostility towards her was personal, or directed against the British in general.

Her sister-in-law invariably took on an air of cultural superiority, whether trying to justify the existence of the two-pin electric plug or the bolster pillow.

How many times had she been subjected to Marie-Christine's refrain, "You come here, you buy our houses, you push up the prices, you bring over your own workmen, you don't contribute to the local economy."

And then there were the tiresome Joan of Arc jokes. Every time she offered to help out with a barbecue in the back garden in Dingy, one of them would ask if she wanted to burn them at the stake. *"Ah les Anglais,"* Marie-Christine would say, wagging a nail-varnished finger. "We can't trust you."

With a bit of luck, she had heard her last in-joke from the Gautiers about *Jeanne d'Arc*. But with Serge gone forever, she had to ask herself whom did *she* trust?

Chapter 9

"MUM YOU SHOULD go online, you know."

"I do go online. I just bought a cut-price sweater through the miracle of global communication."

Susan was juggling a cup of coffee and a bran muffin on a tray when Mimi had popped up on Skype, nose stud glittering in the Stygian gloom of the Wandsworth flat.

"That's not what I mean. You should try Internet dating, it's time you took the plunge again. Everyone does it."

"I know. But everyone's not me."

"I found my boyfriend online," said Mimi.

"You did *what*?"

So that's what accounted for the cheerfulness. This was two pieces of information at the same time: Her daughter had (a) ended a two-year fallow period having declared that she was through with men after being ditched by her last boyfriend, and (b) done so in the murky underworld of the Internet without, apparently, being killed or kidnapped. "When did this happen?"

"About a month ago."

"Okay. So never mind me – tell me all about him."

"There's not much to tell, really. He's a librarian."

Mimi explained that her boyfriend, Josh, was a PhD dropout – a couple of years older than she – who worked at the local library. At least he did until he started "borrowing" more books than he loaned, and now he was unemployed.

"So how often do you… see each other?"

"Well," said Mimi, "he's actually just moved in."

"That was quick, I must say." She squinted into her laptop in case the boyfriend could be seen in the shadows.

"Is he there now?"

"No, he had to go out."

"And what exactly are you going to live on?" A tone of sarcasm crept into her voice. "Because even the most valiant activists have bills to pay, you know. Banner printing, vegan shoes, voice projection…"

"Don't worry, we'll be fine. But look. This isn't about me. I was saying that you should find a man online."

"Look," she sighed. "I don't want to talk about that right now." She didn't have the stomach for another shouting match. She sensed that Mimi had had enough also. Her image disappeared with an electronic groan.

"God!" Susan snapped her laptop shut.

She padded round the apartment, fluffing the sofa cushions and smoothing out the duvet on her bed. Then she went to the bathroom and on impulse opened the cabinet and took out some dark cherry nail varnish she'd bought recently, a welcome sign that the tidal wave of grief might be receding.

But then a tear sprang onto her cheek, and she wiped it away. "How could you do this to me?" she said aloud, slamming the varnish down on the washbasin. Why had she bought this stuff anyway? There are Korean nail bars on every street corner. She took a deep breath, headed for the kitchen, switched on the radio and began painting her nails with an unsteady hand.

"Christ, I need a drink." Susan settled into the smooth leather booth at the Café Deluxe, and craned her neck in case she could catch sight of the cathedral.

"Nice place, right? So what's up?" Jessica crossed her legs and leaned in to listen in one smooth movement.

Susan sighed. She'd met her at Pilates, and the classes were obviously working better for Jessica than for her.

"I've got so much work on," she said. "It's pressure, pressure, pressure." Jessica looked disappointed.

She was a freelance interior designer, and not the slightest bit interested in politics, especially office politics, or the trials of working for a multinational. "I wasn't talking about work. What else is going on in your life, Susie? Are you ready to rumble yet?"

"Are you psychic? My daughter was just telling me I need to start trawling the Internet," she said. "But I'm damaged goods."

"Damaged goods? Don't be ridiculous! What's wrong with finding a boyfriend online anyway? Less chance of running into them when you split up," Jessica said. "You need a man, so check out the man store."

"Really? Have you?"

"Of course."

She was dumbfounded. If the lovely Jessica couldn't find a partner without going online, what hope was there for the rest of us?

"I don't know. Who's going to fall for me and my spare tyre?"

"Are you crazy? You're hot to trot, Susie."

"Aren't all the nice ones either gay or married?"

"Well, you won't know until you try." Jessica looked over the menu. "How does the seared salmon sound?"

For the rest of the evening, Susan probed her friend's knowledge of the various online dating sites, from the specialized Jewish and Christian ones, the uniform fetishists, the bondage consultants, the fee-chargers and the free, the places where the dater's profile is created by a friend, the marriage-or-your-money-backs, the good, the bad and the downright ugly.

Jessica finally admitted she had met her (now ex) boyfriend Randall on Partners 4 U. Susan had never thought to ask her where they met, they seemed so natural together. And then Jessica added that her sister, too, had found a partner in a chat room.

She wasn't expecting the first hurdle when she signed up that evening. She had to make up a name for herself. The ironic MsWhiplash? Already taken. The flirty MadamPerky? What, already taken too? The next task was to describe herself. This was going to take all night.

Signed on as Peek-a-boo, which to her sounded light-hearted and flirtatious, Susan rested her head on her hands. It needed to be witty and cliché-free while conveying her personality and the reason she was even in this cattle market.

They would be able to see her picture, so she wouldn't need to describe herself physically. She carefully picked a photo from before Serge's death, in which she was definitely a few pounds lighter. Oh no, that won't do. She flicked through the few photos she'd taken in DC. Here was a nice one of her in the Botanic Garden, no cleavage in sight. With a click, it was up.

As soon as she entered her date of birth, the pictures of "single" men began floating along the top of the screen. That was already an achievement, she hadn't expected any matches after entering her Washington zipcode. Everybody joked that you had more chance of being shot by a terrorist than finding a soulmate in DC. When did hair make a comeback, she wondered as she examined the photos. She laughed out loud when she noticed the site was automatically putting her desired age match as from 50 to 100.

She began, "Devastated by the death of my husband, 18 months ago" and paused. No, too tragic.

Before she had time to find the Edit button, her words had gone live. A message from a lugubrious guy with a moustache in Ohio.

"Hello dear, would you like to share your pictures?"

She was not getting the hang of this. A few minutes later she found Edit and tried again. Who was she looking for? Someone who wasn't frightened by freckles. Was that too flippant? She rubbed her eyes, wondering why she found this so hard. She was writing an ad, after all.

Tell us something about yourself, the site said. She'd better be honest. So she told the whole world, or at least the single men of Washington DC, about how she'd thought that Jimmy Granger had asked her for a kiss in the school playground because he was after her body. Then she found out all he wanted was to be introduced to her friend who lived next door.

Story of my life. I've always had friends who were prettier than I. Lily would certainly have no difficulty in attracting a long line of suitors if she were to try Internet dating. Maybe she had, already.

She found herself mesmerized by the floating photos. Some of those 50-year-olds were quite well preserved. But how could you judge from a picture? As Jessica had said, there's only one way to find out.

She stood nervously at the end of the boardroom table, looking through her notes. She was about to present the marketing plan for Guilty Secrets, the name of DeKripps' new product targeting rich professionals, to the company's senior executives. The CEO, known to everyone as Bubba, would be watching from DeKripps headquarters. It was a big moment and she had dressed for the occasion, her hair tamed in a switch.

She was excited by the launch. Barney, with the air of a conspirator, had presented the results of Project Candy to the strategy group a couple of weeks earlier. Each of them was given a chocolate, inside which was a piece of fresh fruit. Hers was mandarin. Judy, the communications chief, had a strawberry, and Randy, the lawyer, a blueberry. Barney stood back and savoured their reaction.

"Awesome," said Judy, licking her lips. Susan was equally impressed: "Can I have another? Just for comparison?"

"No. I want you marketing people hungry. Go away and remember the taste of that first bite. Think pleasure principle. An explosion tickling the taste buds."

"But this is fresh fruit," said Ellen, who had bitten into a raspberry chocolate and was holding it up to her eye. Susan, trying to analyse the sweet's slight fizziness which was almost like sherbet, was wondering simultaneously how they'd keep the product from going mouldy on the shelf.

"That's right," Barney said. "Fresh fruit. So how do we keep it fresh? By selling it in *fridges*. Once again, DeKripps has innovated with a special recipe and a very short sell-by date thanks to our technology and our balls. They are the first chocolates ever sold from the fridge. Wait till the folks at Chewers get their heads around that!"

When they were all assembled in the boardroom, Susan described the ad campaign, which would launch the golden boxes of Guilty Secrets on billboards across the country. There would also be a separate TV spot with the slogan: "Forbidden Fruits Taste Sweeter".

They'd agonised over the best outlet for the chocolates and had finally rejected supermarkets in favour of Partridge and Peartree. It was a gourmet grocery store, affectionately known to its customers as P and P, with only about a dozen branches in the major American cities.

It might be a risk but they'd decided less was more, taking into consideration the target demographic. The price was far higher than any other DeKripps chocolate products.

"Everyone has their fingers crossed," Susan said. "After licking them, that is."

The billboard ad was projected onto a screen that descended as the office blinds came down. A glamorous blonde in a blue silk dressing gown and heeled slippers was shining a torchlight on a half-opened golden box. By her side was a tousle-haired little boy in pyjamas. The DeKripps logo was almost invisible in a corner.

"You think of midnight feasts, and you want something you know you shouldn't have," Susan said. "Transgression makes the ad all the more powerful. It should resonate with both parents and their children."

She added, "You'll notice each chocolate is individually wrapped, which amplifies the secret pleasure inside."

The wall-mounted screen crackled. It was Bubba.

"Ms Perkins, I like this."

Every time she saw the elderly Quaker, she was reminded of his resemblance to his grandfather whose portrait hung in reception.

"Thank you sir," she said. "Are there any questions?" She glanced round the table.

"We just need to decide when to rollout, but apart from that, we're good," said Barney, smiling. Once any product had the CEO's approval, the rest fell into place.

"LA?" Barney asked, just for form.

"No problem," said Luke.

Someone wheeled a trolley into the boardroom. It was filled with boxes of Guilty Secrets and Barney beamed. "Help yourselves, folks," he said. They each took a box for home.

Susan opened hers before leaving the office. There were twelve little Guilty Secrets tucked inside. There was no flavour guide because DeKripps had decided to add to the mystery, teasing the consumer.

The first one she picked was strawberry. She ate it in one bite. Heaven. She had never tasted a boxed chocolate so exquisite. Next came mandarin, the flavour she'd first been given. By the time she left work, she'd already devoured half the box. Usually, if she ate so many chocolates in a row she'd feel sick, but she convinced herself she was really eating fruit, real fruit. Customers might even think it's good for them.

She was lifting the lid of the golden box again as she crossed the street to the entrance of her apartment building. A swishing noise made her look up.

"Watch out, dude! Coming through!" It was the leader of one of those annoying Segway tours, shouting out as the group swung past, forcing her to halt in the middle of the road.

"Look where you're going!" she screamed. They swarmed around her, laughing, and she was surrounded by the giant scooters and their upright riders. Their sudden appearance, and the speed at which they moved, could have easily knocked her off her feet. Reaching the safety of the curb, she shouted, "And I'm not a dude!" to their helmeted heads disappearing down the street towards the National Mall.

Susan's resolution to spend more time at the gym had somehow petered out. She needed a new trim figure to go with a new boyfriend, she said to herself, and Pilates wasn't producing results.

She waved Barney away when he offered her a lift in his black SUV one evening just as she'd changed into her running shoes and was setting out with her rucksack for Rock Creek Park, pulling in her tummy and straightening her spine.

She'd mentioned what she called her "social outreach" project to Ellen, who laughed, and said she had several friends who met their partners online. But she hadn't heard of Partners 4 U.

"In the end, it all comes down to chemistry," Ellen said. "That's all that counts, and you will know in an instant when you meet someone whether you're compatible or not. Never mind all those algorithms, never mind star signs, never mind judging a man by his shoes."

"I know, but how can you trust what you see? How do I know the guy calling himself 'Switchblade' on Partners 4 U isn't a knife-wielding serial killer even though he looks charming and lives in Old Town Alexandria, or at least says he does?"

"I guess you just have to be careful before you get an idea what makes them tick."

They lowered their voices as they chatted by the water fountain in the corridor, within earshot of the receptionist.

She asked how Ellen had met Jed. "Oh, the old fashioned way," she said. "We were sitting next to each other at a bar in Georgetown, and started chatting. Boring really. What about you and Serge?"

"He was sitting in my seat on a flight to Paris."

"Neat." Ellen began drifting down the corridor back to her office.

Susan called after her. "Do you think I'm putting on weight?" She smoothed down her pencil skirt and gave a half-twirl.

"It's hard to say," Ellen said. "You're tall, so if you were it wouldn't be noticeable really. Then again, maybe a tad? But voluptuous is good. Some guys like it."

That evening, Susan emptied the fridge of the remaining DeKripps chocolate bars which had provided her comfort over the last few months. They would have to make way for the new supply of Guilty Secrets anyway.

The fridge was always stocked with DeKripps products by the invisible housekeeper, paid by her employer, who also ensured that her carpets were always hoovered and her bed linen always clean.

Every time she logged on to Partners 4 U, she was overwhelmed by the number of men who wanted to interact. After the first week, she learned that 100 candidates for her affections had viewed her profile, had looked at her face and clicked on her goals and interests. And then came the comments.

"You look attractive and I think we would have a lot in common," said one, who identified himself as WorldTraveler77. Deleted! A couple of Brits messaged her after she admitted she was a foreigner in these parts. Some professed to like redheads. Were they fetishists?

Then there were the widowers. Maybe she shouldn't have mentioned Serge's death after all, they all seemed so wretched. And they were fixated with pets. One volunteered that he was looking for another mother for his children. Another, whose profile she viewed after he visited hers, offered "long, nostalgic chats" about their dead partners. She might not feel as cheerful as she sounded, but she couldn't imagine drowning her sorrows with any of them. And finally, there were the cigar smokers. She'd already had one smoker in her life, and look what had happened to him.

Eventually she took the plunge, contacting a mysterious 'Lamartine' with thin lips and possibly a wig, who appeared to have a French connection. After a desultory exchange about Catherine Deneuve and how hard it was to see French films in Washington, the dialogue dried up.

She called Jessica. "Look, nothing's happening."

"Be patient, you can't expect a miracle overnight. It's like buses, first none then three in a row, right?"

The dating site started to feel like homework, checking in as night fell and numbly dashing off the required text.

Then, one evening, Peek-a-boo received a message from

Somebody called Warlord.

"Self-deprecating humor is my favorite thing," he wrote, obviously an American by the spelling. Warlord didn't look like his username. He was trim, slightly balding with grey hair and according to his profile was 6 feet tall and a lawyer from Chevy Chase. He was apparently divorced and admitted to two grown children. "I'm not looking for a soulmate, just someone who lets the good times roll," he said, signing his message Paul. He was 45, two years older than she.

I used to have a sense of humour and a zest for life, she thought. But what a cliché about letting the good times roll. She could add "fun-loving", "free-wheeling" and "laid back" to the most overused adjectives on the site.

What caught her attention about Paul was that he too had an obsessive interest in supermarket labels. Hers was a perfectly legitimate professional curiosity, but what about him? A health nut with OCD?

She scrutinized Paul's photo, which she found strangely compelling. She was reminded of something friends had said when adopting, that a remarkable bonding occurred as soon as they saw a picture of the child who was to be theirs.

But Warlord—really? He wanted to come across as commanding, confident, bellicose even. Would he sweep her off her feet? She'd never gone for that self-assertive kind of guy – and there was no shortage of them at work. But there was always a first time. Maybe it's time to break the mould, she said to herself.

Susan felt self-conscious as she walked to their date at a bar near Dupont Circle. Partners 4 U advised subscribers to stick to public places for a first meeting.

"Go for a drink," Jessica had instructed. It was preferable to a restaurant – all that food to get through, and wasted time and calories if it didn't work out.

She wore trousers rather than jeans, so she wasn't too casual for the encounter. She decided against lipstick, in case he got the wrong impression. Her moss-green jacket highlighted her eyes.

Paul was sitting by the fireplace when she walked in and recognized him instantly from his photo. He was actually better looking than his picture, although he seemed older. He definitely didn't look like a warlord.

When she reached him and stretched out her hand, he stood and planted a peck on each cheek. "The European way," he said. She breathed his heady aftershave and took in his slightly high-pitched voice. Not a promising start. But it was only when he moved to sit again that she noticed the limp. All of a sudden, she was no longer interested in his theories about supermarket labelling.

"So, tell me about yourself."

She was glad the bar was empty and nobody could eavesdrop on their getting-to-know-yous.

"Okay," he pipped. "I do patents for a law firm."

Did her disappointment show?

"Business dropped off a bit in the recession. Law firms are always the first hit as you probably know. But we're bouncing back again now, thank God."

"Hmm, patents," she said, "that sounds interesting."

She clutched at another straw. "And children?"

He had two boys. One was in the army, the other a hairdresser-turned-writer.

"What about yourself?" It was her turn. She ticked off the social CV: Degree in psychology, focus groups, American food multinational, poisoning the world, alienating the daughter, husband dead, moved to America.

"The rest is history," she added with a smile.

"Escaping your troubles?"

She didn't reply. "And were you also in the army? It's

often the way, I suppose, in families."

"I was indeed an army brat. My father moved all over the place with the military." So that was the military background explained. "But I managed to escape Vietnam because of my childhood polio. I had office duties."

Childhood polio? How old was this guy?

And there it was. How could she ever contemplate being intimate with someone so removed from her?

Their conversation faltered towards best wishes for the future and within the hour she was heading home.

That night, she dreamed she was running through a field of eye-level corn. But was she being chased or was she chasing someone? Too late, she realised she was on a cliff edge. Somehow the coastline of Brittany had been transported to the American Midwest.

She saw Serge climbing down over the edge. She opened her mouth to scream, but no sound came.

She was wearing a blue dress with a full skirt, and as she fell, it lifted like a parachute. Her stomach lurched. She pedalled frantically as she dropped.

In the split second before she woke up, her heart thumping, she looked down to the waves, expecting to see Serge's body floating there, expecting to join him, expecting peace. But instead of him, Barney was looking up at her, grinning like the demented gnome from *Don't Look Now*. She lay there in the darkness, unable to shake off the notion that he'd tried to lure her to her death.

Chapter 10

SUSAN WAS MAKING her way down the chocolate aisle at a P Street supermarket. It was lunch hour and she was pushing an empty trolley, pretending to shop but hovering a pencil over a red notebook.

She liked to compare the processed foods on display, to see how the DeKripps products were placed, and to note what the competition was up to. Sometimes after her inspections she would report back to her staff for follow-up action. Sometimes she would go upstairs for a cupcake.

She picked up a bar of Chewers' Ecuadorian chocolate and checked the sugar content. The DeKripps bars, which even she found suspiciously tasty, were at eye-level. That was good. But she noticed a new so-called organic brand on the same shelf. She took one of the orange bars and noted the facts: Only 11 grams of sugar. That was far less than the DeKripps version, and her company was the brand leader. We're giving the customer what they want, she thought, remembering Frank's words, as she pushed her trolley back to the entrance, noticing the Buried Treasure bars at the checkout. DeKripps' marketing studies showed invariably that most people actually don't like healthy food.

She'd persuaded Jessica to accompany her that night to the Politics and Prose bookstore to hear Bill Kramer promote *Sickly Sweet: How We Fell In Love with Toxic Sugars*. Jessica, who was interested in what she put inside her shiny little body only up to a point, had reluctantly agreed. She'd never heard of Kramer.

When they arrived it was standing room only at the back of the store, rows of folding chairs laid out in front. Was there so much interest in this issue? She scanned the room, hoping none of her colleagues had shown up. The audience was mainly young, students probably, which set her mind at ease. Hardly anyone in the audience was overweight. If any of them asked the author about DeKripps, it certainly wasn't going to be her.

Kramer stuck to generalities in his pitch. He was a small guy in his late 50s with a slight stammer, which might make him a less than compelling speaker. But his audience was riveted. They looked as though they were hearing this stuff for the first time.

Kramer said he was interested in taking questions, so he raced through his theories on how added sugars in sufficient quantities are toxic because of the way they are metabolized by the liver, essentially poisoning the blood. He threw in his usual shtick comparing sugar to cocaine.

"Two white powders, but which one's addictive? They both are," he said, pausing. "They're both mind-altering drugs. Does anyone know how many names for added sugar there are?"

He stuttered on *shh-shh-sugar*. Nobody spoke.

"Twenty one! And they're all on the FDA website. Take a look one day. Check the Food Facts on what you eat. Particularly the real villain, High Fructose Corn Syrup. Thanks to the slippery food corporations, the list is getting longer all the time."

As he warmed to his theme, the stammer disappeared. It must have been nervousness, she realised, noticing that he was sweating. He concluded with a crescendo, raising his voice when he talked about the obesity epidemic: "Sugars aren't just empty calories. They're vicious and vile. They're cancer's favourite environment. They're killing us."

She glanced at Jessica. Although she was moving from one foot to another in her stilettos, she was hooked.

Susan was relieved that Kramer had stopped short of accusing added sugars of actually causing obesity and diabetes. Nevertheless it was an indictment of her industry, and the book must be even more virulent. Of course Kramer wasn't the first to identify sugars as the culprit – poor Yudkin had done that in the 70s, the first on the DeKripps hit-list – but she had to admit he rolled out a convincing argument.

The questions came swiftly. There were queries about diet, about legislation, about what should be done. He wanted the FDA to be more proactive, but he also called for more effective self-regulation by the food manufacturers. She noticed one of the audience was typing on his laptop. Was that Alex Levy, the food blogger? There used to be a picture of him pasted on a toilet brush holder in the staff loos at DeKripps London.

Know thy enemy. She picked up a copy of the book before she and Jessica left the store and headed across the street for a pizza. She didn't join the queue for Kramer to sign it.

The sun was sinking behind the apartment block, warming the fringes of the supermarket sign across the street. But this time she walked past the store entrance and took a piece of paper from her bag to check the address, before mounting a short run of steps. She looked down the list of names until she found Jenny Holland. Nervously, she pushed the buzzer and the door swung open.

"Hi, I'm Susie," she told the middle-aged woman who let her in. "Hi. Jenny. Come in and meet the others."

It felt like Alcoholics Anonymous. A group of six or seven women was standing in the living room where light poured in through large windows. "Everyone, this is Susie. Now we can get started," said Jenny, gesturing to a circle of chairs.

"You all know why you're here, but your own experience of grief will be different from the person next to you. You've got one thing in common, though – you're all young widows. Why don't you each tell me a bit about what happened?"

Susan listened to the familiar stories about death and loss from Planet Grief. There was so much with which she could identify. Every one of them was otherwise happy, healthy, lively. There were professional women like her but more recently bereaved. One had watched her spouse die a protracted and agonizing death from cancer.

Another, Lori, said her husband had dropped dead from a ruptured brain aneurysm as they walked to the car together. "Nobody tells you that you don't need to reply to every letter of condolence," she said. Susan glanced at Jenny. You mean you didn't have to write to everyone? That had been one of her most stressful tasks when Serge had died. Lori also mentioned that she used the services of a bereavement company which had sorted out all of her late husband's papers. If only she'd known. Nobody tells you how to grieve.

When her turn came, she prefaced her remarks by saying that her husband had been French. "Well, nobody's perfect," said one of the women, and they all laughed gently. "I thought I was okay, but I'm definitely not okay," she said, "and he's been dead for eighteen months."

She spoke about her guilt over not being there when Serge had driven to his death, so close to their home. She talked about the despair that had torn her apart after the initial period when everything seemed completely pointless.

"I have a psychology degree, so I kind of knew what to expect. We were taught all about the five stages of grief, but I hadn't expected that after denial and anger and negotiation and depression and oh God, what was the other one?"

"Acceptance," somebody called out.

"Thanks, yes, acceptance, they begin to blur and mingle and hit you all at once. I did think I would get through this by myself, but I suppose I'm here because I've changed my mind."

"Don't worry," said Jenny, who kept quiet during much of the session, "there's no right way to handle grief. Everyone's experience is different."

It was what her mother had said after her father was killed. "I know," she went on, "but I just want to know when it will end. If someone had told me eighteen months ago that I would still be crying at night, I would never have believed them."

"That's perfectly normal," Jenny said. "It will take time, believe me. You will heal, but you'll do it slowly. And it will get easier."

She went on to explain how she had decided to come to Washington to reinvent herself, how she no longer trusted her instinct. "My boss said I was impulsive, crazy to extract myself from my support network. Here, nobody knew Serge, which I thought would help, but it also means I don't have anyone to confide in. It's almost as though he never existed, which makes me feel even worse."

"Now, Jasmine, what would you like to share?" Jenny asked the only black woman in the room. She opened her mouth to speak but no sound came out. She began sobbing, her eyes fixed on the carpet.

Another woman began to cry too, as her own memories resurfaced. Then they all struggled to stop their lips trembling.

"It's alright," said Jenny. She took in the others with her gaze, while Jasmine recomposed herself. "But, you are allowed to laugh too, you know. And you shouldn't feel guilty when you do. You've all got the right to a life after death."

Another woman, an outwardly buoyant blonde in a dark trouser suit and heels, told the group how she was struggling so much with grief herself that she was neglecting her two young children who had fallen behind with their homework.

"The school has been great but nobody has a clue how a child is supposed to grieve."

Susan remembered from university that if a child wasn't able to take the necessary time to grieve, emotional problems and learning difficulties could show up years later. If she and Serge had had a child, the brother or sister he had wanted for Mimi, they would have been school age now. But it had never happened, and by the time she reached forty they both knew it never would. It hadn't mattered that much to her because they had each other.

Jasmine was talking about Facebook. She was disturbed by her husband's profile, which was still on the site along with his comments and photos of their last holiday in Orlando. Another said that friends had turned her spouse's page into a shrine, with pictures of candles and recollections. Jasmine had written to Facebook which had offered to "memorialise" the page, effectively freezing it in time. "But it gives me the heebie jeebies to see Terrance's picture. I can't handle it."

"You can ask them to delete it altogether, if that's what you'd prefer," Jenny said.

Serge wasn't on Facebook, thank goodness. That was one less problem to deal with. Like most of the mothers she knew, Susan had joined the site to monitor what Mimi was up to, but her daughter had refused to "friend" her.

She lingered beneath the pink cherry blossom on Logan Circle on her way back to her apartment. I'm normal. So that's okay.

For some reason, her thoughts turned to her mother. How

well did she really know her? She'd suffered the double blow of a divorce from Susan's father, followed by his horrendous death in that motorway accident, but she never talked about her feelings. In fact, had Serge not died, she would never have known about her mother's recourse to bereavement counselling.

Mimi had always called her grandmother the "Merry Widow", but now Susan realised nothing could be further from the truth. She was only just beginning to understand.

As she neared home, she had a sudden craving for chocolate. Luckily, she had exactly what she needed in the fridge.

She logged onto the computer while licking some Delight chocolate ice cream from a spoon. Her mind was on the lessons of the widows' group. She wanted to talk to Mimi. To her surprise, she answered her Skype call. Susan screwed up her eyes to look into the ill-lit flat. Was Josh around?

"Actually, he is."

A figure moved out of the shadows and waved at the screen. She waved back. He seemed open and friendly, not prickly like Mimi. He had a shaved head, a long neck, big round eyes and a pointed chin, a bit like a meerkat. He wore a dark woolly V neck jumper over a T-shirt, although she couldn't make out the colour. At least the pair of them weren't running up electricity bills.

She wasn't used to being introduced to Mimi's boyfriends. But the unemployed librarian had an easy manner. They had scarcely had time for the introductions before Mimi announced that time was up.

"By the way," she said, as her pixelated image vanished, "Josh knows all about Serge and Camus."

Chapter 11

"SO, LOOKING FOR love, are we?"

It was Barney.

"Everyone's looking for love," she said coolly. He had stepped inside her office and shut the door. "What's up, Barney? Do you want to talk turkey? Or salt?"

She stood up and moved round her desk to open the door. That was a mistake. Her boss blocked her path, smiling. He was treating this as a game. But she was increasingly nervous.

Susan cleared her throat. This was America in 2010 after all. "Look Barney, I think there must be some misunderstanding."

He reached for her. She could feel his hot breath close to her cheek. His hand made its way down to her waist to her bottom and he was pulling her towards him. She managed to sit on the edge of her desk and was trying to grab something with which to deter him. She felt a biro between her fingers. Could she stab him with that? Then a picture frame came within her grasp. But her squirming had only increased his ardour. Finally, she managed to push him away with her knees, and he stumbled backwards. She stood up to her full height and glared at him in silence.

"This is just between you and me, isn't it, Susie? Consenting adults. You're not going to go running to HR now, are you?" At least he was aware of the risk.

She walked to the door, opening it with a flourish. She summoned up her most clipped British accent to say, "Of course not. Carry on."

And with that, he smirked and was gone.

Only a few seconds had passed but Susan was panting from stress. She picked up her phone and ran down the six flights of stairs to the street, pushing through the revolving doors.

"He did *what*?" came Lily's reaction. She'd just finished a performance at a music circle in Cheltenham.

"Just bear with me," she said as she moved to a quieter spot. "You must go straight to your personnel department and complain. This is utterly inappropriate behaviour."

"But what can I do? I promised I wouldn't go to HR. Even though he's such a sleazebag, he's got hiring and firing power over me, and it would be his word against mine. And actually, nothing really happened."

"Eew, Susie, gross. What you don't know is that maybe he's got a reputation. He's obviously a predatory male and you might not be the only victim."

"What did he mean by 'looking for love'?"

"Come on. He's on your dating site. He saw your profile."

It made sense. "Oh my God. Miss Peek-a-boo! I could die from shame. But he's married. What's he doing on a singles' site?"

"Predatory male, you see," Lily said.

Susan was aware that people who complained about discrimination or harassment in the office invariably lost their job – not always directly, but eventually they'd enter a kind of unspoken professional quarantine. Having ascended to within sight of the corporate summit at DeKripps, why should she jump now?

But Lily was baffled: Why would Barney be so rash as to make a pass at her in the office? "What is he smoking?"

She agreed that had they been in a bar or restaurant she might have less of a case. Then it could be argued presumably that through her membership of an online dating site she had put herself in a situation where he may have legitimately surmised that she might fancy him.

"It's so reckless. Anyone might have walked in."

"I know. I really think that's the end of it, though."

"Are you going to be alright?"

"Don't worry about me." She switched off the phone and returned to work. It struck her that she was the one who had been looking for a partner online. Was Barney really the guilty party after all?

She tried to maintain a brisk professional exterior in her dealings with him in the days that followed. DeKripps was preparing a relaunch of a popular yoghurt, which had a picture of a fat but contented bear on the pot. But she was starting to have misgivings about the promise contained in its "new improved flavour" which could not reasonably include any more sugar.

She went to see Barney with the results of a comparative survey on the sweetness of yoghurts. He took his feet off the desk when she walked in, put on his reading glasses and skimmed the conclusions.

"Sugar, HFCS, salt, we've got to get ahead of this, Susie, before the regulators start a witch-hunt."

Barney had made things easier for her by showing no outward sign whatsoever that he had the slightest recollection of groping her in her office. He must think he's untouchable.

"Of course," she said. "By the way, did you see that Michelle Obama doesn't want her kids to eat HFCS?"

He raised his eyes to the ceiling, and said nothing. Susan had already guessed he wasn't a Democrat. But at the moment he was actively cultivating a senior Democratic senator in hopes of leading him into a policy U-turn.

"Everyone has their price," he predicted. It wouldn't take long for the senator to lose his scruples and drop like a ripe, genetically modified tomato into his outstretched hand. She couldn't help noticing the size of his hands before turning on her heel. She'd felt the warmth of one of them splayed on her buttock. She shuddered inwardly at the memory.

She'd checked Lily's theory about Barney. Back on Partners 4 U she looked up 50-year-old men looking for 40-year-old women. A picture of him appeared straight away. He was "Silverado" from Georgetown, aged 51, and single. How many other men were cheating on their wives on this site?

Susan's phone rang. It was Frank calling from London.

"How's the flame-haired temptress?" She smiled at the reference from *Private Eye*, and Frank had always prided himself on his cultural onions after so many years in England. "Are you dating?"

If only you knew, she thought. But she couldn't help launching into a description of her experiences online.

"As you can imagine, men are falling over themselves," she said, hearing him laugh. She told him about one email exchange which had led to a drink with an architect named Bill, who had convinced himself that he'd be more attractive if he joked about his other dates. "I mean he was telling me about this stunningly beautiful girl who left via the bathroom of his hotel. Can you believe it?"

Frank was tut-tutting in the background. She told him about Scott, an estate agent who forgot to set a date on the phone because he was so busy talking about his personal influence on the property prices in downtown DC.

"I've actually arranged a meeting with a management consultant from Virginia, but to be quite honest it feels too much like work. You know what, Frank, I'm far too busy to think about dating," she added. "But if Mister Right comes along, I wouldn't say no. Although in this heat, I'm not sure that I'll ever be able to step out of the aircon and actually meet him. I'm wilting."

"I wouldn't worry if I were you. Plenty more fish in the sea, Susie."

"Isn't that a dating site? You mean I should try that one?"

They laughed again and their conversation returned to work. Susan told Frank about the results of her yoghurt study. "The other thing I'm wondering about is bread," she said.

"You want to put sugar in baguettes? Good luck with that. That effeminate French poser would have us shot." She was reminded that for people like Frank and Barney, all European men were "effeminate".

As though reading her thoughts, he asked, "How's Barney?"

She told him he was busy with the Guilty Secrets launch, which by all accounts was going extremely well. She didn't mention the incident in her office.

"But you know Barney. He's terrorizing everyone." She recounted a recent meeting between him and a Congressman from Nebraska. "He actually told the poor man, 'I own you'."

"Well, I guess he does," Frank said, "DeKripps donates enough to keep those guys on the campaign trail in the Midwest. He did good in the Scrutineer, by the way."

The Barbara Miles story had led to an editorial in the New York Scrutineer praising DeKripps for reducing HFCS in soda. "There's been the usual whining on Twitter, of course," Frank added.

She didn't mention that she'd gone to see Kramer, the devil himself, in Washington.

"Barney's calmed down a bit now. He knows it's all publicity. People remember the brand," she said. "Thing is, where do we go from here?"

"Actually, here in the UK, salt's gotten bigger than sugar right now," he said. "We might have to make some gesture on that before too long."

"Anyway, keep cool," were his parting words. "We miss you."

"Miss you all too."

She was standing under the shower, rubbing herself down with a body scrub, keeping an eye on the laptop on her bed in case Mimi called.

She found herself thinking about Barney and his ominous threat about Kramer at the end of the strategy meeting. Could DeKripps really ruin his life? In the light of the incident in the office, she saw a man who felt he was above the law. Look at Bill Clinton and Monica Lewinsky; lies, blustering and denial, in the face of unprecedented scrutiny and public censure.

In the case of Barney, he might just get away with it. What was it he had said to her? "Consenting adults." There went her defence. At least he hadn't called her Peek-a-boo. Imagine that being mentioned in court.

Susan recalled a guy in the London office who managed to escape sexual harassment charges not long after she joined DeKripps. He would grope women at the Christmas party, and because of his senior position was quite open about it. One day, he was walking through the office, plopped himself down on the corner of one of the secretaries' desks and said, "Have I fucked you yet?"

Susan would never forget the woman's reply. She had looked up and said matter-of-factly, "I can't remember." Both had since left the company.

She stepped out of the shower and studied her thickening waist in the mirror. Time to get back into a new fitness routine. She should ring Jessica and join her for a workout.

She was in her dressing gown, emptying the dishwasher, when her laptop brayed. She ran into the living room, and there was Mimi, her face distorted by her proximity to the computer screen.

"Hi Ma, what are you doing today? It's 11 o'clock and you're not dressed."

"Well, it's Saturday, I don't have to do anything if I don't want to."

"In any case," she added, "it's mosquito season. And they seem to have my address. Or my *add*ress, as they say here."

She said she'd be staying in the cool, either at home or at a movie. In fact she had no plans for the entire weekend.

"No hot date on a Saturday night?"

"Give me a break. What's happening in Wandsworth? Are books back in fashion?"

"At least Josh doesn't kill people in his profession," said Mimi. "But to answer your question, yes, he's still job hunting."

"And maybe now you could tell me what exactly Josh knows about Serge and Camus?" Her voice was cold. How could there be something new about someone she and Mimi had known so intimately?

"Well, he looked him up the Internet. And loads of links came up to articles about Camus he'd written. He was also on panels with top French academics."

"Fascinating," Susan said, relieved. "You know, Serge was at a conference on Camus the day we met?"

Mimi went on, "Anyway, it turns out that Serge was one of key figures who helped rehabilitate Camus. That was the word. Rehabilitate."

"You're kidding. Fancy that, he never mentioned it."

She felt a pang of guilt for not having shown more interest in her husband's academic activities.

"But why did he need rehabilitating? Serge always said he was a better writer than Sartre."

"He suffered from negative comparisons with Sartre,

mainly put about by Sartre himself, according to Serge. He told me that himself when I was doing my A levels."

Susan recalled coming home from work to find her daughter deep in conversation with Serge - their *"messes basses"* as the French say - at the kitchen table, where he would sit smoking a cigarette to unwind from school before preparing dinner for the three of them. She, the "Madame workaholic", was always the last to arrive home on a weekday.

"It's funny, I was thinking quite a lot about *L'Etranger* after he died. I'd fallen into a bottomless pit but I felt nothing at the same time."

"Yes. Well you might find *La Peste* even more relevant then, in your new life," Mimi said. It had only taken a few minutes and she was twisting the knife again. Susan hadn't read the book she was referring to, but her daughter was obviously about to remind her that she was responsible for an epidemic.

"Speaking of my new life, are you ever going to come over and see for yourself?"

She heard a door slam shut.

"It's Josh," Mimi said. "Got to go. By the way, did you know you're putting on weight?" And she disappeared from sight.

Susan sat staring at the darkened screen while she calmed down. So Mimi was interested in Camus too. The connection was intriguing. A French Algerian and a young English activist born decades after he was writing about alienation and the absurd. Was that what had attracted her to Josh? Was that Serge's legacy?

It began to make sense, in a Mimi kind of way.

She switched on the radio. It was 'Wait, Wait, Don't Tell Me', the weekly radio quiz show. She looked at the clock on the wall and noticed she had only missed the first few minutes. Getting dressed would have to wait.

For the rest of the weekend she brooded about Mimi's throwaway comment. Having savoured *haute cuisine* in France and left her long expense account lunches behind in London, good eating had been replaced by comfort food. It was hard to resist the delights of her fridge—a box of Guilty Secrets might as well have been glued to her fingers. She polished off the last few while standing in the kitchen. I'm bereaved after all, she thought.

On Monday morning, she made an appointment with her doctor. A nurse checked her blood pressure – 120 over 80 – and weight. One hundred and sixty pounds. A little on the heavy side for someone measuring 5 feet 8. Susan looked peevishly at the nurse.

"I can't even blame my shoes," she said, having taken them off before stepping onto the machine. She had put on nearly a stone in the year since she had arrived in DC. But she suspected that most of it had been in the last few weeks.

She sat in the surgery while Doctor Osborn peppered her with questions. Did she smoke? No. Drink? Five glasses a week, she said, cutting her real alcohol consumption by half. Large or small? Large, she admitted.

The doctor raised her eyes from the question sheet and peered over her glasses at Susan.

"Well, I'm a European, and my husband was French."

The doctor's smile was frosty. They proceeded to discuss her family history. There was no cancer or diabetes that she knew of.

"What's your primary source of protein?"

Susan thought for a moment. "Cheese, probably. But I also eat meat and fish." Susan explained that she worked at DeKripps. "I reckon I have quite a balanced diet, actually, for someone in the food industry."

"What about exercise?"

"I do quite a bit of walking."

"I meant exercise. Cardio."

Susan shrank a little in her chair. She'd been so busy at work. But she told the doctor about her new resolve.

"I did step onto the treadmill yesterday, but..."

"How many minutes?"

"Maybe ten." The doctor wrote it down on her chart.

"Twenty minutes is the minimum if you want to see some benefit."

A few days later, she was back at the doctor's where she was told that her blood-sugar level was "dangerously high".

"You mean I'm at risk of diabetes?"

"If you're careful with your diet, you can avoid it," Doctor Osborn said. "So if I were you I'd watch those carbs. Cut back on bread, potatoes, pasta. Anything starchy turns rapidly into sugar, topping up what you already consume in pastries, ice cream, soda and cookies. And wine."

And chocolates. Wait until Mimi hears about this. I've poisoned the world, myself included.

Chapter 12

THE OFFICE HAD been buzzing for days but now Barney had called a handful of executives to a post-launch briefing on the success of Guilty Secrets.

Susan and Judy were standing by the ficus in a corner of his office, discussing a planned press release, and swapping anecdotes about the launch.

Susan had been in Partridge and Peartree in Georgetown, where she almost got into a fight with a woman over the last box of Guilty Secrets in the fridge.

"It was like she was demented," she said. "She was one of those social X-rays. Skinny. Extremely sharp elbows."

"Did she win?"

"I let her. I think. I knew there would be plenty more at home."

Judy described a similar encounter at the store, where she had spotted a tall, thin woman dressed head to toe Gucci by the fridge. She'd said to Judy, "Have you tried these? My children have been pestering me for more."

"That spells success to me," said Susan. "Families like that are our bread and butter."

They looked round as Barney came in, a wide smile on his face. He noticed them in the corner.

"Susan, Judy," he called out, as he gestured with his index finger to the chairs. It was the first time Susan could remember him treating her as a subordinate in front of colleagues.

"Are we all here?"

The video showed nervous-looking executives in LA and Kansas. As usual, Barney had found a way to stand in the very centre.

"Right, gang, what we have here is a major triumph. It's

huge. Guilty Secrets are flying out of the stores. From LA to the Big Apple. The scientists can barely keep up."

What's it got to do with scientists, Susan wondered, but before she could ask, Barney had moved on.

"This vindicates marketing completely," – he gave the slightest nod in Susan's direction, which she acknowledged – "and has given DeKripps a decisive edge over Chewers who so far are still scratching their asses. It's hard to see how they could respond quickly and effectively to Guilty Secrets. It's the dream product. So what we're going to do now is rub their noses in it."

He turned to Judy and began to read sales figures from Partridge and Peartree. The bestselling Guilty Secret stores were in California and New York, which in the first month had sold more than 18,000 boxes. And the same customers were coming back for more. It wasn't a lot compared to other DeKripps sales, Susan thought. They were selling millions of boxes of cereals and chocolate bars. But given the price of Guilty Secrets and the high end of the market, client loyalty would be an unexpected bonus.

"OK, Judy?"

"OK, Barney."

"Get this straight. This is a story to shout from the rooftops. Particularly in the direction of Chewers' rooftops. And the rooftop of any tree hugger with a food blog. So tweet it, too."

The group was dismissed.

Resurfacing from her office for a break a little later, Susan bumped into Barney at the soft drinks machine. He punched the buttons furiously before a plastic bottle of recycled water rattled into the tub. She chose an apricot Angeljuice.

"Did you go to the White House reception last night?"

"Sure did," he said.

The event had been held outside in the Rose Garden.

Susan asked whether he had met the Obamas.

"They came in together, and worked the room. But they only stayed for five, ten minutes, the usual."

"I wouldn't know. I'm still a White House virgin, I'm afraid."

"I buttonholed one of the First Lady's aides about anti-obesity. She denied of course that DeKripps was being targeted. Can you believe those people? It's like they've all drunk the Kool Aid. And the media assholes swallow it. *We decided from the outset,*" he mimicked squeakily, "*that Let's Move would be a positive enlightenment program. We're not going after anyone. We're setting an example to young people, it's all about education.*" Yadda, yadda, yadda. Education, my ass!"

He turned on his heel. As he returned to the office with his coffee, she heard him mutter, "Black bitch!" before slamming the door behind him.

Susan unscrewed her Angeljuice and stood for a moment, staring into the yellow mouth of the bottle.

Susan badly wanted Mimi to visit – without the unemployed librarian in tow – but she knew it would be weighted with the same tension as their conversations on Skype. So she was relieved when her daughter said she'd sorted out lodgings for a couple of weeks in June with a friend who worked for Code Pink, a group of feminist activists.

They were famous locally for disrupting Congressional hearings by holding up placards calling for an end to the war in Afghanistan, dressed head to toe in pink. Susan had seen them on the news, Capitol police escorting them quietly from the chamber.

She picked Mimi up from Dulles airport and couldn't help clinging to her daughter as she came into the Arrivals hall. Mimi, her hair piled around her face, was as pallid as ever in her boots and black tights.

"I've missed you." Mimi wriggled out of her embrace and she kissed a mouthful of lacquer. She led her to her rental car outside, wondering why she had so much luggage for such a short stay.

"Have you brought Josh in there?" she asked. She suspected it might even be fancy dress for some kind of activism. "Or are you loaded with presents for me?"

"Very funny."

Mimi gave her the address of her friend who lived just off H St, a neighbourhood close to Capitol Hill where Susan had seen reports of shootings and car-jackings.

"It's full of media people now," Mimi said. "Creatives. Keep up."

They crossed the tramline under construction and pulled up outside a shabby house with two wooden chairs on the veranda.

"This is it," said Mimi. "Thanks for the lift."

"So when shall I see you?"

"I'll call you."

After three anxious days, she finally received a phone call. Mimi agreed to join her for supper at her apartment, posing again the delicate problem of what she could possibly cook. Once, forgetting that eggs were prohibited, she'd offered an omelette. "Do you expect me to eat the menstruation of hens?" Mimi had said. It was almost enough to put Susan off eggs for life.

Mimi roamed round the apartment, plopping herself down on the sofa where she plumped the cushions. "It looked bigger online," she said as she took in the living room, pulled a face at the Modigliani and stretched out her long skinny legs.

Before Susan could speak, she made for the bedroom, where she picked up a photo of Susan and Serge, taken on their favourite beach in Brittany, and examined it carefully.

Susan followed her.

"Well, I don't need a big place just for me. And I'm not having many dinner parties these days. In fact, most of the time, I order in."

"That's why you put on weight," Mimi said. "All that fast food. Did you tell the doctor?"

"That's irrelevant now. What counts is what I've been eating *since* seeing the doctor." She didn't mention the new delivery of Guilty Secrets in the fridge. She went into the kitchen and put out a salad of tossed lettuce leaves and beans, and pulled out a chair for Mimi.

"So when will I get to meet Josh? How is he?"

Mimi shrugged. "He's OK. He's finding it tough to find a job, so he spends most of his time online, doing research and stuff like that. He's had a few interviews but so far nothing. Loads of his friends are out of work too."

She knew she should ask Mimi about her work, although she didn't want to pry. Besides, she might be scared by the answer. Sometimes it was best not to know.

"What are you working on at the moment, Mimi?"

"We're mostly crowdsourcing stuff."

"Really? Cutting edge," she said, realizing too late that her tone might have betrayed her. There was a long silence.

"How do you feel really, anyway?" Mimi asked eventually.

"To tell you the truth, I just feel empty inside. It's as though something has switched off. I miss him so much. So many times I've been on the point of speaking to him when I wake up."

It was probably more than she had wanted to admit to her daughter, but Mimi seemed to know what she meant.

"I miss him too. I dreamed about him the other night. It was as though he was there, completely real, it was weird, we were walking along the Embankment together. Then he began moving backwards and when I turned round he'd gone. I felt bereft. But it must be worse for you."

She reached across the table for Mimi's hand, which her daughter didn't snatch away. Such moments were rare. She wanted to fold her in her arms, but carried on holding her hand whose index finger was dwarfed by a pewter skull and crossbones ring.

"Sometimes I dream about him too," she said. "It's so real. But they're mainly anxiety dreams. I don't know if it's worse when I dream about him, or when I don't."

"Me neither." The moment passed. Mimi gently withdrew her hand and took their plates to the sink.

"That's okay, I'll put them in the dishwasher," Susan said.

She asked Mimi what her plans were during her stay. Her daughter was vague, as usual. "We could have brunch at the weekend, if you like," Susan said, adding: "We could have Mimosas."

"You know I don't drink."

"I know, that was a joke. Hey, miss sourpuss, lighten up, will you?" She spoke more sharply than she'd intended.

"Chocolate?" she asked. Mimi shook her head.

"Anyway, it's time I got back." And with that, Mimi picked up her things, accepted the money for a cab without saying thank you, and left for her lodgings.

The sound of Dancing Queen rang out while Susan and Mimi were walking through the Naval Academy grounds in Annapolis.

It was coming from Susan's handbag.

"Why do you have that stupid ringtone?"

"I have to get this. Just a sec. And it's ironic, actually, if you hadn't noticed." She silenced her phone and moved out of her daughter's earshot, standing with her back to her.

Mimi had shown zero enthusiasm for their excursion to the former colonial capital. She was more interested in the capri pants at recession-knockdown prices in a Chicos store than in admiring the deep blue stained glass windows of the academy chapel.

After a few minutes of strained silence sitting in a pew, Susan said: "Right, let's have a bite of lunch. I'll have to go back to the office afterwards."

They found a café on West Street which met with Mimi's approval once she'd scrutinised the vegetarian menu on the door, and she ordered a tomato salad. But after only two bites, she pushed it aside, wrinkling her nose.

"Why do tomatoes in this country have no taste? I don't know how you stand it."

"I suppose it depends where you buy them. I've never had any complaints, but I think you have to buy fruit and veg in season. I'm sure that a tomato in December wouldn't be as tasty as one now. Do you want me to order you something else?"

Mimi shook her head. "I'll make myself a smoothie when I get back to H St," she said. Susan stopped herself from pointing out that smoothies were like drinking a gallon of sugar.

"Mimi, are you sure you're eating properly?"

Another glare.

"What else are you going to do while you're here?"

"Oh, this and that. Some stuff with Code Pink." Susan raised her head from her lentil soup to pick up more information, but none came.

"Why do you love it so much here, anyway?"

"I wouldn't say that I love it. I mean I miss London obviously, but you can't compare the two. As cities go, life's easier here, it's modern, everything works, the Metro's clean and you can get anything delivered to your door at any time of the day or night."

"Big deal," said Mimi. "Everyone you meet seems to work for the government."

Susan smiled. She'd noticed that too.

"They're parasites."

"I wouldn't go that far—"

"How would you describe it then?" Mimi said. "All those lobbyists. I don't know how you can live with yourself out here. But then I wouldn't expect an objective view from you."

Susan bit her lip. Then looked at her watch and suggested they returned to DC. She did have to go back to work, but she also had a romantic rendezvous that evening – with someone who worked for the government. He was a member of Partners 4 U, and his was the mysterious phone call earlier.

As they drove back to Washington in the hired car, Mimi asked her about Obama.

"He's cerebral," she said. "I like him. He makes me feel safe, you know that before he takes a decision he's weighed up everything. Of course that's where his reputation for indecisiveness comes from. And he's already in trouble with Democrats because he's not moved fast enough on their agenda. Did you see the healthcare bill only got passed last month? It took eighteen months."

"Really? I didn't see that, we had the election stuff on and I was up to my eyeballs. I like him too. And Michelle.
It's good she's doing this anti-obesity stuff. Making people feel responsible for what they eat. They need that here."

"Yes, but you'll notice that what she's doing isn't just about food. It's also about getting people off their bottoms. It's not just the additives that you're always attacking, but a lifestyle. There's certainly a generation of couch potatoes growing up here, and they're fat. But they're catching up at home too, believe you me."

Mimi let that pass. "He's still incredibly popular in Europe. He could have given Gordon Brown a lesson or two. And now we've got a coalition of toffs!"

"Did you vote Green again?"

"I campaigned for them actually. The candidate was a mate of mine. There was quite a high turnout in Wandsworth. I'm glad I'm here now to avoid the sickening love-fest between Cameron and Clegg."

Mimi looked out of the window at the trees lining the Parkway. "Mind, they've made my work a lot easier," she added.

Susan changed into a loose shift dress and left home with a familiar mix of curiosity and apprehension. Might it work out this time, she wondered as she walked to the cocktail bar off K St, where her date was already waiting at a tall table, legs wrapped round a stool.

He was called Matt and worked for the State Department, at least he said he did. Susan had become used to daters' flair for exaggeration and wasn't going to be taken in. Did State allow its employees to go on dating sites? They were human beings after all.

She and Matt had emailed before she gave him her phone number. She'd given him a specially-created email address, to be on the safe side. Jessica had warned her that if things went sour, she wouldn't want rejected suitors sending nasty messages to her personal email.

Susan liked him immediately. He was tall and gangly with a mine of funny stories from his postings abroad. He'd done Kosovo and Lagos, and was now killing time before his next job, which could be at the UN mission in New York. He was being considered for first secretary.

"Up or out" was how the State Department worked. Either you were promoted or you left.

"Is that true? Goodness, and I thought my industry was cut-throat."

"I guess you could say I'm doing okay. Like the guy said as he jumped out of the skyscraper and passed the 37th floor, 'so far, so good'."

Matt, who had a dark mole on his cheek, said he used the dating site because he had very few friends in Washington as a result of his foreign service career.

"So, like I said on my profile, I'm looking for good company rather than kinky sex," he said.

"That's good, me too," she laughed, raising her glass to his. "But that means you won't be sticking around for long."

"It sounds like you won't be either, as you're a Brit. By the way, you look slightly different to what I'd expected."

"I don't look like my profile picture?"

"You do, but I can't quite figure out…"

"Slightly fuller in the face, perhaps?"

"That's it, yeah. Well, maybe. I dunno."

He'd said it too quickly. Her appearance was obviously the first thing he'd noticed. She was crushed. He thought she was fat, so why didn't he just come out and say so?

She finished her drink and said brightly: "Well, good to meet you. See you again maybe."

He nodded and stood up.

She left the bar dejected, but by the time she got home she'd convinced herself that the date hadn't gone so badly. He'd seemed keen on meeting up again. Or maybe he was being diplomatic. Non-committal.

She noticed with gratitude that the housekeeper had replenished the neat pile of Guilty Secrets in the fridge.

Chapter 13

THE CABLE TV news was always on mute in the DeKripps reception, although Susan never usually paid attention to the screen unless there was a Congressional hearing into food issues. But after the BP oil spill in the Gulf of Mexico, there was huge interest in the impending appearance of her fellow Briton, Tony Hayward, before the House Energy Committee.

"Hey, Susie, how's your guy going to wriggle out of this one?" Barney asked her, to which she could only say, "He's not my guy." The worst oil spill in US history seemed to have caused a bit of a transatlantic rift, and even Obama repeatedly used BP's former name of "British Petroleum" to make his point.

On the morning of the hearing, a few colleagues gathered round the television out of curiosity to watch the public lynching of the BP chief executive. Just after he began reading from a written statement, a woman leapt to her feet and began screaming at Hayward, her hands and face daubed with oil. But that wasn't the image that caught Susan's attention. It was the face of her daughter, standing right behind the woman, being pinned to the wall by a member of the US Capitol police.

Nervously, she glanced at her colleagues. None of them had met Mimi, so she was safe on that score. They were all engrossed in the session, in which the hapless Hayward, accused of "astonishing complacency" by the Committee, stuck to his talking points, which were varying versions of 'not me, guv'. The DeKripps people watching agreed it was a disastrous performance.

Had Mimi been arrested? How could she track her down? Were these the people she'd been staying with? Struggling to appear relaxed, she rushed back to her office and shut the door. Should she find a lawyer first or try to get hold of the Capitol police? She was trawling through pages of lawyers' offices in Washington on the Internet, and had just alighted on Smithson and Hopkins close to the DeKripps offices, when her mobile rang. It was Mimi.

Somehow she managed not to fly off the handle and wrote down the address of the police station located inside a Congressional building. She took the precaution of calling Smithson and Hopkins who assigned her a lawyer named Palin, and rushed out of the office to catch a cab to the Hill.

Mimi looked sheepishly up at her mother from the chair to which she had been handcuffed. With her nose stud and a new tattoo showing under the strap of her T-shirt, she looked every bit what Americans called a "perp".

"How are you doing, Ma'am," said the officer in charge after Susan passed through security screening. "We understand that this young lady is your daughter. I'm afraid that she's not going to be able to stay in the United States any longer."

Deported? "Just a moment, officer," she said. "My lawyer is on the way, I'm sure we can sort this out."

The man was polite. "There's nothing to be sorted out Ma'am. She's committed a felony."

"Well I'd still like to wait until my lawyer arrives," she said. She looked mournfully at Mimi who refused to acknowledge her mother's concern. She sat down and the policeman returned to his computer. After about twenty minutes, a man in a sports jacket and chinos arrived. Could this be him? It wasn't the image that Susan had expected of a hot shot Washington attorney. He was tieless. Everyone in DC wore a tie.

The man came towards her. "Ms Perkins? Mark Palin, Smithson and Hopkins. We spoke earlier."

He turned to the officer who explained that Mimi's case

had been referred to the immigration authorities, and that she had been working illegally while in the US on a tourist visa. Then he had a chat with Mimi. Susan heard him say "don't worry" as he turned back to her. He promised to ring her as soon as possible once he had looked into the case, but he sounded confident that they could avoid deportation.

By the time she got home that evening, the pictures from the Congressional session were leading the television news. She cringed as the protesters who disrupted the session were identified as Diane Wilson, a shrimper and co-founder of Code Pink for Peace, who had yelled at Hayward, and a British activist who worked for USAway. USAway! So that was her NGO – the most anti-American outfit in London. But at least Mimi's name wasn't mentioned.

She walked to the office the next day, dreading the reaction. As soon as she arrived, she was called into Barney's office. She wanted to fade into the carpet, feeling the receptionist's eyes on her, as she walked along the corridor. He pushed that morning's New York Tattle across his desk towards her.

"Mimosa Fizzes!" was the tabloid's headline. The story announced under a photo of Mimi that Mimosa Perkins, daughter of an executive working for the DeKripps food manufacturer, was being booted out of the country for "anti-American activities" after joining the Code Pink protest about the Gulf oil spill.

"We like to keep DeKripps out of the papers unless it's good news," he said. "Particularly when our senior staff are connected to hostile international activists, who openly campaign against us." She didn't dare ask to see the paper.

"I swear I didn't know anything about it. And I had no idea she worked for that organisation."

USAway was known to have an axe to grind against DeKripps. In fact, she dimly recollected seeing protesters in

London holding up placards saying "DeKripps is Krap", before she left for Washington. She realised with horror that Mimi must have had something to do with that.

"Well you need to get your priorities straight," he said. "This company has been very good to you," – she lowered her head in bitter acknowledgement – "but Christ, Susan, if this is how you repay us, dragging our name through the mud, there are some serious questions to be asked here."

"I'm so sorry," she began, but was cut off as Barney threw the newspaper in the rubbish.

She rang the lawyer. He said he might be able to persuade Homeland Security not to go ahead with deportation as Mimi was only in Washington for another week. But he suggested that she was booked on a flight out as soon as the arrangements had been approved. "So technically, it won't be deportation," he said.

Three days and $5,000 later, Susan was riding with Mimi in a cab to Dulles airport.

"Congratulations on getting yourself noticed again. Big time. Why didn't you tell me you'd joined USAway?"

"I did, but you weren't interested."

"I certainly would have been if I'd have realised that it was that particular bunch. I thought you were with an NGO doing good work in public advocacy, not the most vocally anti-American group in Britain. Have you given any consideration to the consequences? Do you realise this sorry episode cost me $5,000 and possibly my career?"

"It's all about you isn't it?" Mimi sobbed. "You only care about me because I could ruin your reputation."

"I'm sorry. It's not about the money, of course."

Susan reached for Mimi's arm and squeezed it. She was so angry, she felt like squeezing until it bruised.

"Have you no idea how much trouble you're in? You're lucky you have a mother like me, or you'd be out on your ear back in England."

"Okay, okay, now let me go." For the rest of the journey they nursed their mutual resentment, and Susan was relieved when the car pulled up outside the airport terminal.

"Get in touch me when you get home."

With a jerk of her head, Mimi got out of the cab, and took the escalator up to international departures.

In the days that followed, Susan noticed a change in the atmosphere at work. She sensed the critical gaze of colleagues as she walked to the coffee dispenser. She could swear she heard "Mimosa" whispered disparagingly as she passed Barney and Judy by the water fountain. Or maybe it was paranoia. She knew that Frank would be furious with her too, so she didn't call him for sympathy. He'd never stood up to Barney and would have heard already his version, she was certain.

She tried to put the incident behind her. She'd warned Mimi against giving press interviews on her return to London, and she had reluctantly complied. Mimi was going to be out of touch for a while anyway as she and Josh were off to Glastonbury, where for once, sunny weather was forecast.

But she didn't seem to comprehend that she'd gone too far this time, and never gave the slightest indication that she might be concerned about a backlash against Susan.
In fact, she seemed to relish the attention.

"Any luck with the lonely hearts club?" Mimi asked her on one of their Saturday morning calls. Susan turned down a CD of Lily's ensemble and leaned in.

She didn't mention Matt from State. "Oh, delete, delete. How are things with the unemployed librarian?"

"Fine. Actually, Ma, would you mind not describing him as an unemployed librarian? It gets on my nerves."

"Fine. So maybe you could stop calling me Ma. Likewise."

There was an awkward silence as they both stared into their computer screens on each side of the Atlantic. "So, is Josh in today? I hope to meet him properly when I'm in London next month." He was out. "He's gone to the shops because I asked him to. I've got something to tell you," said Mimi.

Even before her daughter told her she was pregnant, and that the baby was due the following March, Susan had a premonition of what she was going to say.

"Are you completely mad? What do you suppose you're going to live on? Dressing up as a corn on the cob in Parliament Square denouncing High Fructose Corn Syrup isn't going to pay the bills you know."

"I'll have you know I don't dress up any more, I haven't done for ages," said Mimi. "I do comms." She added: "And at least this is a baby who'll have a proper father. And it won't be an inconvenience like I was to you."

"What do you mean, an inconvenience? You were never an inconvenience for me, you know that perfectly well."

"You say that now," said Mimi. But she'd landed a blow. Susan knew it was true. She'd never sought to play down the challenges of being a single mother. Unfortunately, to her eternal shame, Mimi had found out from a school friend that her biological father was a married man who didn't want to have anything to do with them. That had been hurtful for them both.

Susan never forgave the girl's mother who'd betrayed her secret, breaking their friendship. But Mimi had taken Rod's rejection personally. When she eventually managed to sit her daughter down, Susan tried to reassure her that she'd only wanted to protect her. But the slammed doors and pointed silences went on for months. Luckily Mimi had never found out that Rod had finished with her by fax. That had hurt her more than anything.

Even then, Susan never regretted her decision to raise a child alone. Then Serge came along. Maybe things would have been different with Mimi if they'd had their own child. But there was no point in raking over that again. Not now.

"Tell me more about this baby. How are you feeling? When did you find out about it?"

"I'm fine," came the reply. "I've got to run, we'll catch up when you come over."

That was that. Susan felt like a boat that had been holed, tossed on the ocean and about to capsize. Not only was her daughter a penniless activist, she was a pregnant penniless activist.

A baby, though. That was wonderful news. She'd been overwhelmed with euphoria herself when she'd found out she was expecting a daughter.

For the first time in ages her thoughts turned to Rod.

Where was he now? She didn't know and she didn't care. But as she picked up her shoes she was tickled to think he was about to become a grandfather.

Chapter 14

IT WAS ONE of those late summer evenings when she felt like her old self again. She was back in London in a Bermondsey restaurant with Lily, reminiscing about their student days over dinner and a bottle of wine. It was a welcome distraction from the work tensions in DC.

"Who was the one who introduced me to that idiot, what was his name?" Lily said, helping herself to the olive oil and bread on their table.

"Brian! The sociologist? You mean who was the one who stole him from me?" Lily sat back in denial. "He *was* handsome. But he kept some strange company. He used to hang out with those chemical engineers."

"Oh yes, the chemical engineers. They were the worst. And thick!" The two burst into laughter.

"That moment when you came into my bedroom, and there was Brian on top of me. He was just wiggling!"

"Wiggling. Like a caterpillar," said Susan.

"Especially with that hairy back! No wonder you shut the door in a hurry."

"I was giggling so much I had to get out. The sex life of the British male. Ugh!"

Lily feigned hurt. "Well not everybody finds a French lover."

"I know. God, that was a revelation for me," said Susan. "Someone who actually knew what to do. Although it must be said that Rod knew how to satisfy a woman, too."

"That's why he's called Rod!" This was getting out of hand. Susan glanced sideways at the table next to them whose diners were staring at their mezze.

"Have you any idea what happened to Brian?"

Lily shook her head. "We didn't have that much in

common, did we? We were pretty innocent then, I suppose. He was into the anti-Thatcher radical politics at uni, and I just wanted to get on with growing up. Do you remember that big scandal when they compiled those files on students with political activities? Brian was in the thick of that. I think he must have been one of those Marxist Trotskyist anarcho-syndicalists. Somebody told me later that he was organizing poll tax riots."

"Oh, that makes sense. Maggie, Maggie, Maggie—"

"Out, out, out!"

They hadn't shared the same group of friends in Brighton, although Susan had introduced Lily to Brian who was in her social sciences faculty. After that, Susan had been wrapped up in her relationship with Rod. He told her she reminded him of the pre-Raphaelite portrait of Ophelia, something which had amused both her and Lily.

"It really could have been you," said Lily. "She posed in the bath!"

She'd disapproved of Susan going out with a married man, of course, and had noted Rod's lack of candour regarding his wife. But Lily hadn't been at home much that year: The university silver jubilee had been one long concert.

Lily, who had switched to music after dropping out of law studies, had quite a following. She was known as the "flutie cutie" with her trademark scrunchie tying back her sleek dark hair. Susan, too afraid of the sun to join other friends who took books to the beach, had drunk bottomless cups of coffee on campus with Rod, a former Sussex student who'd set up his own business and drove around in a flashy BMW. Another trait that hadn't endeared him to Lily.

"Guess what, I'm going to meet Josh tomorrow," Susan said, lowering her voice.

"The boyfriend? The one who looks like a meerkat? Are you going to the flat?"

No, they were meeting on neutral territory in Vauxhall.

"Well find out the name of the baby, at least. And tell me, how are things at work with slime-bag?"

Susan confided that she'd been seriously considering returning to London.

"But what about Matt from State? He might be The One."

"He never called me again. Nothing. And there I was thinking we had chemistry. He said I was fat!"

"No. I can't believe it. Who would do that?"

"Not in so many words, but that's what he meant."

"You could always ring him. Or maybe he doesn't like redheads."

"Excuse me. Who doesn't like redheads?"

"But what were you going to say about Barney?" Lily leaned forward.

"I've got the impression that he's fed up with me. What do they say in America? Three strikes and you're out? Well, I feel as though I've got two strikes against me. If I ask to come home, it could save face for us both."

"Tell me more about him."

Susan leaned on her hand. "Macho, powerful, intimidates people. Sexist. Racist. Scary. There again, if he'd been Mister Nice, he probably wouldn't be where he is today."

"Sounds charming. Married, presumably."

"Yes. Grown kids. He and his wife live in Georgetown. Like Frank and June in their little cottage in Cobham. It's funny to think of these big Americans crammed into such twee places. Barney is like Frank's evil twin. "

"But what would you do if you came home?"

"I'd get my old job back, of course."

"Are you sure?" Lily could spot a get-out clause a mile away.

She hadn't thought that far ahead. But it made sense to her to come home after a year away. And DeKripps had treated her generously until now. Practically like family. In fact, after Serge died, they'd been her lifeline. But from a professional standpoint, now that the Guilty Secrets successful launch was complete, there were fewer reasons to stay in DC.

"Are you emotionally ready to come home?"

"I think of Serge every day. I miss him so much. But yes, I think I'm ready."

At least she could pronounce his name now without tears stinging her eyes. What's more, she missed Frank, she missed Lily, and of course she missed her family.

"Anyway, Mimi's having a baby and I want to be there. I'm fed up of being on my own in Washington."

"Well can I give you a word of advice?" said Lily. She momentarily stopped drumming her fingers on the table.

"Of course."

"If I were you, I'd consider hiring a lawyer."

The young man waiting for Susan in the entrance of Mimi's office building was tall and slim. Rangy. She noticed his sandy goatee which had been hard to distinguish on Skype. From close up he really did look like a meerkat.

"Call me Susie," she said, as they shook hands and waited by the red, white and blue USAway sign. Mimi, of course, arrived late, running down the stairs. Had she intended to leave the two of them alone for a few minutes?

"Hi Ma. Josh, this is Ma. Ma, Josh," she said.

"We've done the formalities," Josh said. He gave Mimi a kiss and squeezed her arm. Her daughter's nose accessory had been replaced by a sparkling ruby-coloured glass stud. Susan wondered whether the future father approved.

She noticed how protective he was with Mimi, as he fussed over her at lunch at a nearby vegetarian café. It reminded her, poignantly, of how Serge had treated her.

"I hear you've been doing some research on Serge," she told him. "That's really interesting, thanks."

"It didn't start out that way. In fact, I'd been reading Camus and started looking up criticism, and that's when his name came up. I'll send you the links if you like."

"That's kind of you. But actually, Serge kept the hard copies at the house anyway. I found the files in a chest recently. But I must say, I never read them, and they're in the attic."

"You must be really proud of him."

"Yes." Susan returned to her carrot and chickpea salad. "He was a hoarder, you know. He kept every single letter that I wrote to him."

"A real Sartre-and-De Beauvoir," said Mimi. Susan chewed on, then, embarrassed for Josh, changed the subject.

"Mimi, do you remember when we went to Brittany, and it was impossible for you to find anything you could eat? The waiters didn't understand when you asked for a salad without chicken, and stuff like that. There was that time when you said you were a vegetarian and they brought you a salmon steak."

"It's *vegan* by the way. The French just don't get it. I bet they don't even have a word for it."

"The last time we went, you just ate chips and salad."

Mimi had rarely been to Brittany, part of her ongoing 'my mother's life is boring' phase. But even as a child she was never made welcome by Serge's family. Susan once overheard Marie-Christine telling a neighbour that she couldn't understand why she had named her daughter Mimosa after a brand of French loo roll. In pious Brittany, where everyone was named after their saint's day, the in-laws knew there was no saint Mimosa.

Susan ploughed on. "It's so much easier in America. But then again, I've seen dinners ruined by people being picky about their food in restaurants. It's embarrassing sometimes."

Another silence. Josh was stroking Mimi's arm.

Susan didn't like to ask him about his job, or lack of one, so she turned to the pregnancy. "I was sick a lot at the beginning, wasn't I?" Josh nodded as his hand moved to his sparse goatee. "But it's settled down now."

The baby was due on March 29th, six months' time. A month after Mimi's birthday. They didn't want to know if was a boy or a girl. "Don't I have the right to know the sex of my grandchild?" she asked, feeling like an antique. Apparently not. After another silence, she glanced at her watch.

"I'd better go," she said, before Mimi had a chance to throw any conversational grenades. "I've got a train to catch. Let me know if you need anything."

"Give my love to granny. And tell her we were at Glastonbury, not Glyndebourne."

Susan found two £20 notes and paid their bill. Oh dear, she thought as she left, dragging her wheelie suitcase behind her, I should have asked about Mimi's latest project at USAway in case it blows up in my face.

Chapter 15

THE CHANGING ROOM at the discount clothing store in Washington was one of those communal spaces that Susan despised. She'd never set foot inside, although she had seen its customers on the Metro carrying bags with *"Grab it while it lasts"* in big letters.

"Don't be so snobbish," Jessica had said, edging Susan into the dress department. "Everyone likes a bargain."

There was always an unspoken rule in communal fitting rooms: Customers kept their eyes on their own bodies as though in a private fashion show, unless it was to marvel at a friend's dress.

She undressed self-consciously in front of the wrap-around mirror, in the company of a dozen other women. She stood for a moment studying herself in her bra and knickers before struggling to hoist a grey size 8 dress, which meant size 12 at home, over her head. Her weight gain had produced flab in unexpected places. As well as developing love handles whose blubber protruded like porridge above her knicker elastic, her thighs had coarsened, and she could swear she had the beginnings of a double chin.

She checked the dress size as she shimmied the garment down to her waist. It was definitely an 8. But from there it refused to budge. She couldn't force it over her hips.

Jessica was standing next to her, trying on a pair of skin tight jeans. Not a trace of cellulite, Susan noticed, as she stole an admiring glance at her olive-skinned friend. She was wearing a sleeveless top that showed off what were known in DC as "Michelle Obama arms".

"That looks great on you," she said to Jessica. "But I think I need the next size up. At least."

"Wait, I'll ask someone to get it for you."

She forced it backwards and up over her shoulders, and hung it back on the hanger. She tried on a second one, a dusky jersey fabric which was supposed to look slinky. Instead it amplified every bulge.

The sales assistant returned with a size 10. Susan thanked her and tried again. It fitted but the neckline was too low for work, and as she smoothed it over her hips she noticed it was too short anyway. To cap it all, her freckles were standing out even more than usual on her tightless legs. Her ankles were swollen and speckled with mosquito bites.

"This is a disaster," she said.

"What's wrong? It's not that bad. It's your colour."

"Not that bad? I just don't know why I'm getting so fat when I'm watching what I eat."

They picked up their things and waited at the cash desk with Jessica's jeans.

"There must be something. Like you can't just put on weight for no reason," Jessica said.

"I did start expanding gently after I came to Washington. I was eating too much chocolate. The DeKripps housekeeper leaves bars in the fridge. I ended up throwing them out. Now I'm ballooning and I don't know why."

As she followed Jessica out of the store, and they began walking towards the Metro, Susan considered her eating habits in detail. She followed all the rules, never skipped breakfast, and was careful to eat salad for lunch. What could it be?

They took the long escalator down to the platform and waited for their train. As the minutes ticked down on the digital screen, she worked through her mental inventory of recent meals. The lights along the platform began to flash slowly, as the train approached. As the doors slid open, Susan said, "Just a second. There's one thing I've been eating that I didn't before. Guilty Secrets."

"What's Guilty Secrets?"

"It's from DeKripps. Fresh fruit covered in chocolate."

"Well stop eating it."

"That's the whole point. I can't!"

A couple of evenings later, Susan tackled Ellen again about her weight. They were having an after work drink at a rooftop bar overlooking the White House. "Do you remember me asking you about my putting on weight a bit ago?"

"Sure. But don't get upset about it."

"Well, I've noticed that now I'm getting really fat, at least for me. I've gone up a dress size and the only explanation I can think of is that I've become addicted to Guilty Secrets."

Ellen sucked the straw of her gin and tonic. "Are you eating that stuff? I never eat chocolate."

"But don't you get the same deliveries I do? Are you throwing them out, or giving them to the kids?"

"No way I'd let Darren and David have any," said Ellen. "But Jed likes them."

"And has he put on weight?"

Ellen put down her drink and looked across the crowded bar to the view below. They could see two snipers on the White House roof.

"Do you know, I think he has."

"Right!" She looked triumphant. "Because with me, it's like a craving. When I was pregnant with Mimi, I couldn't stop eating salted peanuts."

"But what's different about Guilty Secrets, compared to Buried Treasure and the other DeKripps stuff?"

"I don't know. Last night I checked the Food Facts on Guilty Secrets, and there was nothing unusual on the list."

She stirred the ice in her cocktail round and round, knocking the cubes against the glass. "Maybe it's secret."

"You mean DeKripps would hide something from the

FDA? Don't be ridiculous."

"I know. It's certainly unlikely. But Ellen, I'm telling you these Guilty Secrets are literally irresistible."

"Well, obviously if there were something fishy going on, Barney would know."

Susan sighed. He was the last person she would challenge.

"What about R and D? You've been with the company here for a few years, who do you know there? The developers would know the exact ingredients."

"No one really." She ran her finger round the rim of her glass. "Wait. Do you remember that young guy who came to one of the early strategy meetings?"

"The geeky one with glasses? What was his name…Italian sounding."

"That's right. Tony. Help me here, his last name was the same as that artist."

She looked blank. "What artist? Dead or alive?"

"I don't know if he's still alive. Frank Stella, that's it!"

"Tony Stella. The only thing is that he's left the company. I guess that's why he never came to any more of the meetings. Look," she added, checking her watch, "I'd better head home. It's time I stopped Jed eating any more Guilty Secrets."

Susan smiled. They took the lift back downstairs and she waved Ellen off. She took out her phone, was about to search for Tony Stella when she felt her stomach rumble.

She walked across the street to the Mustard Grill and peered inside. It was unusually free of tourists. She found a free place at the bar and looked at the menu. If only she could track down Tony. But the puzzle was beginning to fall into place. Hadn't Barney warned her against blabbing to the compliance department when R and D were still working on Guilty Secrets? Something must have been concealed from the Food and Drug Administration.

"Do you mind if I sit here?"

"Be my guest."

Susan turned sideways to see a shaved head and a pair of glasses. Probably a lobbyist. He looked about the same age as Susan.

"Are you English? Care for a coffee?" He had already detected her accent, so that was to be the chat-up line.

"And you're a New Yorker."

"Hey, how do you know? I was supposed to be incognito in this town."

"Nobody else says cawfee like that," she said. "And I wouldn't expect to find many locals in this place."

"What are you doing here?"

She told him that she'd moved to DC for work after her husband died. Why had she felt the need to introduce Serge and widowhood right at the outset? He expressed sympathy, ordered wine, offered to share some food. They settled on crabcakes.

He was based in New York but worked for a K St lobbying firm and had been meeting with members of the House Banking committee. But their session had run over schedule, so he was staying at the Merchant Hotel and would return to New York the next morning, rather than catch the Acela that night.

"Do you happen to know a guy called Jed Young?"

"Sure I do. All-American straight out of a Polo ad. They have twins, right?"

"Yes. Twin boys. In fact I've just had a drink with his wife, maybe you know her?" He shook his head.

The two of them agreed what a village DC was. And yet, after a year, she had yet to meet anyone born and bred in the city.

"I'm John, by the way." He held out his hand.

"Susie. Pleased to meet you."

Two hours later, they walked, almost leaning on each other, out of the restaurant. Red wine after a gin and tonic had given her a slight headache.

"I'd better get back." She half-turned towards G Street. "But thanks for a nice evening."

"Hey, it's not over yet," he said. "The night is yet young." Is it? She glanced at her watch. "At least come up for a nightcap."

"I believe I've heard that line before," she said with a smile which she hadn't intended to be so flirtatious. "Just a quick one, then."

She followed him slightly unsteadily the few yards down 15th St and into his hotel, where she tried to adopt a casual air of a guest returning to her own room.

The heavy door closed with a click behind them, and they fell onto the bed fully clothed. There was no longer any pretence of a nightcap. He hadn't even offered to open the minibar.

"Don't rush," she said. He began undressing her while his mouth found hers. His eyes, behind his glasses, were hard and dark.

She interrupted him again to point at the harsh glare of the bedroom lamps. "Do you mind?" He reached across her, and the room turned dark as though by magic. She was excited to feel her layers of clothing being removed one by one and dropped onto the carpet.

She managed to cover them both with the heavy duvet while she still had her underwear on. But she was now the one in a hurry.

"Aah, wait a second," he said. Susan realised he was reaching for a condom without being asked. She took off his glasses.

"Hey, lady, now I *really* can't see what I'm doing," he

protested, kissing her again. She liked it. She felt good. What's more, she felt appreciated.

"That was nice," she said afterwards. "Thank you. I don't mind if you switch the lights on again now."

She had taken the precaution of pulling the duvet up to her chin.

"Thank *you,* Susie. Do you mind if I smoke?"

"Sure, go ahead." It was the first thing that had reminded her of Serge. "I think you're the first person I've met in DC who smokes."

He put on his glasses before lighting up. "I don't really. But there are times like this when I enjoy it."

"Do you know you're the first American I've ever slept with?"

"And you're the first Brit." He put one arm around her as he puffed on his cigarette with his other hand.

"So, you're married, right?" He nodded.

"I thought you must be."

Consenting adults. Casual sex. Strangely, she didn't feel guilty. It was the first time she'd wanted sex since Serge's death and she'd enjoyed it. Did that make her a scarlet woman? In the Merchant, of all places? This hotel must have seen a few clandestine trysts in its time.

"You're still wearing your wedding ring."

"Yes, I often wonder when I should take it off. It's a big moment."

"Maybe you should now."

"Yes, maybe I should."

She waited until he fell into a doze before slipping to the side of the large double bed and silently pulling on her knickers and skirt. She was creeping to the door with her shoes in one hand, and jacket over her arm, when she heard a growl.

"Hey, Freckles, where are you going?"

John switched on the bedside light. "You can stay if you like. We can have breakfast in the morning before I catch the Acela."

She turned, like a thief caught in the act. "No, really. I have to go. This wasn't a good idea."

"Buyer's remorse?"

He jumped out of bed and held her hand. "Look, it was a good idea. You're an impressive lady. I know what you must have gone through. I'm glad I met you."

Still naked, he performed an elaborate bow with a sweep of his left arm and led her to the door. A notice was displayed on it threatening legal action if guests smoked in the room.

"Shall I call you a cab?"

"No, it's fine. I only live a few minutes away. I can walk home."

"At this time of night?" She glanced at the time on the giant TV set. It was 11.16 p.m.

"Good night, John. You're nice," was all she could think of to say, as she gave him a light peck on the cheek. His shaven head was as smooth as polished mahogany.

He squeezed her hand. She put on her shoes and the heels sank into the thick pile carpet as she walked down the corridor towards what she hoped was the lift.

She headed straight for the shower as soon as she got home. She felt a mix of elation and relief. Gratitude, even.

John was right, she shouldn't feel guilty. She hadn't been unfaithful to Serge. In fact as long as she'd known him, she'd never been attracted to another man.

So why were feelings of guilt intruding now? Oh yes! John was married. Just like Rod. But that was different. What had just happened at the Merchant was probably exactly what she needed, and for the first time in two years, a real man, not one of those losers on the Internet, had told her she was lovely. And with that satisfying thought, she fell asleep.

Ellen was the first person she ran into the next morning.

"Sorry I had to rush off last night, Susie."

"Oh don't worry. You'll never guess what happened to me, though."

Ellen's eyes widened when she learned about John. "What, he's married? And are you going to see him again?"

Susan told her that John was supposed to work with her husband. She looked even more surprised, and promised to check with Jed, although Susan was starting to have her doubts about whether her date was really called John after all. In fact the more she thought about it, and the way she had sneaked out of the Merchant like a prize whore, the more ashamed she felt. Maybe she shouldn't have confided in Ellen after all.

But she had more pressing concerns. As soon as she was home from work, she searched the Internet for all the Tony and Anthony Stellas in DC. Less than a dozen work pages or personal profiles popped up. She then widened her search to include the wider metropolitan area, casting her net across Maryland, Virginia and even West Virginia.

She quickly collected about 15 names, along with several emails and telephone numbers.

She sat on the sofa with a box of Guilty Secrets beside her. Of the 15, three calls went to voicemail, two emails bounced and the other Tony Stellas denied all knowledge of DeKripps. It was discouraging. Of course, he's a geek!

The Tony Stella she was looking for probably didn't even have a landline. If he even lived in the area. He might be in geek paradise in Seattle for all she knew.

She considered the alternatives. Could she sneak into R and D and see if she recognised anyone? Then what would she do, invite them out for coffee? It would only raise suspicions if she asked for Tony's contact details. What about confronting Barney? If he were innocent, he'd think she was ridiculous, making such a fuss about a little weight gain.

Damn. She had no hard evidence of anything. She plunged her hand into the box once more.

Chapter 16

THE FIRST SIGN that something was really amiss at DeKripps was when Barney called a strategy meeting without her. Ellen and Judy were talking in lowered voices by the drinks dispenser, and Susan heard the communications officer say "see you at eleven" as she went off with a bottle of water. Susan had no such meeting on her agenda.

On a couple of occasions over coffee with Ellen, she had been on the point of revealing Barney's sexual assault in the office, but each time decided against it. Meanwhile, Ellen had told her that Jed had no idea who "John" was. She thanked her, and said she wasn't surprised. But she now knew for sure she'd been played.

She emailed more Tony Stellas. As the evenings lengthened, she began keeping a diary of profiles and numbers of interest, and in the margins she noted her diet in more detail than before. That should keep Doctor Osborn happy.

But her jottings only seemed to confirm her suspicions about Guilty Secrets. It had become so automatic to return from work in the evening, and open the fridge door to pick up a golden box, that she hardly noticed any more that she was lifting the lid several times an evening. When she checked her diary, there was no denying it. One evening, as she unwrapped a Guilty Secret absent-mindedly, while watching an episode of Mad Men, the truth finally hit.

She threw the chocolate against the wall where it popped and left a raspberry dribble on the beige paint. She tipped the box upside down and the remaining chocolates fell onto the carpet.

"I don't believe this," she said out loud. "Bastards! I'm addicted to this stuff!"

She stood up and picked up one of the chocolates from the floor. She hurled it at the Modigliani woman who looked down at her disdainfully.

"Take that!" she said. The chocolate smacked the swan-necked figure right between the eyes before bouncing off the picture.

She remembered the countless empty boxes of discarded Guilty Secrets, her obsession now recorded in incriminating detail in her diary. But why would DeKripps wilfully deceive her? Not only her but the rest of the department, the whole company. Was it conceivable that someone in the corporation would have deliberately developed an addictive product, concealed it from the FDA and had her market it?

By the time she went to bed, she'd half convinced herself that she must be deluded and soon she'd find the rational explanation.

She spent a restless night with work-related dreams in which Barney played a major role. She awoke anxious and tense, one pillow kicked to the bottom of the bed. But she remained determined to confront him with her suspicions. She constructed her line of attack over a bowl of Crunchaloosa and a banana, switching off the radio for better concentration. Arriving at the office, she marched straight past the receptionist and into Barney's office.

He was stretched out behind his desk on the phone, but beckoned her inside.

"Look, like I said, you've got to get those French faggots in line." She feared he was talking to Frank. "You've seen the sales, there's only one way to go, and that's up." It was definitely Frank. "Gotta go. Talk later."

He hung up loudly, shaking his head. "Goddamned French," he said.

"Barney," she began. Her careful plan was already unravelling. "Look, I'm starting to feel I'm being left out of the loop."

"How so?" He seemed distracted.

"Well, I wasn't invited to the last strategy meeting, for example."

He screwed up his face. "Ah poor baby. Didn't get invited to a meeting and comes crying to Daddy."

Not a good start. Unconsciously smoothing her pencil skirt, which was straining at the waist, she took the plunge.

"Look, could you tell me please what exactly is in these Guilty Secrets? Letters and emails of praise are falling like snow in my department."

"Why do you want to know, Susie? Eating too many of them, like everyone else?"

"Judging by the mail down in customer services, there are quite a few out there reporting a weight gain which they explicitly link to Guilty Secrets." She was bluffing but it was worth the risk.

"I'm dealing with that." His eyes narrowed. "And I would remind you that customer services come under my jurisdiction."

"It's more that I've been thinking that everything might not be above board. For example, why did you say that the *scientists* couldn't keep up? What's it got to do with the scientists?"

First, he adopted innocent misunderstanding. He trotted out the company line about DeKripps products being developed "in partnership" with the FDA.

"Barney," she repeated, in a voice that meant 'don't give me that shit', "I'm asking you for an explanation."

"And that's what I'm giving you, if you'll just listen."

He began speaking very slowly as though addressing a particularly obtuse child.

"Guilty Secrets were developed by the DeKripps R and D. They are involved in all new products, as you know perfectly well. So on that score I'm afraid I don't see what you're driving at. On the other hand if you are insinuating that something underhand or *illegal* has been going on, I would ask you to leave my office."

Susan said nothing, and folded her arms. Seeing that she wasn't going to let the issue drop, he took another tack. Loosening his yellow silk tie, he stood up, gaining the further advantage of height as well as status, and cleared his throat.

"Actually Susie, I'm glad you stopped by. I'd been meaning to call you in for a chat. The fact is that there are going to be some changes round here anyway. We've found your presence extremely…stimulating, but all good things must come to an end. And I would remind you of your role in the success of Guilty Secrets, for which we are all extremely grateful." He smiled.

Had she heard him correctly? "You mean you want me to go back to London?"

Her arms dropped limply to her side. She'd been outmaneuvered. So much for being the company strategy queen.

"As you said yourself, DeKripps can't keep up with demand for Guilty Secrets. That's going to hit profits." She fixed him with a hostile stare. "And if profits are down—," she started to say.

"You understand me perfectly. Like I said, we're going to have to make some changes."

She was dumbstruck. He hadn't invited her to sit down, so she remained standing in front of his desk. "So what happens now? I'd be happy to go back to London. Shall I call Frank?"

"No, no, that's fine. I'll take care of it. Or at least HR will. How long have you been here now? It's more than a year, isn't it?"

She nodded. "Just give me some time and I'll see what I can fix up."

Barney sat down, as though to signal the end of their exchange. He was picking up the phone as she closed the door behind her.

She couldn't face a whole evening alone in the apartment but needed to sort things out in her mind. On impulse, she walked down to Pennsylvania Avenue as it grew dark and caught a bus straight to Eastern Market, where she treated herself to dinner at Montmartre.

She was shown to a corner table and got out her diary to marshall her theories. She already regretted confronting Barney, who was obviously ready for her: Guilty Secrets and the dip in profits must be a smoke screen, an excuse for getting rid of her. Of course there was his clumsy grab but was that the real reason? She'd noticed the change in the way she'd been treated at work since the incident with Mimi in Congress.

"Bonsoir Madame." For a moment she was back in France. The waiter handed her the menu. She chose an omelette, instructing the waiter to hold the French fries, and ordered a large Merlot.

What else had she done wrong? She couldn't think of a single thing. She had an unblemished record as a trusted corporate worker, had made untold millions for the company over the past 13 years. If they wanted to fire her now she could sue for unfair dismissal and walk away with a packet. But she also knew she'd have to say goodbye to a job in Big Food for ever.

That's what had happened to a banker friend from London who'd sued her employer for discrimination. Lucy might be a millionaire today, but it had cost her her health, her husband and her reputation. And she was only 43, the same age as Susan. She looked down at her diary. She'd written only one word: Mimi.

Where could she find a lawyer? There was no shortage of them in town. She needed a proper corporate attorney. There was the one from Smithson and Hopkins who had helped Mimi after her arrest. Maybe he was specialised in immigration. She scanned the contacts on her phone. How could she have forgotten his name? Mark Palin, like Sarah Palin. She resolved to try him the next day.

She hopped on a bus home, where she opened the fridge door, took out the gilded box lying there, and rested it on her knee. She had consumed half of the twelve chocolates inside in the time it took her to switch on her computer and open Facebook. Somebody wanted to 'friend' her.

She gasped when she saw who it was. Looking straight at her from the screen was Rod, the father of her child.

Chapter 17

SHE WAS PACING round the apartment and decided that she had to ring Lily despite the late hour in London.

"Guess what? It looks like I'm being fired from DeKripps!"

"Don't be ridiculous. Why would they?"

"Let's just say that apparently I'm no longer flavour of the month." She recounted every detail of her exchange with Barney.

"So why don't you go to HR before he does?"

"What for? I don't see what difference it would make."

"Don't you see that what you know about Project Candy could be your meal ticket?"

"What do you mean?"

"What would it be worth to DeKripps if you went public with that?"

"God, Lily, you can't be suggesting that I turn whistleblower? I'm a senior corporate executive. Are you mad?"

"You love your job, but your job doesn't love you. How many people do you know who've been made redundant at a moment's notice? Why would you be any different? It's up to you to get the best deal you can. You need to think of yourself."

"But what if they end up transferring me back to London after all? I was thinking about complaining to HR to get a sweetheart deal, not break the law."

"Whistleblowing isn't breaking the law. It's doing good. If you are seriously telling me that DeKripps has invented a secret food ingredient they know to be addictive, *that's* breaking the law," Lily said.

"I still don't have any proof of that. That's the whole

point. I have suspicions, and a bloody weight problem."

"Get some proof then."

"Come on, you know that's easier said than done."

"Well, sleep on it anyway. Did you get a lawyer yet? If not, get one, pronto."

"Funny you should say that." She told her about Mark Palin. Lily approved. "Was he the one who got Mimi off?"

"Yes, it cost me a cool $5,000, mind. This is going to be astronomical if I end up fighting DeKripps. David and Goliath springs to mind."

"You don't know where things are going yet. But wow."

They were about to hang up when Susan said, as casually as she could manage: "Actually, Rod has just got in touch with me on Facebook."

She sensed a chill drift across the Atlantic.

"And did you answer?" She walked to the fridge and took out the Chardonnay, closing the door with a foot.

"Not yet. I'm curious, of course, but I'm not sure how I feel about him."

"How can you not be sure? He's a bastard, that's what he is. And a married one at that. Have you forgotten what he did to you?"

"That's a lifetime ago. I need to check with Mimi. She might want to be in touch with her biological father. Particularly now that she's going to be a mother herself."

Mimi had replied to her message. Yes, of course she was curious to meet Rod. But, equally predictably, she didn't want her to be present.

Susan considered carefully how to respond to his Facebook invitation. She examined his profile: He'd aged quite well, only slightly heavier, just a few grey hairs. But she certainly didn't want him snooping around hers so she decided to send him her email address in response to his friend request. That way, the ball would be back in his court if he wanted to pursue things. But she had to keep cool; the last thing she wanted was to reopen old wounds.

His response came that weekend. The email said:

"Dear Susie

"It's been a long time but I've often thought about you over the years. How's life treating you? You look as lovely as ever. I realise I was a bit of a prick all those years ago, but it would be good to catch up if you have the time and the inclination. I'm still doing import-export stuff and am based in Chiswick.

"Best regards

"Rod"

She parsed the email carefully. She was surprised by her anger. Of course, he'd seen her photos on social media which were there for any casual observer. He might have seen a photo of her with Mimi. Why hadn't she been more careful about her privacy settings? As for "a bit of a prick", that's the understatement of the century. She supposed it was only natural that he would tell her what he was doing now. He was obviously running his own company, near Heathrow, for a quick getaway. And he wants to meet up. That's obvious too.

She immediately forwarded the message to Lily for comment.

Then she started typing.

"Dear Rod,

"I'm well, thanks. I noticed that you don't mention our daughter, Mimi in your email. She is now 22, and working for an NGO in London."

Should she mention the baby? No, that was sufficient for an introduction.

"As for me, I'm with DeKripps Foods Inc." She signed off saying "Yours, Susie," and hit Send.

There were no smoke signals from work. Barney continued to maintain a professional distance, and was civil when they met by the coffee machine. Christmas was approaching and Susan knew she would soon have to decide about travel again. But she was aware that the pre-Christmas period was always the time when corporate pink slips came flying and suspected that might not see out the season of goodwill at DeKripps.

She waited for Mark Palin at Caribou Coffee in central DC. He showed up five minutes late, apologetically tapping his watch. For a split second she was transported back to the moment she'd met Serge, when he had tapped on his watch before demanding "damage". She stood to shake his hand and offered him a cup of coffee.

"So are you related to Sarah?" she asked. "I suppose everyone must ask you that."

"As far as I know there's no connection. My family is from Indiana, not Alaska," he said, taking off his overcoat. He was casually dressed again. But she liked his informality.

She took a moment to study him. He was tall and athletic, with the slim build of a basketball player. He had big ears, a long face and the slicked-back hair favoured by the young professionals of DC. She noticed with appreciation that he switched off his Blackberry as he sat down in the brown leather chair.

"So what can I do for you, Ms Perkins? How's Mimi?"

"Please call me Susie. And thanks again for all you did for her. She's still causing trouble, of course, but she's back in London. This time I'm the troublemaker."

Susan briefed him on her predicament. He didn't need to be told that there seemed to be a connection to the incident with Mimi and her boss's loss of trust in her.

"But so far you may be over-reacting, right? After all, DeKripps hasn't done anything yet."

Susan went on to explain about her suspicions about Project Candy and Guilty Secrets. His long face darkened.

"You mean they're deliberately putting an addictive substance into the food we eat for the sake of increased sales? Without the FDA knowing?"

"I know it sounds incredible. And can't prove it yet," she said. "I've tried to track down one of the scientists, but that's not worked out so far. I can hardly point to a weight gain as the proof in the pudding, as it were. And that's me in the starring role of pudding."

He examined his fingernails, which she noticed were bitten down to the quick. Do all lawyers in Washington bite their nails?

"The sales stats have been amazing," she went on. "The boxes of Guilty Secrets are flying off the shelves. They can't meet the demand. But the thing that got me thinking is that Barney said the scientists couldn't keep up. It was like a Freudian slip."

"Listen Susie, this could be big," he said, leaning forward. "If what you're suggesting is true, *if* it's true, I'd put it on a par with tobacco and nicotine."

"You don't mean we could put Big Food on trial, like they did Big Tobacco?"

"Why not? But we must have a smoking gun."

"Or a smoking chocolate. I know."

"I can't believe they called it Guilty Secrets," he said. He looked at his watch again.

"So what happens now?"

"Let me think about it. Tell me if there are any more developments."

She took his proffered business card. She watched him leave with the loping gait of a sportsman and sat back in her chair with a smile.

She studied the embossed lettering on the thick white

card. She'd been about to give him hers before deciding that would be pointless. He had her number anyway. For the first time in a long while, she didn't feel alone.

Susan and Rod had agreed to meet for coffee after Christmas in Hammersmith. She was looking forward to going home for the holidays.

Jessica invited her to a performance of The Messiah. It wasn't Susan's first choice but provided an opportunity to recount her story about "John from New York" with a few embellishments for effect. Jessica referred to him for the rest of the evening as "American Gigolo".

Three days before her departure for London, she received the email she dreaded. It was from HR, inviting her to a meeting.

She had only met the head of HR, Lynn Proctor, once before when she'd just arrived in Washington.

"How are you, Susie? Please sit down."

Lynn had a spacious office on the seventh floor. Susan sat obediently in front of her desk, feeling like a junior employee.

"Barney asked me to look into transferring you back to London at the end of your time here. I've spoken to Frank, of course, and others about how best to use you. Your job in London has of course been filled while you've been here. Let me see." Lynn pulled up a file on her computer. "Your immigration status."

Susan knew that DeKripps had renewed her visa for another year so it was valid until the following September.

"So," said Lynn to herself. She turned back to Susan, who was waiting for the verdict.

"Regrettably," – the word was heavy with doom – "it's proved impossible to find you something commensurate with your pay level, despite all our efforts and the best will in the world."

She smiled complicitly before adding, "As you know, DeKripps execs aren't exactly underpaid."

"So we're talking about redundancy?"

Lynn smiled again but her glossed pink lips had tautened.

"You do know that I'm about to leave for England on holiday? It seems very unfair if you expect me to leave Washington and never come back."

"Oh there's no suggestion of that, Susie. No rush. We'll just get the paperwork done and then let's say you'll be on gardening leave for a while."

Susan understood there was no more to be said. She got up, wanting to throw out a devastating one-liner, and longing to say "My lawyer will be in touch," but that was Hollywood. Here, DeKripps was king, and she wasn't even sure she *had* a lawyer.

"Happy holidays," said Lynn, opening the door.

Susan's legs were trembling as she took the stairs down to her office. She called Mark Palin but was put through to a secretary who said she would pass on the message.

She couldn't face ringing her mother to tell her about her humiliation. She shut the door and rang Lily, who was at home.

"This is how they treat me after 13 years' loyal service!" She could hear music in the background. "What am I going to do? DeKripps has been my whole career."

"What does the lawyer say?"

"I don't know. I'm waiting for him to ring me back."

"Sit tight. You'll be fine. You've had a shock. Even though you knew it was coming, it must be a shock."

As she returned to the apartment after work that night, carrying a heavy bag of shopping and trying not to slip on a dusting of snow, her mobile rang. She put down the bag carefully on the pavement and stood under a streetlight. It was Mark, who said he was sorry to hear her news but wouldn't be able to meet before she flew home for the holidays.

"In any case, we need to wait until DeKripps makes you an offer. You've only had a preliminary conversation so far."

Swallowing disappointment, pretending to be caught up in the bustle of Christmas and work, she promised to email as soon as she had some news.

"See you next year," he said, and rang off.

She picked up her bags and walked slowly back to her apartment.

Chapter 18

A FEW DAYS LATER, she awoke with a stomach ache like the grinding of a blunt instrument. It was so painful she curled up in bed, rubbing her tummy.

It took her a minute or so to remember that she wasn't in the artificial darkness of her apartment in DC. She'd spent her first night back in London on the sofa bed in Lily's tiny Bermondsey flat. Then she remembered her arrangement with Rod and knew why she was so consumed by anxiety.

"Lily?" She heard the tinkle of a phone from behind the closed kitchen door, then a hushed voice saying, "Hello."

"Morning," Lily said as she came into the main room, and opened the curtains. "That was Daniel. I hope I didn't wake you." Susan knew she was still in touch with her estranged husband, a documentary film-maker, but Lily rarely mentioned him. Susan suspected that they'd never divorced because of her Catholic background.

"What time is it?" It was already 9.30 a.m. She'd slept well despite the jetlag. She was supposed to meet Rod on the other side of London at 11.

She threw off the bedclothes, ate half a slice of toast with Lily, had a quick bath, and dressed carefully. She decided on professional skirt rather than jeans. She sprayed herself with her Coco Mademoiselle, which hung heavily in the airless flat.

She headed out, only just hearing "Good luck" as she opened the front door. She breathed in crisp London air and felt exhilarated. How many years had she carried this grudge on her shoulder?

She rehearsed what she would say to him as she walked out of the Tube. Would she mention Serge? Why would she? She didn't want her ex-lover's pity. He would not even know she'd been married. She hadn't said anything about her work or relationship status on Facebook. What about Mimi's pregnancy? That was none of his business. Or maybe it was. She would have to see.

Rod was already waiting for her when she arrived at the café on King Street. He wore a brown Barbour jacket with a woolly mustard scarf draped around his neck. He was restlessly turning the pages of the Times. Maybe he's as nervous as I am. Good.

He only saw her when she began dragging a chair towards his sofa. He stood up.

"Here, let me do that. You look good, Susie."

"Thanks," she said, sitting down, "a little heavier, but then..."

"Are you?" he said. "It suits you, anyway."

She was gratified that they'd neither kissed nor shaken hands. They went to the counter and brought back a couple of cappuccinos.

It was weird, it was as though she'd seen him only yesterday. She was no longer looking at a middle-aged man with greying hair and the beginnings of a paunch, but a dashing boyfriend who'd simply taken longer than expected to keep this appointment.

If she closed her eyes and listened to his slightly breathy voice, she could whisk herself back to their romantic evenings in the flat in Brighton, to Devil's Dyke and the leather seats of his BMW. She noticed the crow's feet and the eyebrows flecked with white, but his grey-green eyes were as hypnotic as ever.

She was determined to show no sign of familiarity with this person who had deserted her, fearing that his wife would find out about their affair. But she had to admit despite herself that he did look rather distinguished.

"So how are you?"

"Fine. Very well, thanks. And you?"

"Yes, fine." She started to feel awkward. What was she doing here anyway? What was she expecting from this? Did some part of her hope for the old Rod? Now he was here, what was she meant to be doing about it?

"What made you think about me, then?" she asked.

"I've never stopped thinking about you. I suppose I wanted to make amends."

"Well that would cost you. Your child is now twenty two years old," she said. The words sounded harsher than she intended.

"No, I don't mean financially. I guess I just wanted to see you again to say sorry. I know I behaved badly."

"Badly." Susan considered the word. "To abandon your lover who was seven months pregnant with your baby? Yes, I suppose you could describe that as bad."

She was swallowing her coffee in gulps. How could he have any idea of how it had felt? Fearing to go to ante-natal classes alone. Bringing up a crying baby whose party trick was to throw up like the girl in *The Exorcist*. Susan never knew where the projectile vomit was going to land. Then there were the lonely evenings spent watching television or reading baby books while listening for sounds from the cot, the lack of a loving and reassuring presence when things went wrong.

"You fired me. By fax. How could you do that?" She shot him an accusing glare.

He looked downcast. "I had to tell you. And I didn't want a scene like this."

Susan kept her eyes on a corner of the sofa, and Rod waited patiently to meet them.

"So she's called Mimi," he tried again.

She was silent. And the spitting image of you, she wanted to tell him. How she'd missed him in those early years, when she'd been so jealous she'd been tempted to track down his wife to confront her. Finally, she asked the question that had been on her mind since he first got in touch.

"And are you still married?"

"Yes I am."

The violence of her reaction surprised her.

"So exactly what is the point of this charade? You walk in here after twenty two years, saying you want to make amends, but we can't exactly pick up where we left off, can we? You broke my heart, Rod," she said, "I brought up our child on my own, never knowing whether I would ever see you again. You ran off like a coward! And now you say you're still married to the same woman you refused to leave in the first place. Just tell me what is the point of all this?"

Her voice came back at her from the wooden floorboards like a squash ball. A few of the other customers looked their way.

"Susie, listen," he began. But she didn't want to hear it. She stood, picked up her bag and said to anyone within earshot: "Don't you *ever* get in touch with me again."

She strode out of the café, ignoring astonished looks. Oh God, I screwed that up, she thought.

Back on the sofa at Lily's, a mug of tea in one hand and her phone at her ear, she was listening to Mimi screaming at her.

"It just came out that way. I didn't mean it to," she said. "And he'd just said he wanted to make amends."

As she'd feared, Mimi made her feel as though she'd committed treason. According to her, the sole purpose of their encounter was to engineer a meeting between father and daughter. "And I couldn't even trust you to do that!"

When Susan protested that it wasn't an easy situation, Mimi started screaming that she'd just lost the only opportunity she would ever have to meet her real father.

Lily came in and heard the shrieks coming down the line. She made a cut-throat gesture. "I'll call you later," said Susan, and rang off.

Co-habiting with Lily in such a small space proved a challenge, despite their closeness. Lily insisted she didn't mind practising in the bedroom, although Susan knew that she usually set up in the living room, now her makeshift bedroom. Lily was preparing for a concert by her ensemble at the Royal Festival Hall but was already worrying about the stage fright which might, or might not, strike at any moment. And she was complaining about a pain in her arm.

Through the door, she could hear the trilling, meandering flute. She could imagine Lily playing, didn't recognise the melody but sat still enjoying the music. Lily stopped and started again. She repeated the same bars. And again. Eventually, the repetition forced Susan outside in search of some quiet.

On her last morning in Bermondsey, she received an email from Lynn Proctor. She sat staring at the screen of her laptop on Lily's dining table while she read. DeKripps was offering her a redundancy package which, including three months' pay in lieu of notice, would amount to a full year of her London salary. In other words £125,000.

"DeKripps believes that these terms are exceptionally generous," Lynn wrote. She also said that as Susan came under the purview of the London office, she should discuss any issues about terms with HR there.

Susan was astonished. A full year's pay to walk away!

"Lily, listen to this!" she called out, forwarding the email to Mark Palin for advice. She was tempted to accept on the spot.

Lily was as amazed as Susan at the terms.

"Goodness, imagine what you can do with £125,000."

"I know! And the first £30,000 is tax free."

She realised that figure must seem monstrously unreal to her impoverished friend. "It'll give me a breathing space while I consider my next move."

"More than a breathing space, I'd say. This calls for a celebration!" Lily returned from her bedroom with her flute, and pretended to be the Pied Piper of Hamelin. Susan followed behind, giggling, kicking her legs in the air.

Picking up the phone, she called Mimi. Once again, it went straight to voicemail. She could just imagine her checking the caller before coldly switching off.

Mimi had made it quite clear that she didn't want to see her while she was in London. She certainly wasn't going to plead with her for an audience. So in the end, she appealed to her mother to intercede.

She'd reacted sympathetically to Susan's double disappointment: The loss of a job she'd loved, despite the generous payoff, and the tense confrontation with Rod, which her mother diagnosed as his "permanent mid-life crisis." Susan didn't go into details on the phone about Mimi's role in her downfall, or the cloak and dagger drama at work.

"I've spoken to Mimi about your leaving work," her mother said. "But as I don't know all the details there wasn't much I could tell her."

Susan heard the dog barking in the background. She wanted to know more about Mimi's state of mind, but she wasn't sure she had her mother's full attention.

"Hard to say, really. You can't tell on the telephone. She was surprised, obviously, but you'll have to tell her more about your decision yourself," her mother said.

"Yes, but will she speak to me?"

"I hope so, dear. You're losing friends like a hedge fund manager."

She rang off. Now that the effect of Lynn Proctor's email

had worn off, she was angry at DeKripps, and hurt by the company's treatment of her.

But she would have to accept it. Didn't they say that redundancy was like a bereavement?

Chapter 19

"I WOULD RECOMMEND you accept these terms, Susie," said Mark.

She was seated in his plush office at Smithson and Hopkins, an imposing red marble building on 11th St NW. "If you sued for unfair dismissal you'd stand to get much less. It's capped at £80,000 anyway in the UK. The only way you'd get more is if you claim discrimination, sexual, racial, etc. But we're not talking about that, are we?"

He looked surprised when she began to fidget. "*Are* we?"

"Well, I should probably tell you this in case you hear about it in the future, but my boss tried to seduce me in the office last year."

"Really?" She could almost see the dollar signs flashing in his eyes as she recounted the incident in her office.

"No witnesses, of course."

"It's his word against mine. And there's another thing. And you will really think I'm an idiot when I tell you this."

She went on to tell him about Peek-a-boo, her online dating experience and her suspicions about Barney's predatory behaviour. He digested the saga without comment.

He asked whether she was a permanent employee of DeKripps in Washington, or on secondment from London. It was the latter.

She didn't even know if she was on three months' notice or six, which could make a difference to a settlement. He offered to put her in touch with someone in his London office who could review the redundancy paperwork for her.

She was relieved. If she didn't want to have anything more to do with Barney and Frank, she wouldn't have to.

She was still thinking about the conversation with Mark

as she descended the long, steep escalator at Dupont Circle.

It was a cold night, and people were wrapped up warm. A young man wearing a Peruvian woolly hat and wire-rimmed glasses brushed past her as she reached the bottom. He looked vaguely familiar. After a few seconds, she'd made the connection: The geek! She began chasing after him as he swiped his travel card.

"Hi, excuse me, I'm Susie from DeKripps," she said.

"Yes, I remember you from a marketing meeting." He stopped to wait for her.

"Tony, isn't it?"

"Tony Stella."

"Yes!" she beamed. "Tony, I know you've left the company but I've got something really important to ask you." He looked uncomfortable. Did he know what was coming? She wasn't sure he could hear what she was saying over the noise of an arriving Metro train.

"I'm just worried there's something in Guilty Secrets that makes people fat," she said.

He looked around distrustfully. "Why do you ask?"

"Let's just say that I know there's a secret ingredient." He wouldn't know she was bluffing.

"You know I left the company months ago, right?"

"Of course. But can't you help me, because what's going on is wrong. It's bad. We can't play with people's health like that. And you were the key person on the R and D team."

He stood there silently, looking at his feet, as a group of evening commuters passed by. They were in the no man's land behind the ticket office, and she worried he might flee in either direction.

He hesitated. "I can't help you, I'm afraid."

"What do you mean?"

"It's not my problem."

"It may be, though. Because now it's the whole world's

problem, and I intend DeKripps to pay for it."

He turned his head to look at the time of the next Glenmont train. One minute.

"I've got to catch this," he said.

"Can't you see that you've got a public responsibility here? DeKripps has done wrong, it's harming American children and frankly it's unacceptable."

"Excuse me." A man in a hat bumped into Tony Stella as he ran towards the Glenmont escalator. He recovered his balance and said, "Look, really, you didn't hear this from me, because that's the reason I left. It's an enzyme."

She suddenly wished she'd paid more attention in biology class.

"But how can I find out more without going to the scientists who would never tell me?"

"The others don't know. Barney's the one," he said. "And now, I must go."

Out of the corner of her eye, she could see the flashing lights on the platform and knew they had run out of time. Before she could ask him for his contact details, she saw the two woolly strands of his hat flying down the escalator to the platform, where he jumped inside the train. "Wait!" she called out lamely, but he was gone.

Susan worked late the next evening. She had two presentations under way, on a crunchy cereal and a new ice cream, and out of a sense of professionalism she wanted to complete them before having to clear her desk. She was standing by the window when she saw Barney's black SUV crawl out of the underground car park.

The cleaners arrived. Was she alone on the sixth floor?

She strode purposefully along the corridor towards the coffee machine and noticed that Barney's office door was slightly ajar.

As though drawn by a magnet, she wandered in, after checking the coast was clear. His computer stared at her insolently from his desk. She touched the keyboard and the lock-screen flickered on. A half-formed idea swung into focus.

First, she had to crack Barney's password. She tried the same password protocol as her own, substituting her own initials for his. It worked first time! She was so taken aback she realised she was unprepared. She practically ran back to her office in search of a flash drive. A cleaner looked up from his hoovering.

"Sorry, Ma'am."

"Please, carry on," Susan said as she headed back to Barney's office.

She inserted the storage device, and mentally crossed her fingers. Now to find Project Candy. Her heart was beating so hard she could almost hear it. There was so little time.

She flicked anxiously through press releases, spreadsheets, a disconcerting folder called "Family" and there, deep in a file called "Launches", was a document entitled simply, "Candy".

Was he ridiculously careless, or mindlessly arrogant? Quickly, she clicked and copied the file onto the flash drive, speed-reading the longest document as it transferred. It was written in a technical jargon mostly about enzymes. She hoped this was the one, but in any case, it would have to do. There was no more time to check.

She stood up. She hadn't noticed that the hoover had gone quiet along the corridor.

At that moment, in came the cleaner, clearly surprised to see her in Barney's office.

"Just watering the plant," she said, grabbing a bottle of water from her boss's desk and walking towards the ficus in the corner.

The cleaner said nothing. Susan cursed herself – why was any explanation necessary?

Putting on a false grin, she dropped the plastic bottle back on Barney's desk and crept out of the office towards her own.

Chapter 20

SUSAN COULD HARDLY contain herself. As soon as she got home, she cleared the kitchen table and sat down to devour the Project Candy file.

She knew a bit about enzymes, because the food industry used them perfectly legally as a catalyst to turn starch into sugar. The FDA didn't expect the enzymes to be announced in the food facts on products, although as far as she knew the regulators were supposed to be informed about what was being done with them.

As she read the document it became clear to her that the DeKripps scientists had been working on the effects of sugar on the brain. The enzyme amylase, which Susan knew was commonly used in food, had been synthesized from genetically modified microorganisms.

The modified enzyme was released by being soaked into the fresh fruit in Guilty Secrets, which according to the document "produced a variant of the normal fruit sugar (or fructose) breakdown", dulling receptors in the brain. As she read on, she realised that the more sugar was consumed, the more would be craved.

She could scarcely believe her eyes, leafing again through the pages. This is like nicotine! No wonder Barney said Guilty Secrets was revolutionary. At last, there it was, in black and white, the reason she'd become so reliant on those little sweets and gained a stone.

She couldn't wait to tell Mark about her discovery. But when she phoned him the next morning he could only see her the following week.

She began to clear up her things in preparation for her departure from Washington. It had been five weeks since she had heard from Mimi, which meant she was increasingly anxious and upset.

She's punishing me, she said to herself. And the baby – my grandchild – will soon be born. She wanted so badly to help bring up that little boy, or little girl. She envied Ellen and her twins who were changing so quickly.

When she'd almost given up hope of hearing from Mimi, her laptop buzzed when she was packing a box of books one Saturday morning. There she was, looking heavily pregnant in a pair of blue dungarees.

"How are you? I've been so worried."

"Josh kept badgering me to call. I'm fine, but they've brought forward her birth by a couple of weeks."

So the baby is a girl. And this is how I find out.

"But is everything alright?"

"Yes, of course."

"So have you forgiven me?" Susan didn't dare mention Rod's name.

"I've been thinking about it. You did the right thing."

Susan sat back in her chair. This was quite a moment.

"No, really. You did. When Josh and I talked about it I told him that Serge was my real father."

Susan had a lump in her throat. "Oh Mimi, thank you."

"There's nothing to thank me for." At least they were talking.

"So tell me about the baby. What's her name?"

"There's not much to tell. We've not decided yet. Anyway, what about you?" She seemed to have found Susan's question awkward. "Granny says you're leaving DeKripps? Could it be that you have finally become aware of the fundamental cynicism, hypocrisy and corporate greed of the multinationals?"

If only she knew. Susan took a sip of coffee. She couldn't share her shock news with Mimi and therefore USAway.

She explained that the time had come for her to return to

London, but that she'd accepted an offer of redundancy as she fancied a change.

"What, really? You're leaving marketing? It's been your whole life. You can't be serious."

"Probably. We'll see. I've not had much time to think about it really. Where's Joshua?"

He had nipped out to do some shopping and was just coming up the stairs. He came to stand beside Mimi when summoned.

"Hi Susie," he said, waving. Was that an egg carton in his other hand? Could it be that Mimi had finally seen sense?

"Look, please, please let me know about the baby," Susan pleaded. "You're so far away."

"I will. Got to dash now."

She did a mental calculation of the remaining time before the baby was due. Only five weeks to go.

She resolved to go home for the birth, even if Mimi didn't want her around. Unlike Mimi's birth, at least this baby would have her father there.

The day came for her meeting with Mark. She walked into his office with a file under her arm and a smile creeping over her lips.

She threw it down onto his desk. "There you have it," she said. "Project Candy!"

He raised an eyebrow when she told him how she'd obtained the file. Then looked at her expectantly. "And?"

"And… I was right."

"Wow," he said. He sat back heavily on his sofa and raised a mangled index fingernail to his mouth.

"Like, wow. This could be big, Susie. You've read it, of course."

"Twice, just to make sure. It's all there. It's a bit dry and scientific, but you don't need a microbiology degree to be able to understand it."

"You mean there's a clear indication about the addictive ingredient?"

"It's an enzyme. It breaks down sugar in a different way, so the brain's normal response to high blood sugar levels is impaired. It basically starts asking for more instead of holding up a red flag. It multiplies the opiating effects of the sugar."

She described the fresh fruit covered in dark chocolate, and how each fruit was marinated with the enzyme.

"So that would explain why Barney said the scientists couldn't keep up. They need to make the stuff to use in the marinade, and the enzyme is the result of a genetically modified microorganism. What's more, the files make clear that it's very hush-hush. It's got 'confidential' stamped all over it."

Mark said nothing for a moment. "You mean it's like a sugar bomb that explodes in the brain?"

"Exactly. And the brain can't do anything to stop it," she said. He made a sucking noise through his teeth: "And they were deliberately concealing it from the FDA."

"Looks like it."

"And does it say it's addictive?"

"It was obvious to me. But not in so many words. Is that a problem?"

"It might be. Who wrote it?"

"I don't know. It's unsigned."

She was starting to feel that she'd let him down. The two of them looked at each other.

"I'm going to have to read this very carefully," he said. "But you know what this means, don't you?"

"You mean, am I going to be a whistle-blower?"

It was beginning to dawn on her that she was setting in motion events she wouldn't be able to control.

"This might not seem like a big deal to you, but I must tell you that this is a completely new situation for me."

"I understand."

"It's just that I'm not used to being in this position. You see, I'm a model corporate employee."

"That's what everyone says until they're screwed by their company," he said. "But you've got balls. Not everyone would go into their boss's office and steal from his computer."

She didn't know whether to smile at the compliment.

"Strictly speaking though, you're not a whistle-blower. You won't be protected by the legislation or DeKripps because you'll no longer be a company employee. I'd expect DeKripps to hold you to waiving any claim against them. And don't forget that confidentiality clause."

"How do you know there's a confidentiality clause?"

"There always is. Don't worry, if this goes to court, we would argue that you violated confidentiality in the public interest and in order to disclose illegal activity by the company.

"And in any case, DeKripps is going to have the FDA crawling all over them, so your breach will seem like small potatoes. But let's not get ahead of ourselves here."

"Mark, I don't like to mention this, but am I going to end up spending all my redundancy money on this?"

"If a case like this does go to court, Smithson and Hopkins would work pro bono. We'd of course defend you in case of any counter litigation from DeKripps. You're going to need all the help and protection you can get."

They agreed to meet again on her return from London to discuss strategy.

But he also advised her to make a clean break from DeKripps and wait until the end of her notice before revealing anything.

"Take care," he said. "And from now on, be *extremely* careful about what you say on the phone."

Chapter 21

THE NEXT FEW weeks were a whirl of packing, trinket shopping for a baby girl, and a couple of carefree farewell dinners. Susan shut down her Partners 4 U account without regret. Indeed, why hadn't she closed it earlier? She knew that after so long there was no chance that Matt from State would be in touch. The entire dating exercise had been a failure.

She didn't set foot in the Washington office again after receiving another email from Lynn Proctor informing her that she could keep the Penn Quarter apartment until the end of her stay. DeKripps was behaving decently. Good riddance to Barney: All she had to do was sit tight and wait for the cheque.

Susan hesitated to contact Ellen to say goodbye in case she said too much. The younger woman reminded her too much of her own former total commitment to the company and its corporate values.

Had she been taken in by the company propaganda? Probably. It was obvious that DeKripps and the entire industry had every interest in pushing their line about food and healthy eating, and she'd bought into it for years. In fact she had repeated it to shareholders, journalists, colleagues. It was part of the job. She'd been their tool even when the clamour about the health risks of HFCS had become deafening.

But she felt strange about walking away after so many years. "It's been such a big part of my life," she told Jessica one evening over a drink. "It's daunting."

Jessica was flicking through beach photos of herself on her phone. She looked up.

"What, you're complaining?" she said. "Get over it.

You've got a house in London, and a huge payoff from the company. You're a woman of means. The guys will be beating a path to your door."

"You think?" She took the phone. "The next photos you see will be of the new baby, by the way," she said.

"And what are you going to do with the rest of your life?"

She sensed that, as usual, Jessica was more interested in her love life than her professional future. "I don't have a clue," she said. "I might go back to university if I can afford it, but honestly, I need to think about it."

A waiter stopped at their table to top up their wine glasses from the bottle.

"Actually," she went on. "I've been thinking about doing French. I might teach. You know, like Serge. It's what he would have wanted."

"You, a teacher? Gimme a break."

Jessica was staring into her wine glass as though it were a crystal ball. Then she turned her brown eyes on Susan. "I don't mean this to sound cruel, but you're not living Serge's life any more. He's dead. You're on your own. You've gotta do what you want to do."

Next morning, Susan remembered Ellen again, the one person in the company who'd gone out of her way to make her welcome in DC. Eventually she decided that she couldn't just vanish without saying goodbye, and rang her at work.

"Susie, what's happening? I've been so worried about you."

"Can we meet? I can tell you everything then."

"When?"

"It'll have to be in the next day or two. I'm going back to London at the end of the week."

"I see."

Susan imagined her at her desk, a photo of Jed and the

twins in front of her. But the warmth in her voice had vanished.

"That's going to be difficult. Why didn't you call me before?"

"I'm sorry. I know I should have. I'll be back again but I'm rushing off now because Mimi's baby is due."

They agreed to meet for lunch at an Asian fusion restaurant in Penn Quarter on Thursday night.

She waited nervously for her friend who rushed in a quarter of an hour late and dropped her phone onto the table.

"It's crazy at work," Ellen gasped. Susan recalled Jed's earlier concern about his wife, whose workload must have increased even more now she was leaving.

"Well at least I'm not having work-related dreams anymore," Susan said. "Or should I say nightmares."

"But why are you leaving the company? I didn't believe it when Barney told me."

"I'm sorry, I should have told you. But it all happened so quickly. They ended up making me an offer I couldn't refuse when it turned out that my old job in London had been filled."

She decided to leave it at that. She hadn't even had to lie.

"Well, I suppose you were only here temporarily. But I'll miss you, Susie. It was fun."

"I'll miss you too." She meant it.

"But how are you really? Are you sure it's the right time to go back?"

"I do miss my family, if that's what you mean. I want to spend time with Mimi after she has the baby, and I feel that we're getting our relationship on an even keel for the first time in, well, probably since she was a girl."

"That's good. I understand. It's exciting."

"And it's possible, although not yet confirmed, that she

may have given up her vegan diet during her pregnancy."

Susan shifted in her seat. She could see that Ellen too was mystified by why she would give up her job on an impulse, knowing how much it meant to her.

She told her that emotionally, too, she was ready to return home. She described her loneliness in DC, the nights crying herself to sleep, the overpowering grief and her embarrassing experience at Tiffany's freckle cream evening.

"Oh Susie, I had no idea. You should have told me." Ellen's angelic face creased with concern.

"Yes, I know. I'm sorry. People kept telling me how well I was doing, but inside I was really hurting." Susan paused to think. "But you did help me. It was thanks to your friend Tiffany that I went to that widows' group. And I found out there that I'm normal!"

She held up her hand to attract the waitress's attention.

"Anyway," she added, "I think I'm over the worst now. But listen, keep in touch. Here, let me get this, it's my treat."

"You can't be serious. You're calling her Meadow?" Susan's mother was on the phone to Mimi, who had given birth the previous day to a baby girl weighing 6 pounds 8 ounces. Josh had been with her in the hospital for the natural childbirth. At least Mimi had agreed to hospital.

The phone was passed to Susan while her mother settled into an armchair with Nellie on her lap and contemplated with disapproval the future with a grand-daughter called Meadow. She said in a stage whisper, "It's a baby, not a picnic spot!"

"Is this true? Meadow? Has Josh agreed to this?"

"Of course he has. We wanted something Green and so we came up with Meadow. She's adorable."

What a right-on baby this would be. Susan suspected the name might have something to do with Glastonbury. It must have been around that time last year that the baby was conceived.

Susan didn't dare tell Mimi that she too had been conceived in a tent at the festival, where she and Rod had happily wandered round in their wellies for three days of magic despite the miserable weather. On occasions the sun had come out. It had been one of the rainiest, coldest Junes on record. She could vividly remember Elvis Costello, and swaying with Rod in a kind of mystical waltz to New Order.

How happy and carefree they'd been. She'd been so wrapped up in her relationship with Rod that she hadn't noticed the drugs and the travellers people asked her about back in Brighton. Glastonbury had been in the news and they'd had no idea.

How had Rod got a 'weekend pass' from his wife? Susan never asked. She knew nothing about Rod's spouse, and he never volunteered any information. It was as though she didn't exist. Lily wasn't the only friend who took a dim view of the relationship. But she was so bewitched by Rod that she couldn't tear herself away.

Susan had convinced herself he would leave his wife, but in retrospect she realised that if she were brutally honest he hadn't actually made that promise. Ever. How self-deluded she'd been.

Seven months after Glastonbury, Rod was gone, and that was the end of her festival days. Serge had enjoyed music, but had preferred the comfort of the concert hall.

There's nothing to stop me going back to Glastonbury in the future, she thought.

She was allowed to see the baby twice within a few days while she was in England. Her first glimpse was in the hospital. A little face with closed eyes and tufts of hair.

"Your hair was just like that," she said to Mimi, as she stroked the baby's head. The second time, Mimi was back at home, breast-feeding of course, and Meadow was suckling noisily, breaking off from time to time to gurgle or burp. But she seemed to be a cheerful soul, and Mimi was confident and efficient as she winded her on her shoulder.

Susan was surprised by how easily Mimi settled into motherhood. She showed unusual patience when the baby cried, and seemed to know instinctively whether the distress was due to hunger, tiredness or tummy pain. The maternal bonding was in stark contrast with her own experience: Mimi had been a miserable baby to nurse, and seemed to reject her whenever she could. It had taken weeks to diagnose an allergy.

Josh fussed around, cradling the baby, changing her, tending to their every need. Another contrast she couldn't help but notice.

She saw that a cot which she had bought for them, ready for later use, had been installed in the dark living room which was cluttered with Josh's books piled on the dining table and in floor-to-ceiling bookcases. There was just about room for a small sofa, an armchair and the TV.

"How long is Mimi going to stay off work?"

"She's going back in a month."

She stopped herself from saying that surely the struggle against America could wait for one more month. Why cast a shadow? The two of them were obviously happy.

"Have your parents seen Meadow yet?" she asked him.

"My father's in Devon, and he's not been up yet. But my mum came yesterday. She's in Chigwell."

"That's not too far," she said. "They're divorced?"

"Yes. My mother remarried after dad went off with a younger model, as they say." Classic. "But they both get on fine. It just means my family became six times bigger."

"A typical English family. When was that?"

"They split up when I was still at school, so that was

tough for us all." She noticed the glottal stop when he said "split up." The whole country seemed to have adopted estuary English since she'd left for Washington.

"And the new family?"

"I've a younger brother, who stayed with my mum. David, my mother's husband, had two of his own kids who are grown up now. And let's see, my step-mum had three kids from her first two marriages."

"Christmases must have been fun."

"In fact, we were rarely all together at the same time. But yes, you could say that. We had to have a pact about Christmas presents though, or we'd have gone bankrupt."

She'd often wondered how different her life would have been had she not been an only child. And of course she'd run out of time to give Mimi a brother or sister.

"Well let me know if you need anything," she said. "It'll be a wrench for Mimi when she goes back to work. I hope her workload isn't too bad."

"We'll be fine, Susie," he said. She never mentioned the warning from the lawyer. DeKripps was a world away from Wandsworth, and she had a grandchild.

Chapter 22

"YOU'RE BACK. GREAT!"

She'd rung Mark as soon as she returned to Washington.

"You feeling strong?"

"DeKripps had better be ready for a fight." She flexed her muscles and inspected her fist as though about to enter a boxing ring.

"How's Mimi's baby?" He liked Meadow's name. Susan told him she was as cute as anything, that Mimi was fine, and that Josh was a considerate and helpful father.

"But let's get down to business, shall we? This is a strategy meeting after all."

"So tell me about DeKripps," he said, moving his chair next to hers in front of his desk.

"Well, we – I mean they – are powerful. The food industry is nearly one fifth of the US economy. High Fructose Corn Syrup is cheap thanks to the government subsidies," she said. "Actually, it probably shouldn't be called HFCS as it's not really fructose."

What was it then? "Fructose occurs naturally, but HFCS is man-made. It's corn stalks put through a process with enzymes which makes a new compound of fructose and glucose. Stop me if I'm boring you. What else?"

He wanted to know about the corporate structure, and the company values. "Would you say DeKripps' culture is based on rules or principles?"

Rules, definitely, she said eventually, thinking of the company's lobbying efforts and its relationship with the regulators.

"I'm afraid to say that we've been trying to persuade the FDA to let us call HFCS corn sugar, which sounds more natural, but it doesn't look like they'll let us."

She also described her role at DeKripps which had helped the company diversify by drilling down into the focus groups which had been her speciality. The face to face interviews had yielded a rich seam of information about family habits, what they're thinking, from workplace to supermarket to dinner table, she said.

But now, the majority were conducted online in the US. "It's a shame. You don't get the same dynamic. Anyway, never mind, I can't do anything about that now."

"So what's the DeKripps brand best known for now, Susie? Excuse my ignorance." Mark said he'd never paid much attention to food brands until now, and admitted to ordering in on most nights.

The core product remained the breakfast cereals. But that had broadened to include yoghurt, and even biscuits, although she admitted that she wasn't particularly proud of their added sugar. Then chocolate bars, desserts and ice-cream had been tacked on. And then Guilty Secrets. Frank had always said that we gave the consumer what they wanted, she went on. "But I used to remind him of Henry Ford. 'If I'd asked people what they wanted, they would have said faster horses.'"

She told Mark how she would identify with the public service aspect of DeKripps, as exemplified by Frank, rather than the power aspect as embodied by Barney.

"But why do you want to know all this?"

"We need to know who we're up against. Can you remember any time when DeKripps made a concession to the consumer, or whether they would brazen it out in the case of a bad product launch?"

She was twirling a strand of hair round her ear. "You mean like Coca-Cola when they pulled New Coke and then brought in Coca-Cola Classic?" He nodded.

"I'd have to think about that. Yes, actually we did the

same. Of course we had the FDA on our heels, and I wasn't in Washington at the time, but a few years ago we withdrew Kookies because they had undeclared peanuts in them. We were deluged by customers complaining about their faces swelling up because they were allergic.

" I don't remember how it all ended, but DeKripps said there was a slip-up. I certainly didn't think at the time that concealing the additive was deliberate. And we were able to turn it to our advantage by talking about our values."

"That's interesting," he said. "A slip-up. There might be a pattern to explore here. And where do you stand on sugar?"

Which kind of sugar? I don't know, he said, you tell me.

"We're talking about refined sugar, really." Susan explained how the miracle sweetener HFCS had led their scientists to the Project Candy experiments and Guilty Secrets.

She described the positive consumer reaction to Delight when they began adding HFCS. And the cultural differences when branding products. Less sugar added to UK foods than in the US, and even less in France.

"And is the consumer told about added sugars?"

"Yes and no. The FDA let us put the total amount of sugars on food labels, but doesn't distinguish between natural and added sugars. But then on the food facts it lists the different types."

"Which presumably most people wouldn't know about, right?"

"Yes. Probably." She remembered Kramer and his rant at the bookstore. "But I should say all that's totally legal."

"And is there a link to diabetes and obesity?"

"That's the hundred million dollar question," she said.

"Personally, I didn't think so before. But if you just think that the average American consumes sixty pounds of HFCS every year, compared to zero in 1980 before the food manufacturers began using it, and during that time obesity and diabetes have exploded, you have to wonder."

She held up a hand as though to stop him. "I know, Mark, don't tell me, I should have asked myself earlier. But surely there's a difference between improving taste by adding sugar, and *addiction*."

He was concentrating and didn't respond immediately. He must have noticed she was on the defensive.

"So finally, tell me, let's say this goes to court, and the DeKripps executives are put on trial. What do you want to achieve. Why are you doing this?"

"Revenge."

"Wrong." He shook his head in mock dismay.

"No, no, I'm joking." She took a deep breath. "I want to expose how DeKripps has done wrong, is deliberately playing with public health to boost profits."

"Exactly."

They were sitting in the corner of a dimly lit coffee bar in Georgetown. Susan hadn't wanted to take the risk of bumping into anyone from work. She ordered coffee for Mark – whose presence she had insisted on – and for the journalist from the Washington Gazette.

Barry Pringle was the Gazette's health and science reporter. It was one of the few surviving beats on a paper in retreat. Mark had suggested contacting Barbara Miles from the Scrutineer, but Susan worried that she was too close to Barney. She handed the documents to Pringle and sat in silence as he worked through them, underlining sections with his pen as he read.

He didn't look like he heeded the advice in his own reports, judging from the solid paunch.

Eventually, Pringle put the papers down.

He looked at her, then Mark.

"This is dynamite," he said. "At least it could be. There's certainly enough here to smoke them out. Is there anyone on the record about this being addictive?"

"Not yet," she said. "Apart from anecdotal stuff. Obviously they're being very careful."

He started quizzing her about her role at DeKripps, but Mark interrupted. "Look, we have to be really careful about this. If you attribute any of this to a former DeKripps executive, the company is immediately going to know it's Susan. This leak can't have any fingerprints on it, I'm afraid."

"Okay. You can trust me," the journalist said. "This is on background. You didn't give this to anyone else, did you?"

"No, it's exclusive to you."

Pringle wanted to know how the company had got round the FDA.

"We, I mean they, didn't tell them. It was secret," said Susan." Criminal, in fact."

After nearly an hour, they separated, and Pringle agreed to let them know about the publication plans.

"Don't forget, if you have any more questions, contact me," said Mark.

"Sure. Thanks again."

"Okay Susie. Listen up," he said as they watched the reporter disappear down the Metro escalator. "When we get the heads up about this article, you'd better be nowhere to be seen."

"Where should I go? London?"

She turned over the possibilities. Her London house was rented out. Wandsworth was out of the question. Lily's place was too cramped for the two of them for more than a couple of days, and she couldn't think of anyone else who could take her in. That left her mother. If only Serge were here, she might have found a bolt-hole in Brittany.

"I could stay with my mother in Dorset. Even if the paparazzi start looking for all the Perkins in the phone book, they're unlikely to narrow it down to there. But I also need to protect Mimi."

"Perfect."

They chatted for a while longer before she asked him again, "Are you sure it's necessary for me to go underground? Have you been watching too many cop dramas?"

"All I watch is Mad Men," he said. "And even Don Draper couldn't help us here."

Mark said it would be wise to take precautions, as situations could develop that were unpredictable. She locked eyes with his seeking reassurance.

"So, thanks again." She stood up to leave. She might not see him again for a while, she realised, but didn't want to appear needy.

"I'll be in touch. See you."

He opened the door to show her out. "Oh, and there's one more thing. Get a new phone when you get back to the UK and change your number. We don't want anyone from DeKripps pressuring you."

She looked surprised.

"Susie, get this straight. If you expose DeKripps after leaving the company, you're in contravention of their whistle-blowing policy which precludes contacting the press. They'll try to discredit you if you're suspected of the leak. They'll come after you and your family. It won't be pretty. And they'll set the press pack on you."

She remembered Barney and his threat to bring down Kramer. "Well, there's only me and Mimi," she said. "And my mother, of course."

She saw the lawyer's gaze settle on her ring finger.

"Oh. My husband died three and a half years ago. I've

never got round to taking it off. "

"I see. I'm sorry."

"Anyway, I'd like to see them come after Mimi – she can take care of herself."

A few days later Susan headed for the airport, with hardly a farewell glance at the characterless apartment she'd called home. She grabbed one last box of Guilty Secrets from the fridge, steeling herself to ignore the others in the pile.

As she waited for a cab outside the apartment, she glanced nervously behind her and tried to damp down the stirrings of paranoia. Why was that guy leaning against a streetlamp with his hand in his pocket?

She turned again to stare defiantly at him and watched as he pulled out a phone from his raincoat. Who was he calling? He seemed oblivious to her presence but isn't that part of the training?

Her thoughts were on fast-forward on the ride to Dulles. The taxi crossed the sparkling waters of the Potomac on the Arlington Memorial Bridge then climbed up through the trees lining the Spout Run Parkway.

This is it, first Big Tobacco, now Big Food. A trial. People may go to jail thanks to her. The idea was simultaneously terrifying and exhilarating. Barney in jail! Then she thought, dismally: What if *I* end up in jail? I stole company property and violated a confidentiality agreement.

Her thoughts turned to Mark. He'd seemed genuinely pleased to see her. She closed her eyes to picture him better. She was just thinking about his bitten fingernails when the cab driver interrupted her reverie.

"That's fifty five dollars, please, Ma'am."

She dropped her suitcase at the airline counter and headed for the gate. As she glided down the escalator towards the immigration controls, a full screen ad caught her attention.

She saw the lady with the lamp, on her way to the fridge with the tousle-haired boy. It was a giant billboard for Guilty Secrets.

Chapter 23

SUSAN LET HERSELF quietly into Lily's flat and listened for the sounds of flute practice in the bedroom. Nothing. She placed the velvet-lined black leather flute case on the table and crept away.

She'd only got as far as the sofa when the bedroom door opened and Lily came out, stretching her arms, dressed in a turquoise tank top and jeans.

"What's this?" She noticed the case on the table straight away.

"Open it and see."

"Oh no. You haven't. You couldn't have."

Lily snatched the case and opened it to reveal the glittering silver instrument inside. "I can't believe you've done this! This has cost you a fortune!"

"Do you like it? I was so worried about picking the wrong one. I should have asked you, but I wanted to surprise you. I hope that's okay."

"Are you kidding? Of course it's okay!" Lily examined the instrument carefully before giving Susan a hug. "How can I thank you enough? You'll be first on the list for free tickets to my next concert."

"How can I thank *you*?" said Susan. "You've been such a support for me. Aren't you going to try it?"

Later, she said, glowing with pleasure. She put it away carefully.

"And now, will you let me buy you a drink?"

"You'd better be careful or you'll have spent all your redundancy money before you even get it."

They walked to a pub near Borough Market, where traders were putting away their stalls. Lily appeared not to notice a wolf-whistle in her direction from a vegetable stallholder whose belly hung over his jeans. At least Susan assumed it was for Lily. It usually was.

She wanted to warn her that any day now, there would be an article in the Washington Gazette denouncing DeKripps for illegally developing an addictive food ingredient.

She needed to get to Lymington in a hurry, and who knew how long she would have to stay with her mother and Nellie.

"You mean you're the whistle-blower? You managed to get the incriminating evidence?"

She nodded.

"This is so exciting! It's like Russell Crowe in *The Insider*!"

She smiled grimly. They'd seen it together, the film in which a company executive goes public with internal documents to expose malpractice in Big Tobacco. "I suppose so. Actually it might be more alike than you think. It's all about deliberately working on an addictive ingredient. I'd imagine that investigators are going to have to know who knew what and when. Who gave the order. That kind of thing."

Lily whistled in admiration.

"Better not get ahead of ourselves though." Susan raised her glass, beaming. "But guess who's in the line of fire? It couldn't happen to a nicer person."

"Barney? Cheers," said Lily, clinking her glass against Susan's. "Okay, who's going to play you in the movie? Julia Roberts?"

"Stop it, Lily. This is serious. She's too old, anyway."

"Have you told Mimi?" Lily had put her finger on it, as usual.

"Not yet. I have to find the right time. The baby, you know."

"How is she coping with Meadow?"

"Incredibly well. But Josh is the real revelation. When I was at the flat, there he was changing nappies, bathing her, winding her, completely unfazed."

"Earth to Susie. Guess what, men have changed since we were their age. Not everyone runs off scared in the middle of a pregnancy. But wait a sec," she said. "Isn't anyone at the company going to suspect you?"

"I don't see how. I'm being so careful. I've covered my tracks and I trust the Gazette guy to protect me. I've gone over it again and again, and I can't see that there's a trail leading to me, so fingers crossed and touch wood," Susan said, tapping the table.

They picked up an Indian takeaway on the way back to Lily's flat. It was one of the things she'd missed in DC, where Ethiopian cuisine had definitely not been a substitute. Later that night, wishing she hadn't had a second helping of chicken masala, she checked her emails before going to bed. There were a couple of phishing scams and a message from Mark.

"Lily," she called out after a quick calculation. "Oh no. The Washington Gazette. It's going to be online tonight!"

She'd put the sofa bed away and was making breakfast in the kitchen when Lily came through and switched on the TV. She heard her shout, "Susie, Susie!" and rushed in.

Despite Mark's warning, Susan hadn't anticipated the firestorm the Gazette article could ignite. Project Candy was already the top story on the main TV news channels, and running along the bottom of the screen was a ticker that announced "FOOD GIANT ACCUSED".

There was no sign of any reaction from DeKripps, as it was still the middle of the night in America.

She ran to the computer on Lily's dining room table, read the Gazette story carefully, twice, then printed it off. The headline read: "Multinational accused of adulterating food: addictive ingredient allegedly developed by DeKripps." It was the main front page story and continued at length in the news section.

Pringle had done a good job, nothing in the article could be traced to her, although he did mention marketing and the targeting of children. A DeKripps spokesman, contacted by the Gazette, queried the authenticity of the documents, but there was no outright denial. She wondered idly whether the spokesman was Judy. She went back to the sofa where Lily sat, mesmerized, in front of the television.

"Thank God nobody's mentioned you," she said. "Well done."

There were experts already comparing DeKripps to the tobacco scandal, and saying that the leaked document could only have come from an insider. Other specialists, who were talking about possible links between sugar additives and diabetes, were also wheeled in. One was Kramer. He must be lapping this up.

"Oh my God," she said to nobody in particular. She had to warn Mimi about keeping a low profile. But just as she reached for her phone, her daughter rang.

"Ma, have you seen the news about DeKripps?"

"Of course I have. Lily and I are watching it now."

"Fantastic. We're just putting out a press release, and getting the 'DeKripps is Krap' campaign rolling again. It's just as well you left that disgusting bunch of hypocrites."

"Just a minute. You're doing what?"

Susan's heart sank. The news about DeKripps was a gift for USAway, of course. "Mimi, I want you to take a leave of absence, extend your maternity leave, whatever. But I don't want you at work at the moment."

"Are you out of your mind? Look, I'm far too busy to talk about this right now," she said. "Anyway, what do you care?

You've left DeKripps and I'm glad you did."

She rang off, leaving Susan holding the phone saying "Hello? Mimi?"

"Doesn't sound like that went too well," said Lily. "Here, let's have that coffee."

"And I haven't even told her it's me! What am I going to do?"

They agreed that she should confess to Mimi at the earliest opportunity, but Susan worried that she wouldn't answer the phone for the rest of the day.

"I'd better go to her office. I need to speak to her directly."

"But didn't the lawyer tell you to lie low?"

"He did, but you know what Mimi's like."

"Let's just take it one day at a time. Stay here, and talk to Mimi tonight. She'll be on your side, I'm sure."

They returned to the living room where DeKripps was still "Breaking News". By lunchtime, there were protesters outside her old office in Covent Garden, holding up "DeKripps is Krap" placards, "GUILTY Secrets" and "USAway". Maybe she would see Frank leaving the building.

"God, look at that, it's Mimi's NGO," she said. "Quick work."

"Where *does* she get her talent for strategy?"

She remembered with horror the incident in Congress. "What if somebody remembers about Mimi being forced to leave Washington? It said in the articles she was the daughter of a DeKripps executive. Oh shit, I'd better warn her now before something else happens."

She swallowed, picked up the phone and rang Mimi at the office.

"Listen mum, I've already told you. I'm really busy today with this DeKripps thing."

"Mimi," Susan said. The tense note of urgency in her voice ensured that she would pay attention. "That's what I'm calling about. The whistle-blower – it's me. That's why I want you to keep a low profile. People might make the connection between USAway, me and the leak. This is too important to mess up."

"I see." She could almost hear Mimi thinking.

"All they would have to do is google USAway and DeKripps, and it's right there. Please Mimi," she pleaded. "I'm an Internet search away from exposure."

"Why didn't you tell me before?"

"I was going to. But you were busy with Meadow. And I didn't know how you'd react."

"Well that's pretty cool. I never would have dreamed it could be you. But don't worry about me, Mum. I have to do my job. There are only five of us in the office, and I can't let them down."

"Mimi, you don't get it, do you? There is a big risk that my cover could be blown if you keep up your silly activities."

"Don't be ridiculous. And they're not silly. Exposing the lies of a multinational is a civic duty, and we're supporting you. I've really got to go now. But Ma - you rock. "

As she sat down again next to Lily, she realised it was the first time she had ever heard any words of praise from her daughter.

The DeKripps story ebbed and flowed in successive news cycles over the next couple of days, feeding Susan's anxiety. The Daily Scrum – generally known as the "Scum" -told its millions of readers: "Kids hooked on 'magic' chocs" before punning on DeKripps with its "hand in the cookie jar".

Predictably the paper also picked up the "GUILTY Secrets" line.

The French papers were also covering the story. Le Monde had one of its typically impenetrable headlines which seemed to go on forever, and promised a special *dossier* on Big Food in the coming days.

Susan felt trapped at Lily's but was thankful for a bed while the media storm passed over. She spent her time on the sofa in front of the TV, the muted sounds of a flute in the bedroom next door. She paced around the living room, unable to get DeKripps out of her mind, worrying whether anyone in the office had made a connection to her, and wondering what else she could do.

DeKripps was hitting back, filling the airwaves as much as they could with spokespeople who stressed how they had consumers' interests at heart and that was what had prompted the scientific research.

Somehow they had deflected attention from the incriminating information in the Project Candy files. Once she saw Barney on the TV, looking smooth and reassuring, his thick grey hair combed back. She leapt up and shouted at the television: "Fucking asshole!" For a few seconds, she felt a lot better.

The days rolled on. Mark told her to sit tight, that DeKripps was big news in America and being followed by the main cable news networks. The FDA launched an investigation, just as he'd predicted, and slapped an injunction on Guilty Secrets pending the outcome.

"I bet the top dogs at DeKripps are having heart attacks," he said during one of their calls. "They'll be subpoenaed by the FDA from the CEO down."

But, he added, the DeKripps fightback had begun in earnest. "DeKripps has lawyers too," he said. "The last time I saw Barney on TV, he was holding up a sheet of paper and asking them to point to a single instance of the word 'addictive.'"

"You mean it's not the smoking gun?" Her stomach lurched and her mouth felt dry.

"I'm saying it's one thing to accuse DeKripps of having intent, and quite another to say they deliberately developed an addictive product and hid the dangers. That's what all the Big Tobacco cases came down to."

"What about Tony Stella?" she said. The elusive scientist had been on her mind. "He's the one with the inside story. They'll have to get him to corroborate the document. Can't they track him down?"

"I heard the feds are after him," he said. "You doing okay?"

"I'm holding up, don't worry," she said. "But this thing is doing my head in."

She was wrung out from the combination of long hours of boredom and moments of pumping adrenalin, the days spent concealed behind the green curtains and closed windows, lit by the screen. She'd also had time to examine her own role at DeKripps.

Sometimes the self-interrogation kept her up all night. Had she been right to take so little interest in the products she'd marketed? Was she culpable to have promised Barney she'd sell anything he came up with? People in marketing were dream-makers. But surely they had responsibilities too. What about all those sugary drinks and chocolate bars she'd sold in her career? It was a public health issue. She couldn't hide any longer behind Frank and his happy customers.

She waited and watched. Once, she and Lily went to the local pub, but even there the TV was on, and she kept checking the live ticker every few seconds.

On the evenings when Lily was performing, she watched every newscast, channel hopping as she jerked the remote for a new wrinkle in the saga. Apart from the occasional shouts of "DeKripps is Krap" from a handful of protesters in

Covent Garden, Mimi's NGO had gone quiet.

A week passed in which she hardly set foot out of the flat, she felt so paranoid. Lily stopped her from going to the supermarket wearing a borrowed headscarf and a pair of sunglasses.

"Are you deliberately trying to draw attention to yourself?" she said.

If left to her own devices she wouldn't even have bothered to roll up the sofa bed. Before Lily got up in the mornings, she would carry some coffee and toast back to bed, and switch on the TV. She feared her presence must be burdensome for her friend, having never intended to stay for so long. She resolved to go to her mother's as planned, confident that her cover was intact.

"Keep in touch," Lily said. They embraced quickly and she headed for Waterloo.

She was wheeling her suitcase across the station concourse when she heard a deep American voice from behind her, calling her name. She swung round, and immediately recognised Frank. She was so pleased to see his portly figure that she gave him a spontaneous hug.

"Frank! How lovely to see you. Were you following me?"

"I was just about to catch the train home, and there you were. What about you?"

"Lymington, although I'm not sure how long I'll be able to stand my mother's new dog. Have you got time for a quick drink?" She immediately regretted asking.

"Sure. With pleasure. We've got some catching up to do."

He steered her out of the station. It was early enough for them to get a seat in the nearest pub on The Cut, and she ordered a gin and tonic at the bar. Frank had his usual half pint of lager.

"Hey, Susie, it's just like the old days," he said. "Tell me about Washington. How's Obama doing?"

"That's not fair. Fill me in on the office gossip here."

Frank told her that Martin and his wife had a new baby, whose name was Sarah. "At last, somebody with a sensible name," she said.

"Ha! And this from the woman who named her daughter Mimosa!" She grinned.

There had been some changes in the team but nothing major. He didn't mention who, if anyone, had replaced her, that being the official reason for her redundancy.

"But how did you like Washington? Did you make friends? Have you come back with a lover boy?"

"Certainly not the latter," she laughed. "I did make a couple of friends, but you know how it is there," – Frank nodded -"people seem friendly. And they are. To everyone. It's so superficial. I don't think I'd ever have close friendships." She admitted though how much she had appreciated Ellen's company.

"She's a diamond," Frank said.

They sipped their drinks and ordered another round, sitting in companionable silence. Susan relaxed. Finally, she cleared her throat and said, "Look Frank, I'm really sorry about the thing with Mimi."

"Don't worry about it," he said. "It was a bit awkward at the time, but…"

"I presume that you got the whole story from Barney. I didn't dare tell you, I was so ashamed. I never expected to see my own daughter on television in circumstances like that."

"I bet. But did you really not know she worked for USAway?" Susan shook her head.

"Honestly, all I knew was that she worked for some NGO as an idealistic do-gooder. You don't know Mimi but I can tell you that if you start grilling her, she either clams up, barks at you or flounces out in a huff. She always has."

Frank smiled.

"How are June and the kids, anyway?"

"They're great, thanks. Nothing to report. Just preparing for school after the holidays."

The talk of his family reminded Frank that he had a train to catch. They'd been in the pub for a nearly an hour.

"Time to go. Can I carry your bag Ma'am?"

They walked slowly, Frank pulling her suitcase. "You know we're in a fix," he said. "All this fuss about Project Candy. It's a damaging leak and it came from someone inside DeKripps. Someone wanted to hurt us big time."

She hoped he would leave it there. She followed him up the escalator to the concourse. He knew which platform his train usually left from, but she needed to buy a ticket.

They faced each other to say goodbye under the echoing vaults. Looking her straight in the eye, he said flatly, "It was you, wasn't it?"

Susan said nothing. She was kicking herself for having dropped her guard. Why had she been so trusting of him? She couldn't lie, but she couldn't admit it either. There was too much at stake.

What should she do? Apologise? It was too late for that now. She was casting around for an appropriate and convincing answer, when he looked at her again. He wasn't angry, but deeply sad. Disappointed by her betrayal. Her disloyalty. He'd been her partner in so much. In crime even.

"Goodbye, Susie." He turned to make his way to the platform. She realised she would never see him again.

Chapter 24

SHE OPENED THE curtains in her mother's dining room to a hail of flashlights. The front lawn had been trampled by photographers and the rose bushes bent aside.

A neighbour walked past, staring at the window where Susan was standing in a flowery dressing gown belonging to her mother. God, she thought, I'm Cherie Blair, remembering the photo of the prime minister's wife opening the door of Number 10 in a nightie the day after Labour won the election. The reporters shouted her name but she ignored them.

"Mother!" she cried out. "If you're coming downstairs, make sure you're dressed. We've got a media circus outside."

She heard the sound of the bath being run, and headed upstairs. She knocked on the door. "Mother, did you hear me? I said there's a media circus outside!"

"Coming, dear."

She pulled the curtains closed again, and fumbled for the blinds switch. They came down slowly – too slowly. She ran round the other downstairs rooms to make sure that all the blinds and curtains would protect them from the paparazzi. How had they traced her to Lymington of all places?

She found her phone and sent a text message warning Mimi to stay at home. She had only just hit send when she received the reply. "Daily Monitor – coming down", was all it said.

Mimi was telling her to read the paper and was on her way, she guessed. Her mother didn't have a computer so her only Internet connection was on her phone. The Monitor headline blared: "The Widow Whistle-blower".

She was starting to feel physically sick, but followed the

link. What dirt had they dug up on her?

"The marketing executive who has exposed alleged malpractice at the food giant DeKripps is a red-haired widow who haunted Washington bars by night looking for men and dated online under the nickname Peek-a-boo, according to former colleagues."

She reached for the kitchen chair and sat down. She forced herself to read the whole article over two pages, dotted with photos of her taken from the Internet. One was from her Facebook profile, taken a few years ago by Serge, her frizzy locks flying in the wind as she posed on the sloping red rocks of Perros-Guirec against an emerald sea.

The other looked like a group photo taken at a party – surely not Frank's garden party one summer in Cobham? Her face was circled in red as though she were a bullseye.

Finally, of course, there was a picture of Mimi, apparently taken from her NGO website, nose stud and all. The story recalled her fateful trip to Washington the previous year, and even quoted "former colleagues" – the same ones? - who suggested that mother and daughter might have been working together on the DeKripps exposé.

She was relieved that there was no mention of Serge, apart from a cursory reference to her "dead French husband."

Her mother came down carrying Nellie and found Susan with her head in her hands. "My dear girl, what on earth is the matter? Who are all these scruffy people outside and what's going on?"

She gave Susan a long hug which brought tears to her eyes.

"This is so awful, I don't know where to start. I'm the scarlet woman from DeKripps and now the whole world knows about it."

"Give me that," said her mother, in full battledress

makeup and wearing a light blue summer frock and high heeled shoes. She'd obviously noticed the cameras. She set Nellie down gently in front of a bowl of dog food before taking the phone and wincing. "I don't know how you can read anything on this thing."

After a few minutes, she put the phone down, shaking her head in disbelief. "But darling, is this true? Or is it all made up? Are you really Peek-a-boo? It certainly doesn't sound like you."

"Yes, it's all too true, that's the trouble! It's exaggerated, but basically, it's true."

"You mean you picked up men in bars while you were in Washington?"

"Look, mother, I picked up one man in a bar, as you describe it, and had sex for the first time nearly two years after Serge's death. And unfortunately I told a colleague from work about it, when I believed she was my friend. Now look what's happened. This is exactly like Mark said."

"What is? Who's Mark?" The whole story was making no sense to her mother. How could turning the tables on DeKripps cause the world's media to be trampling her Queen Elizabeth roses?

"Mark Palin. The lawyer who helped Mimi when she misbehaved in Washington last year. He told me that DeKripps would come after me, firing with all barrels, if they found out I was the source of the leak about Project Candy."

Her mother sat down at the table while she digested the news. This was clearly too much information at once.

"Mimi's on her way down now. She'll want to know everything too. Why don't we just wait until she gets here, and I'll tell you both the whole soap opera. It'll be too long and confusing otherwise."

"That sounds like a good idea, dear. Now, let me make

you some coffee."

"I don't want any. I don't think I could eat or drink anything."

"But look at you. You must eat. Keep your strength up. You can hardly stand."

"I've never been so humiliated in my whole life."

"But may I ask you one more question?" She nodded. "What will they write in part two tomorrow?"

"What do you mean?" Susan hadn't noticed that at the end of the article, the Daily Monitor promised a second day of revelations.

What else could there possibly be to tell? She needed to talk to Mark. Maybe they could obtain an injunction against the Monitor and prevent publication. Without thinking of the time, she picked up the phone and dialled his number. It went straight to voicemail.

"I'm going back to bed, mother. Can you let me know when Mimi comes with the paper, and I'll get dressed then."

"Of course, dear."

"And don't open the door to anyone else."

About an hour later, there was a hubbub outside. Susan, who was lying prostrate on the bed, heard a man's voice shouting, "Bitch". Mimi must have arrived. But what could she have done?

She ran downstairs to open the door discreetly, accompanied by Nellie who was yapping violently. A young woman who resembled her daughter was pushing a stroller along the drive.

She was dressed from head to foot in black, dyed black hair framing her pale face. She was wearing black lipstick and black nail varnish. Susan could see the "daughter of Dracula" headlines already.

"Oi, turn round this way, Miss," one of them yelled.

There was some sort of commotion among the

photographers. Susan noticed people climbing up on step ladders with heavy zoom lenses, while others tried to push them aside. As Mimi reached the door, one group with furry microphones broke away from the rose bushes and stood at the end of the drive.

"What did you do to that poor guy to upset him like that?" She beckoned at Mimi so she could get inside.

"Oh, I just spat at him," she said. "He deserved it, the prat."

"So, can we unpick this?" Susan asked. "I just want to be clear in my own mind how they got all this stuff for the article."

The three women were in the sitting room behind the drawn curtains. Mimi had refused the leather chair – veganism *oblige* - and was cross-legged on the sofa. Nellie was in her basket, and Meadow on the floor beside the dog, playing with a moist baby toy chewed beyond recognition by the Yorkie. Four generations of Perkins together for the first time.

Susan, leaning forward in the leather armchair and speaking almost in a whisper in case the microphones outside caught the sound, spent two hours telling her family the full story of her downfall at DeKripps.

The narrative began with Mimi's visit to Washington and ended with her last conversation with Frank. From time to time, one or the other would ask a question. Mimi, who finally seemed aware of her share of responsibility, was holding Susan's hand in an odd sign of contrition.

Neither Susan nor her mother had dared say anything to Mimi about her fashion transformation. After all, they'd put up with dreadlocks when she was a teenager. And the goth look had been all the rage at Sussex. Her mother had made one remark, however, when she brought her in.

"Do you have to stomp around in those boots inside, sweetie? It's high summer you know."

Mimi had removed her platforms to reveal black nail varnish on the big toe poking through a hole in her tights. Later, Susan's mother asked how Mimi could take parenting seriously while dressed so outrageously. Susan had stuck up for her, saying that as far as she was concerned, she was showing signs of being an excellent parent. She was more worried that she seemed to have returned to strict veganism so soon after the birth.

Slowly it began to dawn on her that she might have been responsible for leading the media to her mother's door. Mimi was looking at her strangely when she finished telling them about Frank at Waterloo station.

"Wait, you told him you were coming here," she said.

"Yes. He knows about Lymington." She stopped. It was Frank! What a naïve fool she had been.

"I'm sorry. Of course I made a huge mistake."

It wouldn't have been hard to locate all the Perkins in Lymington once they had a name and a place, and her mother's number was in the directory. She connected the rest of the dots. Barney knew all about Peek-a-boo. And Ellen must have spilled the beans about her one night stand at the Merchant. Under pressure from Barney, no doubt. But still her friend had betrayed her.

"But why didn't you confide in Ellen? Why didn't you tell her about Barney making a pass at you?"

"I was embarrassed. If I was going to tell her, I should have told her straight away. And then the scene at the Merchant happened, and I felt so ashamed. I think she would have misunderstood. In fact, come to think about it, she might have thought I brought it on myself. So I guess that's why I kept it to myself."

She looked at the others for reassurance.

"It's obvious that you should have blown the whistle on DeKripps long ago," said Mimi. "Using a genetically modified microorganism on genetically modified crops to get people hooked on chocolates. Honestly! It gives death by chocolate a whole new meaning."

Nobody laughed. Mimi paused, then said: "Do you know what this reminds me of?" Susan and her mother looked at her warily. "Iraq. Group think! That's why it's so hard to break out and challenge prevailing opinion, particularly in a corporate context."

As Susan struggled to see the connection between DeKripps and the Iraq war, the phone rang. Her mother picked it up.

"Hello, 290 3941. Yes, good afternoon. Just a moment please." She handed the receiver to Susan. It was the lawyer from Smithson and Hopkins. Susan had left a message for the woman who'd helped with her redundancy payment, explaining her plight and inquiring about the possibility of obtaining a gag order against the Monitor.

"Do you know what they are going to print tomorrow?" the lawyer, Laura Melrose, asked.

"No I don't, but judging by today's paper, they must think they can get away with murder. I can only expect something extremely damaging to me and my reputation." Susan had to acknowledge that the story in today's paper was broadly true.

The lawyer explained that succeeding with an injunction before publication would be extremely unlikely, given the fundamental freedom of the press. She suggested that Susan waited to see what was printed. It was already clear that the paper had not attempted to get in touch with her before going to press, to at least enable her to give her side of the story.

That would be taken into consideration if she decided to

take subsequent action.

"Also, I'm afraid that if you do try to obtain a temporary injunction, there is a risk that the paper will get even more excited and advertise the story as the one you tried to ban."

"I understand. In the meantime, would you be able to contact Mark Palin in Washington via your internal system? I need to talk to him urgently but I'm worried about talking on an open phone line. If you could ask him to let me know a time he'll be available today I can ring him from a public phone box, assuming I can find one in working order here."

She hung up. What would the next morning's papers say? She contemplated her family gloomily in the darkened room.

Her mother stood up. "Well, there's only one thing to do in a situation like this." She went into the kitchen and came back with a shopping bag in which to carry Nellie.

"I'm going to Waitrose for a bottle of gin."

She put on a silk headscarf and a light jacket, and from behind a crack in the curtains Lily and Susan watched her wave politely to the rabble of journalists as she marched down the drive.

Chapter 25

"I'M SORRY MUM," Mimi said as they watched her go. She never apologized. This was major. Susan hugged her close.

"Don't worry. I've got to be strong to get through this if there's going to be a trial. And the same goes for you. Mark warned me that DeKripps was bound to launch a smear campaign. It's my fault, I shouldn't have given them the excuse."

"You know perfectly well that companies can dig up dirt on anyone if they set their mind to it," Mimi said. "If anyone's to blame, it's me."

"Look, we're all in this together. But what a total mess."

"They've certainly won round one."

"You know from marketing, and I know from USAway, that whoever gets the first version out there is likely to be believed," Mimi added. "People think there's no smoke without fire. So the issue will be your credibility as a witness if we're looking at the big picture."

Susan reminded herself to discuss this with Mark. Laura Melrose had rung back to say he would be available at 5 p.m. Washington time.

"You're right," she said. "Do you know you sound just like Mark Palin in DC? We need a battle plan. And he can help us."

It was dark when she left the house to find a phone. Only one or two photographers were lurking behind the rosebushes.

"Miss Perkins," one of them shouted.

She closed the gate behind her, intending to ignore him. Then against her better judgment, she said sharply, "Haven't you got anything better to do than to harass my family?

"Can't you see that there's a baby in there, and my

elderly mother?"

"Only doing my job, Miss," he replied. and kept on firing his camera trigger. A couple of reporters appeared from nowhere, and ran behind her with their notebooks. The photographers followed them. "Why Peek-a-boo, Miss?" one of them asked. She turned round, furious. It was exactly what he'd intended. The flash was like a strobe light on her face.

They fell back as a police car rounded the corner, and she strode towards the high street. Little did they know she had no idea where she was going. It was a balmy evening with a whiff of salt air being blown from the Solent. She usually loved evenings like this, but she worried she'd be followed as she wandered down the streets in search of a payphone.

She checked behind her every time she turned a corner. She might be recognized if she dropped into a pub to ask for directions. When she finally found a phone at the station, she grabbed the receiver and dialled. She was relieved to hear Mark's friendly voice.

"So, you've heard about my predicament."

She was shouting down the line, which had a disconcerting echo. She cupped her hand over her mouth, hunching her shoulders. Was there someone behind her in the empty ticket hall? "As you can imagine, I'm a bit upset about it all."

"I'm sure you are. But listen, we can get through this. DeKripps is on the case right now. The Daily Monitor story has been picked up here by the networks and it could get ugly."

"The worst thing is we don't know what they'll publish tomorrow."

"No. We'll have to ride it out. I know you spoke to the London office and I agree with Laura that it wouldn't get us anywhere by trying to obtain a temporary injunction. Why don't you call me again tomorrow when we can see how things stand there?"

His cool professionalism reassured her. Despite her anxiety, she smiled for the first time that day, before hanging up and returning to the house via the riverside quay. When she reached the house, the paparazzi had gone.

The next morning Susan was awoken by a barking dog and a crying baby. For a moment, she couldn't remember where she was. Then she pulled the bed covers over her ears and eyes, wishing she could make her ghastly reality disappear.

When she went downstairs, where the curtains were still drawn, Mimi was breast-feeding Meadow on a kitchen chair, having got up early to smuggle in the morning papers.

She watched them tenderly for a moment from the doorway. They were so sweet together in silent communion like a Madonna and child. The baby's eyes were closed tight as she suckled, and one tiny hand reached upwards towards her mother's breast. Mimi, a flannel laid over her shoulder, was looking down adoringly at the ruffled little head which she cupped in one hand. But she stiffened imperceptibly when she noticed Susan.

"Morning," said Susan, bending over them, and kissing Meadow on the cheek.

"How are you, Mum?"

"Awful. I've just had the worst day of my life. Correction, the second worst day of my life." They both knew she was referring to Serge's death.

"I can't even bear to switch on the radio in case they're talking about me. Do you want some toast?" Mimi gave a nod. "How much longer will you be breast feeding?"

It was an innocent question, but she regretted her words immediately. Mimi raised her eyes towards the ceiling.

"Okay, sorry I spoke."

She busied herself, running the water to make some coffee and popping bread in the toaster.

"Have you seen mother?"

They both swung round as she entered the kitchen, bleary-eyed.

"Oh dear, I seem to have had one glass too many last night." She pulled up a chair and looked sharply at Susan.

"Could you please stop clattering around?"

The morning papers brought a fresh catch of headlines. Mimi's picture was in the tabloids, printed in the Daily Scrum under the headline "PUNK FOOD!", her mouth twisted into a tight O. Her worst crime, apparently, was to have targeted Fleet Street's finest with a gob of spittle.

The short article recapped her shock appearance in a Congressional hearing and described her as the "mastermind" behind the "DeKripps is Krap" campaign.

She turned to the Daily Monitor story, headlined "Dark Side of DeKripps Whistle-blower". It was a hatchet job in which she was described as a seductress who had harassed her immediate boss.

They'd turned the incident with Barney on its head. And there was the photograph of her opening the curtains in her mother's dressing gown. Susan was too embarrassed to cry.

She dragged herself back upstairs and lay curled on the bed, feeling like a hunted animal. Then she sat up bolt upright as though electrified.

"That's it! I'm being punished for not crying at Serge's funeral!"

She called Mimi's name. There was no sound. She must be playing with Meadow.

She shouted her name again. This time, she heard heavy footsteps and the light came on, forcing her to shield her eyes. She felt the baby being laid down carefully at the foot of the bed, and Mimi sat beside her. She couldn't get used to her crow-black hair.

"Can I open the curtains?"

"If you have to. Do you remember the guy in *L'Etranger*? What was his name?"

"Ma, what are you on? The narrator of *L'Etranger*? It was Meursault."

"Well it's exactly what's happening to me!"

"What is? You're being executed for killing an Arab? Don't be ridiculous."

"Mimi listen to me. He didn't cry at his mother's funeral. That's how it starts. They would never have sentenced a French person to death for killing an Arab if it hadn't been for that. Meursault was smeared! It was a character assassination! That's what's happening to me now! And I didn't cry at Serge's funeral. What was it he said about *L'Etranger* – that we must all play the game? And if we don't we're punished? As I see it, Meursault wasn't a stranger, he was *estranged,* that's why he was an outsider. Can't you understand, with this DeKripps smear campaign against me, I'm an outsider, not an insider. Ladies and gentlemen, *L'Etranger,* c'est moi!"

Mimi looked at her curiously.

"But that's fiction, and this is real life. Get a grip. Please." She stood up and picked up the baby. "Listen, I'm going to have to take Meadow back to Wandsworth today. There's a train about eleven. Are you going to be okay?"

"To be honest, I feel like going out there and telling them that the Monitor article is a monstrous lie and that I've contacted my lawyer about legal action."

Mimi seemed genuinely concerned.

"Yes, but you know that if you do that, it'll give them another day's story and another news cycle on the TV. There'll be even more ravenous journos outside tomorrow. Thank God granny hangs up every time one calls the house."

Susan fell back against the bed with a groan.

"By the way, I'll be back at work, but I'm going to ask to be taken off the DeKripps campaign," Mimi said over her shoulder. "I'm going to do fracking instead."

Susan heard the sound of Nellie barking at the reporters as Mimi took the pushchair out of the house.

"Hello, is that the Red Widow?"

Susan's mother passed the phone. It was Lily.

"Very funny. I was going to ring you but I have to go out to a payphone. We tabloid celebs have to take precautions."

"I was starting to get worried after you didn't reply to my voicemail or texts."

Susan had kept her mobile phone switched off since the story broke. She dreaded to see how many messages or missed calls might be there.

"How are you coping? Is there anything I can do? Are you coming back to London?"

"Honestly Lily, I really don't know. I'm just taking each day as it comes at the moment. At least the Scum didn't put me on Page 3 as a 'Scrum-ptious' girl. But the most upsetting thing is the betrayal by people like Ellen. And a friend like Frank. I knew he would be disappointed in me, but I never would have expected this. They want to destroy me."

"I saw that bastard Barney on the news, the smarmy beast. He looks exactly like the sleazebag you described."

"But did you read the Daily Monitor pieces? Basically I'm a loose woman who sexually harassed my boss. How about that for starters?"

"Anyone who knows you would realise it's not true. I'll testify for you myself if that's any good."

"Bless you. If I need a character reference I'll bear you in mind. As long as you promise to stick to an agreed script," she said, then realised she shouldn't have made a joke like that on the telephone. "Listen, I'll call you again soon. But thank you."

She wondered how much longer she could stay at her mother's. She was a liability as long as she continued to be a media target. But she was fed up with Nellie's constant barking, and the fighting over the TV remote. Not to mention her mother's decision to take cups of tea out to the diminishing band of reporters who'd become emboldened by her generosity, approaching neighbours for quotes every time one of them stepped outside.

Could she go back to Lily's? She didn't want to overstay her welcome in Bermondsey. Her best option would be to move back into her own house in Hackney as soon as possible.

That evening, she sneaked out of the house again and rang Mark from Lymington station.

He told her that the New York Tattle was highlighting the fact that the "widow whistle-blower" was a Brit. "That's not good," he said. "Americans come over all patriotic when foreigners criticise them."

Susan was reminded of the Tony Hayward incident and 'British Petroleum'.

"But I've been on the point of giving those reporters a piece of my mind. Talk about blatant lies!"

Mark warned her that it could be counterproductive if she gave her version of the story.

"We need to let things die down for a while," he said.

"Then at some point, it would be helpful if you come back to Washington so we can start working on the next steps."

She liked that idea. But at that moment her mobile rang. It was Mimi. She ended the call and listened to her daughter screaming down the phone. Her flat had been ransacked.

"Oh my poor baby! I'm at the station now, Mimi, I'm on

my way. Call the police. Mother can take care of the paparazzi."

For once, Mimi didn't object. Susan looked at her watch. It would take her two and a half hours to reach Wandsworth with two train changes, so she was looking at a five-hour journey even without spending time at Mimi's. She would have to stay at their flat for the night.

She paid no attention to the New Forest ponies as the train sped through the English countryside in the dusk. She twisted her wedding ring, looking out of the window. How could this have happened? Had she placed Mimi in danger with her actions? And the baby? She took out her phone, wondering whether she could risk calling her daughter. Better not. But she had time to check her messages.

"You have one hundred and twelve voicemails."

She began working through the most recent, all of which had been left by journalists. One, from Fox News, had left several, each sounding more aggressive and urgent than the last. She hit the "clear all" button.

By the time she reached Waterloo she was almost sweating with anxiety. But what she saw when she reached Mimi's street and climbed the steep staircase to the little first floor flat made her blood freeze.

Chapter 26

THE DOOR WAS hanging off its hinges. A white liquid dribbled out of the flat onto the top stairs.

"Mimi, are you there?"

As she spontaneously hugged her dishevelled daughter she could see the full scale of the damage over her shoulder. Every drawer had been emptied, bookcases had been knocked over, the cot overturned, papers were scattered across the living room where Meadow was propped up, giggling. The baby had adjusted to the makeover already.

"Have the police been?"

"They said it looked like a professional job. He, or they, kicked their way through the front door."

"Of course it was professional. One might even say DeKripps."

"That's what I thought. But there were no fingerprints. The police dusted the door. So we'll never be able to prove it," said Mimi. "At least they didn't smash or steal anything. They just left the place in a tip. They might have been watching us and knew when we were out."

"The main thing is that the three of you are okay."

Josh was busy in the bedroom putting clothes back into the wardrobe, which had been emptied of its contents, dumped in a heap on the floor.

"I haven't got anything they want, have I?" said Mimi. "They just want to intimidate me. But if that's what those bastards think they've done, they've got another think coming!"

Susan opened her handbag. The flash drive was concealed in a zip pocket. She was the one with the incriminating evidence.

"But you've not seen the worst yet," Mimi said.

They followed the trickle of white liquid into the kitchen. She gasped when she saw that several litres of soymilk had been emptied onto the kitchen floor. A thick ruby-coloured fruit spread was smeared on the walls.

She put her arm round Mimi. She was struck by how she appeared to be taking the whole thing in her stride. There were none of the histrionics she'd expected.

"I'm so sorry. I feel responsible. Without me this would never have happened."

"Without *me* this would never have happened," said Mimi.

"We don't know that. But let's face it, we can't say we weren't warned. We're going to have to be so careful after this."

She looked around the kitchen again, where the milk pooled at the bottom of a broom cupboard. "Okay," she said. "Put me to work."

"But from now on, for God's sake please be extra careful."

Although Susan was looking forward to recovering her home in De Beauvoir Square, it was strange to wander through the rooms where she and Serge had lived together.

The kitchen where Serge and Mimi would drink tea while he helped her with her homework.

The sitting room where he and Susan had cuddled and watched TV, Serge seated on a floor cushion at her feet.

His upstairs study, overlooking the long back garden. She felt like her own ghost, trapped behind a viewing screen. The place even smelled different.

It was three o'clock in the afternoon. Serge always used to quote Sartre to announce that particular time of day was "too late or too early" to do anything, before leading her by the hand to the bedroom.

The furniture showed signs of wear from the family who'd rented the house, and there were scuff marks on the walls. The place would need a coat of paint, she decided. I can paint the bathroom white now, there's nobody to stop me. She could still hear Serge demanding aquamarine. "It's a bassroom," he would say, "it must be blue."

As her footsteps echoed to the living room, she was reminded that the year before he died they'd hosted her 40th birthday party here. It was also a celebration of her promotion to Marketing Director, and the house was filled with friends, colleagues, neighbours. Mimi had refused to come because of all the "old people" who'd be there. They had a disc jockey with dance music, and sang along to bands like Crowded House that brought back university memories.

Serge, of course, was perplexed, and stood in a corner talking to Lily until they put on "les Stones". Frank had arrived with June and planted a wet kiss on Susan's cheeks, taking glitter away on his lips. He handed her a gift instructing her to wait until later before opening it. When she eventually broke open the silver wrapping, she discovered a watch, engraved on the back with "DeKripps Susie" and a heart between the two. She had no idea what had happened to that watch, whose corporate buddying now repelled her.

Martin was also at the party, with his young wife Katy. She was glad he'd come as the two of them had been in competition for the job, and Susan knew he was disappointed. In fact she'd expected him to leave the company after she was made Marketing Director. She'd heard that according to Frank, Martin had stayed on as her assistant as a tribute to her 'professionalism'. She'd been surprised to get the job at all.

She stepped out of the French window, where Serge used to smoke by the open door, inhaling slowly and half closing his eyes, before casually casting the butts outside.

She caught sight of the next door neighbours over the wall as she inspected the back garden, which was somewhat overgrown. The barbecue was still standing on flagstones under a green plastic cover in the far corner, next to a wrought iron table and chairs.

She waved to the couple who were dead-heading roses. They looked surprised to see her.

"I'm back. Tell me what I've missed," she said, approaching the wall.

"We had a narrow escape during the riots," said Larry. He worked in an accountant's firm or a big insurance company, Susan could never remember which.

"Really?"

She'd been glued to the TV at Lily's then, obsessed by the news about the DeKripps scandal. She'd never realised that the arson and shoplifting that had followed the police shooting of a suspect had been just up the road from her own house.

"Forgive me, I've had a load on my mind recently."

"You should have seen it here. A gang of yobs came along there—" he pointed towards the main road "—and tore through the square. They chucked a couple of firebombs into the garden."

"What, into our front gardens?"

"Next door." He gestured again. "They were away. But we were in, and so were your tenants, so the lights were all on."

"It was terrifying, Susie," said Larry's wife, Meredith. "It was as though the whole country was on fire."

Susan shook her head in disbelief. She looked beyond them to the neatly-tended gardens of London N1. It was hard to imagine their middle class tranquillity being disturbed by anything.

"But what are you doing now? Moving back for good? Or off to another glamorous place?"

"At the moment, I'm trying to figure out what to do. I'm not going to rush into anything."

"Nice to have the choice," said Meredith, a note of envy in her voice. They were a couple in their 50s with three children at university. Mimi had been quite friendly with the eldest girl. Susan sensed that with Meredith staying at home, they were probably finding it hard to make ends meet as empty nesters. "You must find it quiet without the kids," she said.

"Yes, but they come back for the holidays."

"And so does their laundry," said Larry.

Maybe the house would be too big for her too. There had been three of them before Mimi left home. A fear of loneliness was creeping to the edges of her mind. But she was determined to see it off.

"You must come round for a drink soon." She forced a smile, and went back inside, wondering whether they knew she was the "Widow Whistle-blower" and were mocking her behind her back.

She was at the kitchen table one Saturday afternoon, stirring a cup of tea while Radio 4 droned on in the background, when the doorbell rang. It was Mimi, her hair still as dull as soot, and Meadow waving from her pushchair. They wheeled her into the house and installed her on the kitchen rug.

"Do you want an infusion?"

Susan had soy milk in the fridge in case Mimi chose tea. She couldn't even think of it now without recalling the break-in, and Mimi noticed the look on her face.

"We've had the locks changed, and got window locks fitted a couple of days ago."

Susan switched off the radio. "I've got some soothing camomile from Sainsbury's."

The two of them settled cross-legged at the table, just like the old days. A bluebottle circled drunkenly around the kitchen.

"I've got some news, Mum," Mimi said. "Do you remember what you said about Camus, and being the outsider, when we were in Lymington? Well, it's inspired Josh! He wrote a piece for Granta Magazine and they accepted it. It's called, "The Smear – interpreting Camus for the modern world.""

"That's fantastic! Good for him," she said. The meerkat was growing on her. The article would enhance his job prospects anyway, and he was hoping to land a temporary contract at Granta as a result, according to Mimi.

"Did I ever ask you what his subject was at university?"

"French."

"And what was his PhD on?"

"Sartre." That's why he'd been so interested in Serge's work on Camus. "What a shame he didn't finish his thesis."

"I know. He says the research for it kept on expanding and actually prevented him from getting down to the writing. I don't know how long he spent on it, but eventually he decided to turn what he'd discovered into something more concrete. The librarian job seemed perfect."

"He probably found it easier to write short pieces, like the one on Camus."

"Anyway, everything's worked out well for him now."

Susan wondered whether she dared broach another subject: "Do you mind if I ask you something?"

Her daughter looked wary, eyes darting to the baby. She carried on thumbing her smartphone.

"Mimi, I'm speaking to you." That sharp tone had crept into her voice. "Do you mind?"

She put down the phone and waited, sullen as ever.

"Do you know how hurtful it was when you blamed me for Serge's death? Just because I sent him out to get the papers? Was it my fault he was on the wrong side of the road and not wearing a seatbelt? I was just thinking there must be more to it than that. Why have you been so resentful about what happened?"

The expression on Mimi's face was impermeable. Then she frowned, checked that Meadow was still happily sitting on the rug and said, "Well, there was the baby."

"What baby?"

"Weren't you trying for a baby? The brother or sister that he said he wanted for me?"

"Yes of course, but it didn't happen, and he didn't seem to mind."

"Didn't seem to mind? How could you say that?" said Mimi, her voice becoming strident.

"Well, we didn't really discuss it much. I had my work, and—"

"That's the point, Ma. Did it never cross your mind that there was more to life than work?"

"Just a moment, young lady. Did he ever say anything to you about it? And frankly I don't see why he would confide in you and not to me on such an important issue."

The hostilities flared across the table.

"And another thing," said Mimi.

Susan's heart sank.

"Are you aware that he gave up a transfer to Rennes to move to London to be with you? He uprooted himself. You know how important Brittany was to him."

"Yes of course I do. He wanted to be with me. Of course he could have had a transfer to Rennes, but he could have done lots of other things too. He could have taught at university – he had an *aggrégation* after all. But he decided he wanted to be a school teacher. Am I to blame for that, too?"

She got up and picked up one of Meadow's ecological wooden rattles and began shaking in front of the baby. Mimi followed her and snatched it away.

Susan turned round. "But, Mimi, the main thing is that we loved each other – and he loved you too, remember? Love. Isn't that the most important thing? It's exactly what you were just saying about there being more to life than work."

She was breathing heavily. "In fact he loved us both so much that he was trying to get us back together again. He was upset about what happened between us the night before he died. Remember, when you started going on again about Big Food? Maybe that's why he was driving on the wrong side of the road the next morning. "

Mimi stopped shaking the rattle abruptly. Susan sat down again. Meadow's eyes were trained on the clicking yellow and red discs and she was oblivious to their conversation.

"So why should I be the only one to feel guilty?" She could feel years of seething frustration exploding.

"I'm afraid that you're exaggerating this baby stuff out of all proportion. But then that's what you do for a living, isn't it? DeKripps is Krap! How many years did I have to put up with that? God knows I did my best with you, Mimi, I really did, and you never gave anything back. You always used to put up a protective shell, and I could never get through. In fact I still can't!"

Mimi picked up the phone, then Meadow, put her back in the pushchair, grabbed a grubby canvas bag marked with the Campaign For Disarmament logo, and walked out.

"Mimi, I love you!" Susan called out to her back.

She collected the tea cups and dropped them noisily in the sink. She switched the radio back on, but silenced it after a few seconds.

She was staring across the sink into the back garden when her phone rang. It was Mark. What was he doing calling her on a Saturday?

"I've got news," he said. "They've got Stella."

Chapter 27

"STELLAR, WHO'S GONE stellar?"

"The DeKripps scientist. They've got the R and D guy. That Stella."

For a moment, she didn't react.

"Who's got him?"

"The cops. He's been arrested in Seattle." She might have known.

"When?"

"It must have just happened. I heard last night." Mark promised to find out more and to give her a full briefing on her return to Washington.

The next day, she returned to repainting the bedroom. Once all the furniture had been moved into the middle of the room, with the neighbours' help, she found decorating therapeutic. She needed to take her mind off things

She was half way up a step ladder, paintbrush dripping onto a square of newspaper, when the phone rang again. Half expecting to hear Mark's voice, she instantly recognized her brother-in-law's cough. She hadn't expected to hear from her in-laws after their last meal in Rennes.

Jean-Louis sounded cordial, but she detected an edge to his voice.

"Suzanne," he said. "We think you owe us an explanation. We have been contacted by a reporter from Paris Match investigating your activities in Washington."

That sounded ominous. Susan laid the paintbrush on the tin on the ladder's top step and climbed down.

"And what did you tell them?"

"Nothing. How could we? We know nothing," he said. There was a slight pause while Jean-Louis handed the phone to his wife, who took over the conversation.

"Suzanne, what is this Peek-a-boo? You have shamed our family. You have dragged us all into the gutter!"

"Well, all I can say is that if you know about Peek-a-boo, you already know everything. And I don't see why I owe you any kind of an explanation, frankly. I suggest that we all calm down and wait to see what Paris Match publishes."

"*Belle de jour*!" shrieked Marie-Christine, "a prostitute in the family. A fallen woman. Poor Serge must be turning in his grave. *Pff*!" Susan could hear the stifled sounds of a struggle. Jean-Louis eventually wrested the phone back from his wife.

"My wife is a little upset about this, I'm afraid," he said. He was coughing aggressively now.

"Listen, Jean-Louis, I don't know what to say. I'll wait to see the Paris Match article, and in the meantime, why don't you take a pill? And maybe give Marie-Christine one as well." And with that she rang off.

Why was Paris Match was on the trail? It must be the "dead French husband" connection. The French journalists must have gone through the official records and come up with their wedding in Dingé.

The whole village had turned up that afternoon to ogle the "*Anglaise*" their local boy was marrying. The ceremony at the village hall, in which the mayor proudly wore a tricolour strapped across his chest, was followed by a *vin d'honneur* offered by Serge's family to the locals. The youngest were in their seventies. Susan told Serge afterwards that she'd felt like an animal in a zoo. And, of course, even at her own wedding, she'd felt inadequate compared to the impeccably groomed and manicured Marie-Christine.

She put aside her painting to go online. Skimming through the headlines, she saw: "From Brittany to the US: A double life". The French journalists had essentially recycled the information from the original British tabloid stories.

The article ran under the unflattering picture of her opening the curtains at her mother's house. It painted a lurid portrait of the double life of Susan Perkins-Gautier.

Her Breton husband, a French specialist on Camus who moved to London to be with his perfidious spouse, had his life cut short when tragedy struck only days before Christmas, it said. It was her turn to say *"Pff."* There wasn't a single line of original reporting in the entire piece.

The landing at Dulles was bumpier than usual. Susan had often wondered about the winds that swept towards Washington from the heights of the Shenandoah National Park. But this time she held on tightly to the arms of her economy class seat for fear of wind shear and a catastrophic drop in altitude, wishing she'd paid attention to the flight attendants' patter about oxygen masks.

The young woman sitting next to her reached for the sick bag and vomited silently, wiping her lips afterwards with the back of her hand.

Susan was pretending to reach for the airline magazine in the seat pocket, while searching for the sick bag herself, when the plane banked for its final descent, and she heard the reassuring bang of the landing gear being released.

She had to produce her return ticket at immigration, to prove that having worked previously in Washington, she didn't intend to overstay her welcome without a visa. She resisted the temptation to crack a joke to the uniformed agent.

She wasn't expecting anyone to greet her, but experienced that twinge of disappointment as she finallyemerged through the Arrivals doors and saw the waiting crowd.

No one was holding up a sign, a bunch of flowers or balloons for her. It was little things like that which pinched her heart. Serge had always been there waiting, at railway stations or airports. She wheeled her suitcase to the Washington Flyer, which deposited her at the Metro. Within an hour she had arrived at the hotel in downtown Washington.

She was due to meet Mark the next morning. She got up early after a sleep disrupted by jet lag and swirling questions. When she awoke at 3 a.m., she had no idea where she was. Then she remembered she was back in DC, the scene of the crime. What were the chances of running into someone from DeKripps, even Barney, in this village? She decided to give DeKripps as wide a berth as possible during her visit, but the Smithson and Hopkins offices were uncomfortably close to her former employers.

She called room service for breakfast and dressed to please, aware that she was doing so. She wore a light grey woollen trouser suit, black bootees and a white blouse with a chunky necklace of emerald-coloured stones. She grabbed her navy raincoat as she left the hotel for the short walk to Mark's office on 11th St.

She had taken every precaution to be discreet about her arrival in DC, in line with his instructions. Mimi had even done her the favour of telephoning Mark on her own phone to arrange the meeting. After their heart to heart, Mimi had been unusually circumspect and they appeared to have reached some sort of a truce, presumably thanks to Josh's influence. But Mimi had wanted to know why she was going back to Washington so soon.

"Why are you always on the move?" she'd said. "What are you escaping from?"

In her own mind she wasn't escaping from anything.

She'd resolved to go back to college to study for a law degree. In the meantime, she had to return to DC to clear up the mess she'd created. And, although she would never admit as much to Mimi, she wanted to see Mark again. As Susan strode along to the lawyer's, she fished out her phone to talk to her mother, who hadn't realised she'd already returned to Washington to discuss battle plans with him.

There was a crosswalk on 10th St, a block away from the Smithson and Hopkins building. Remembering that she was back in DC where jaywalking is forbidden, she waited impatiently on the corner of the street while the red signal was on, even though there was no traffic in sight.

She barely looked to her right as she stepped off the curb, listening to her mother on the phone. Then she heard a faint revving from around the corner. A lone Segway came into view. She paid it no attention until she noticed the driver's shiny black helmet with skull and crossbones. His face was masked and he was dressed entirely in black.

The man, who was tall and muscular, was staring in her direction. She stopped walking halfway across the street to let him pass and was on the point of saying goodbye to her mother, when a gloved hand reached towards her.

She darted sideways to avoid his grasp, then screamed as he grabbed her and began dragging her by her hair behind him. She broke into a run to keep up and began tugging frantically. Her handbag slipped from her shoulder and into the street. The rider was struggling to remain upright as they wrestled for control.

As they passed the Ford's theatre where Lincoln was assassinated, she was running parallel to him, a foot-long clump of her hair in his fist. The pain was bewildering.

"You bastard, let me go!" she screamed. Could she pull off his helmet and unmask him? She was aware of people stopping to stare and point, some laughing. They must think she was part of a stunt.

She felt the vehicle slowing as it rolled towards a red traffic light, her scalp yielding as his grip tightened. Had he really intended to hurt her? She saw her chance. With all her remaining strength, she yanked her hair to free herself, causing him to slightly lose his balance, while she went flying into the gutter.

"Help!" she yelled. But before she had time to pick herself up and give chase, he'd turned left and was lost in the traffic on Pennsylvania Avenue, leaving her panting on the corner.

"Miss, are you alright?" An African American couple saw her rubbing her head by the side of the road and helped her up. She noticed the man was wearing a Nationals baseball cap.

"My bag," she murmured. "Never mind. I'll be okay, thanks. I've got to get my bag and my phone," and started retracing her steps unsteadily.

The bag with all its contents was still lying by the side of the road. Quickly she checked that her wallet was inside. But finding the phone took ten more anxious minutes. She worried it had been flattened by a passing car, but eventually she found it in the middle of the road just north of F St.

It was still working. She rang her mother who answered immediately. "I've been so worried about you darling. I heard you screaming and then there was a wooshing noise and a crash and the phone went dead!"

"A man just attacked me. I can't believe it. I was on my way to see the lawyer when he grabbed me." She was struggling to stay on her feet. "I'll be okay. I'm just a bit shaken but nothing broken. I'll call you later. I'm late for the appointment now."

She hurried to Smithson and Hopkins where she was shown straight into Mark's office. He'd got up to greet her, then saw her distress. Her trousers were stained with grime where she'd fallen to the ground.

"Has something happened?"

"I've been attacked. It was a man on a Segway."

"A Segway?" The corners of his lips began to twitch. "Death by Segway! Only in DC, right?" He was trying not to laugh.

"It's not funny. This is deadly serious. A masked man grabbed me by the hair and if I hadn't pulled myself away in time I could have been killed." She was rubbing her scalp which was still tender.

"Was he armed?"

Of course, this was America. "How should I know? I don't think so. Do you think he was going to shoot me?"

"Sit down, be comfortable. I'll get you something to drink. You look shaken."

"Tea please, if you can." Her eyes brimmed with tears. But she managed to compose herself by the time he returned with a plastic cup filled with foaming tea from the beverage machine.

"What I want to know is how he knew I'd be crossing the street at that very moment."

He sat down in front of his desk beside her. After a few moments he said, "The only thing I can think of is that they hacked Mimi's phone."

"What? After all the precautions we took? That's not possible."

"These people aren't amateurs, Susie. Remember I told you to get a new phone when you left DC?"

"Yes, I did."

"Well maybe we missed something."

She was stunned. She didn't believe him. How and why could anyone hack into Mimi's phone?

Then she let out a moan.

"Of course, the hacking scandal. Journalists listening to celebrities' messages. They got the passwords. Do you think that's what DeKripps did?"

"It seems to be easy enough. Most people keep the default password," he said.

"I should have warned Mimi, but how was I to know what they'd do? It was bad enough when they broke into her flat."

"Susie, it's okay. Don't beat yourself up. You did everything you could. But this is another warning from DeKripps. Who knows where they'll stop."

"I refuse to be intimidated," she said. "It's going to take more than a man on a Segway to keep me down."

"We should probably think about getting you some police protection. Particularly if there's a trial."

Police protection? "No, I'm okay," she said. "Really. I'm not going to let DeKripps turn me into a victim."

He sat back while she took a sip of the flavourless tea. "Actually, I've got some good news for us," he went on, breaking into a smile. He held up a finger to make sure he had her attention. "And I mean *really* good."

He had been contacted by a top firm of lawyers who had decided to launch a class action against DeKripps in federal court on behalf of several clients who believed that they had become addicted to Guilty Secrets.

"What, bigger than Smithson and Hopkins?"

"I know it's hard to imagine, but bigger than Smithson and Hopkins." He grinned again. "What DeKripps didn't realise when they launched this product is that the greedy rich have greedy lawyers for when they get mad."

"I see. How many people?"

"A dozen have come forward, the best cases, suing on behalf of others. There'll be thousands of them."

Mark explained that in the case of Guilty Secrets, the customers would have to prove a direct link between cause and effect. "In other words, prove they were addicted. And prove that they bought the product, you know, credit card receipts from P and P, that sort of thing."

She rubbed her head slowly and crossed her legs. "But even if they have the receipts, it's going to be incredibly hard to prove, isn't it?"

"We've got the nicotine cases as a precedent there. In the early cases against Big Tobacco, which tobacco won, they were accused of failing to warn smokers of the cancer risk. Like you say, it came down to whether they knew about the health risk or not. But in the later cases, it came down to whether they'd known nicotine is addictive. They could no longer claim they had no idea about that after certain documents came out."

She nodded. "Just like DeKripps. And we've got the Project Candy file."

"Then, of course, for the class action, there's a whole procedure to go through," he said, tapping his pen on the coffee table. "There'll be a discovery phase, just how many people feel they've been affected. But our plaintiffs are ready for that."

One of his friends who worked for Bradley, Steinfeld and Moore had told him that one woman had gained 60 pounds in six months, exactly the time that Guilty Secrets was on the market and before the FDA had slapped an injunction halting their sale.

"Wow. The poor woman. I wonder how many boxes she bought." That's ten pounds a month, thought Susan. Thank God I left the country in time. The weight had been dropping off her since she'd left Washington and could no longer get a box of Guilty Secrets, despite the cravings.

"You can imagine how she felt. Now she and the others want to wring DeKripps dry. Because, boy, are they mad."

He put down his pen.

"I see," she said slowly. "It comes down to proving that DeKripps was knowingly selling an addictive product, and these people having the receipts over that period of time to prove a direct link."

"That's about it. And don't forget that they never told the FDA either." Mark looked at his fingernails before proceeding. "The thing is, Susie, they want you to be a witness for the prosecution. In fact *the* prosecution witness."

"Of course." She didn't hesitate. She'd been preparing mentally for this moment for months. "As long as DeKripps doesn't kill me first."

"Atta' girl."

He thought for another moment. "Do you think there might be anyone else you know at DeKripps who might help?"

"What about Tony Stella? You told me he'd been arrested," she said. "He should actually be the star witness."

"He's not talking."

"But he's *got* to talk!" She raised her voice. "Where was he, anyway?"

"He was living in a commune." She smiled, remembering his Peruvian hat. "It seems he told one of the residents he felt bad about Guilty Secrets. Of course they're all health nuts and denounced him to the police who came knocking on the door."

Stella wasn't the only one arrested that day, apparently. The police found all the occupants stoned out of their mind, and a stash of dope on the kitchen table.

"But if he'd confessed to developing Guilty Secrets, why won't he tell police?"

"The guy he told now denies it," Mark said. "I guess he must have been under pressure. Now he'll feel a lot worse because the whole commune is being prosecuted for drugs possession and possible distribution. So none of them are going anywhere in a hurry."

She thought back to the scene in the Metro when Stella

had been so reluctant to talk. Seattle was probably a good hiding place for a geek with a guilty secret. She cast around for anyone else. "What about Ellen?"

"Who's that?"

"The company's Brand Manager. I thought she was my friend."

Susan quickly filled him in on the background to Ellen's role in her exposure. "To be honest, I never want to see her again. I might scratch her eyes out."

"Is there anyone else? The problem with this case is that obviously DeKripps was taking pains to keep as few people in the loop as possible. And to cover their tracks."

Susan shook her head. "Leave it with me. I'll talk to Ellen. But she probably won't see me."

"You may have to think of a subterfuge."

"Okay." She'd had enough. She was overwhelmed by weariness. "I'm sorry. Is there anything else?"

Mark updated her on the FDA inquiry which was now in the hands of the agency's Office of Criminal Investigations. "This could be a long fight," he said.

"They've got their own enforcement arm, right? Couldn't they fine DeKripps?"

"Of course. A lot of money. Right now I'm not sure whether they're looking at both civil and criminal action, but I figure the whole FDA process could take at least a year. They may want to talk to you too."

"But what about the class action?"

"That won't take so long. Like I said, when rich people get angry, they get impatient. But the discovery phase could take time. The lawyers will want to see every last email."

Susan stood up to go, rolling herself sideways out of the chair. Her bottom was sore. She held out her left hand to shake his, but he ignored it and kissed her on the cheek, squeezing her left shoulder. She felt a warm stir inside her.

Then he stood back as though she'd bitten him.

"Bye. How long are you planning to stay in Washington?"

"Not long. Probably only a week or so. It depends."

"Maybe we could get together again before you leave?"

She was glad he'd said that. But the words seemed to have slipped out despite himself. He held open the door for her as she made her way to the lift, reaching up to massage her scalp.

"Oh God, I just thought of something," she said, turning. "The media will have a field day when all those fatties turn up in court."

Chapter 28

THE KIDS DEPARTMENT at Macy's was overflowing with clothes, toys and books, which meant Susan spent much longer than she meant to choosing presents for Meadow. In the end she picked a sweet designer outfit and a red hooded down jacket for winter. She couldn't wait to see the reaction when she took them home.

She'd decided to take it easy and make the most of her time back in DC. She slept late at the hotel, behind a carefully locked door, to recover from the shock of the attack and flicked idly through the TV to put it out of her mind. But everywhere she went, she was looking over her shoulder. Should she go to the police? An online search told her that it'd be impossible to trace the driver because Segways had no visible licence plate. She also wondered whether she was wise to continue to stay at the same hotel. What if her every move was under surveillance?

She slipped into the National Portrait Gallery, located perilously close to her former apartment and the DeKripps offices, and stared at the picture of Obama.

She'd always found his "Hope" campaign poster on the ground floor inspiring, and today with his fiercely determined eyes he seemed to be praying for her, hold tight, you'll get through it. She strolled across the Mall to the Freer Gallery where they flung open the shutters of the Whistler Peacock Room at noon so she could marvel at the proud birds in the daylight.

She'd never been able to escape from work for the monthly viewing when she was living in Washington, and was startled by the glistening gold in the natural light. The swirl of plumage as the two magnificent peacocks prepared to scratch each other's eyes out. Did their proud strutting gait contain a lesson for her?

She went shopping in Georgetown. And she went to the theatre. Jessica, predictably, turned down her invitation to see the *Heir Apparent,* saying that French farce wasn't her idea of fun, so she went alone to the theatre and laughed so hard that the people in front turned round. Yet despite such moments she couldn't rid herself of the suspicion that someone might be watching her.

She was heading to dinner at Jessica's after finishing her shopping. She might even take her up on her invitation to stay. After she'd paid for the gifts for Meadow, she just had time to look for some makeup for herself. As she examined the foundation creams at a cosmetics counter, rubbing the testers on the back of her hand, she was surprised to see a ginger box decorated with gold glitter called Freckle Free. This must be one of the creams she had tested with the focus group in Chevy Chase.

"Would you like to try Freckle Free? It really works." The sales assistant must have noticed her complexion.

"No, thanks. I think I did already," she said, putting down the box, and walked away. She took the escalator downstairs into the basement and wandered through the bedding department towards the exit that led straight to the Metro.

It was rush hour at Metro Center. She needed to take the Red line to Cleveland Park, which was only a few stops away. But the station was crowded with commuters with their heads down like the workers in Fritz Lang's *Metropolis*. The lights in Metro Center were as dim as in all the other stations, and she had to adjust her eyes to the gloom as she came out of the store. She'd never understood why the Metro was so dark, although it was so much cleaner than the London Tube.

She swiped her Smartrip card at the gate and checked she

was on the right platform. A train to Shady Grove was due in three minutes. The stone seats by the concrete wall were taken, so she waited on the platform as close to the front as she could. But the travellers were three deep. Out of habit, she glanced around her, but saw nobody suspicious.

Still, why would an attacker look suspicious? She was probably more at risk from a pickpocket. She held on tight to her red and white Macy's bag as the crowd around her thickened. The overhead sign on the platform said the train was due in one minute. She looked behind her again and saw people getting up and moving forward.

The lights began blinking white on the platform edge. She felt the warm crush of people behind her, and reached the front as the train roared towards the platform. Then suddenly, she was pushed sharply from behind. She tried to steady herself, causing a man standing next to her to stumble. But as he recovered his balance, she was thrust forward into the space that opened up. As she tumbled towards the track, still clutching her Macy's bag, she saw the yellow headlights of the train approaching in a scream of metal.

When she opened her eyes, everything was pink. She was in a pink room with pink blinds and matching pink sheets and blankets.

Was she still dreaming? She tried to lift herself out of bed, pushing pillows aside, and found she was too weak to move. She noticed a drip attached to her arm. She lay back, falling again, falling. A nurse came in and told her she'd been rushed to hospital after breaking her shoulder, and had been given morphine for the pain. She reached towards her right shoulder, felt a searing sting, and drifted back into wild and colourful dreams.

After more than a week, her arm was still in a sling.

She'd managed to keep her injured shoulder dry without having to ask Jessica for embarrassing help in the shower, but she was right-handed and found it awkward to eat with her left hand. Jessica had chopped up her food into biteable chunks every evening so far. Susan was sure she must be regretting inviting her to stay for as long as she needed.

She'd been sleeping naked to avoid having to tie herself in knots taking off pyjamas, or worse, getting a nightie stuck at shoulder level. Jessica had already left for the day - she was supervising the redecoration of a house in Virginia - and she went straight across the landing towards the bathroom. What a pathetic sight, she thought as she caught a glimpse of her bruised, freckled right side in the full length mirror, a yellowing mark on one cheek glowing next to her hair. The Botticelli Venus she wasn't.

They'd told her at the hospital she was lucky to be alive. The driver of the incoming Metro train had seen her fall and slammed on the brakes, stopping with only a few feet to spare. Her fall had been cushioned by the clothing in the Macy's bag, which had prevented a serious head injury. But all her weight had been on her shoulder which was smashed by the impact. The emergency ward had alerted Jessica to the accident after finding several text messages and voicemails on Susan's phone.

Her friend had thoughtfully left the coffee warming and a blueberry muffin on the table. How considerate, she could crumble it with her left hand. She was unable to spread butter on toast because it kept slipping off the plate. Jessica had also left a note promising her return at six and urging Susan to "chill."

But she couldn't forget that moment when she was pushed in front of the train. Although the memory was a little hazy, disbelief was replaced by fury when it sank in that DeKripps really had wanted her dead.

Over sushi that evening, she tried to interest Jessica in plotting her next move. Susan wolfed down the rolls of tuna and salmon with one hand, while her friend took a little longer with chopsticks.

"So let me get this straight," said Jessica. "You've got to find a way of luring this DeKripps woman out of her office to talk to you. Have you thought of just calling her? You're hardly in a state to go chasing after her."

"She wouldn't answer her cell phone, I'm sure. And she'd alert the bosses if she knows I'm back. She's like a young version of me, that's the trouble."

She hadn't gone into all the intricacies of the plot. She knew Jessica was only concerned about her personal welfare and hadn't been aware of the DeKripps scandal at all.

"And what about the love interest?"

"God, Jessica, you're incorrigible. I told you I don't have a relationship with Mark," she said. "He's my legal adviser."

"But does he give you smouldering looks over his legal documents?"

"Please, this is DC, not Hollywood. Of course he doesn't."

"He's a nice guy though, right? Don't you have the hots for him?"

"Possibly. I don't know. I don't want things to move too fast."

Mark had been following up with the police since the accident. It turned out he had a vague connection with the main witness, a lawyer, the man she'd knocked against as she fell towards the track. Police were studying CCTV footage for clues as to the identity of the attacker, but she had asked Mark to make sure the investigation stayed out of the media. She didn't want Barney to have the satisfaction that she'd been injured.

She steered the conversation back to Ellen.

"I could always follow her out of work and into the Metro. But what if she doesn't stop?"

She'd been terrified of taking the Metro ever since the attack. Since leaving hospital, she'd been waking up in the middle of the night with a recurring nightmare that she was falling down the escalator at Dupont Circle under the Walt Whitman inscription, her face heading for the slicing escalator steps. She'd never been able to read past "the hurt and wounded I pacify with soothing hand" before descending into the escalator tunnel.

"Hey, I've got an idea." She remembered Ellen's twins. "What if you pretended to be their teacher, and arranged to meet her outside the school?"

"Are you nuts? Anyone would think that you've been hit on the head." Jessica pointed out that Ellen would know the teacher's name and probably even the phone number, so she'd be outed instantly.

"Okay, so what if you were a replacement teacher?"

The conversation went round and round, with each new idea more outlandish than the last and no solution in sight. In the end, they decided Susan would have to take the risk of ambushing Ellen on her way home from the office.

"Wait, you're going to jump out of the bushes when she gets home?" The idea of Susan doing any such thing with a broken shoulder made them both burst out laughing.

The FDA investigation was now confined to the business pages after the company shares took a big hit. It wouldn't take much for the scandal to be back on the front pages. If only she could persuade Ellen. If only Tony Stella would do the right thing and talk.

A couple of days later, she found herself posted at a bus stop from where she could see the entrance to the DeKripps building in Penn Quarter. The signage outside told passersby that the company was the maker of Delight Ice Cream. A banner was unfurled around a tub of ice cream, with the creamy vanilla dripping from a scoop, and the slogan "More, Please."

The poster had replaced a Guilty Secrets ad. DeKripps would have had to pull all promotion for the chocolates under the FDA injunction.

She pulled the collar of her coat around her shoulders with her free arm, to keep out the cold. An hour went by, after 6 p.m. the offices began to empty. She began to shiver. The garage next to the entrance opened.

Susan recognized Barney's black SUV. Would he see her? She quickly turned her back on the building, and counted to ten, pretending to look at the menu of a restaurant behind her. Had he gone yet? She was too nervous to look.

Barney's departure would mean that the other executives would feel safe to leave the building. Slowly, she turned round. The SUV had gone. Moments later, she caught sight of Ellen, who crossed the road and headed straight towards the bus stop. It saved Susan the ignominy of trying to hasten after her.

"Ellen," she said quietly when she was within earshot. She was aware that other workers were scurrying home, and didn't want a scene in public. Ellen looked towards her in horror. Then her eyes showed fear.

"Jesus. Susan. What do you want?"

"I wanted to see you. You need to know my side of the story."

"What story? There's no story." Ellen continued on her way without stopping. Susan was again struck by her resemblance to her former self. Now here she was in the role of Mimi. But before she could say anything else, Ellen said, "What happened to you? Are you okay?"

Was the old Ellen still there?

"You'll never believe this, but someone tried to kill me by pushing me under a Metro train."

"What? Jeez." Her mouth fell open and she finally came to a halt.

"Look, I don't want to pester you but I only need a few minutes. Can you spare me that?" She'd been practising a whole speech with which to confront her friend, but now her mind was a blank.

"Well." Ellen was clearly reluctant. "I have to get back. You know, the twins..."

"Please. Just a quick coffee."

They headed towards Metro Center and Caribou Coffee, the place where she'd first met Mark Palin.

They sat in the same leather chairs with their drinks, Ellen carrying Susan's. "You know it's over for DeKripps, don't you?"

"Thanks to you," Ellen said. She sounded bitter. Susan bit her lip. She wasn't going to revisit her own feelings about Ellen's treachery at this point.

"I just wanted to warn you, as a friend, that the FDA is crawling all over Guilty Secrets."

"I am aware of that, thank you, Susie. I'm the one working at DeKripps. Yes, it's crazy." She paused, waiting for her to go on.

"But do you also know about the class action?"

"I saw something about that in the Gazette recently."

"Well I can tell you that one of the biggest law firms in the country is going to war with DeKripps over Project Candy. It's illegal, Ellen. You and I know that. It shouldn't have happened. I'm offering you the chance to do the right thing."

Ellen said nothing. Her face was impassive.

"Listen, I don't expect you to believe this but I was forced into leaving DeKripps after Barney tried to seduce me in my office. I've been kicking myself ever since for not confiding in you, but it's the plain truth. The thing with Mimi was the trigger, but what happened between me and Barney was the real reason."

Ellen looked confused. Then awkward. Had she been troubled by her own role in the smear campaign?

"So he tried to seduce *you*? Not the other way round?"

"That's right. Can you imagine what it's been like for me to have my name dragged through the mud around the world? You know how much DeKripps meant to me. And now look at me. My former employer has not only smeared my reputation but they've tried to kill me. Did I deserve that?"

Susan leaned forwards, hunched in her chair. She hadn't intended the conversation to go this way. This sounded like self-pity. But her arm hurt. Ellen reached forward. "Oh Susie. Why didn't you tell me? "

"How could I? I was too ashamed. I didn't even know if anyone would believe me."

"Didn't you think of going to HR?"

"Of course. But after that Peek-a-boo business that you knew about, and Barney talking about "consenting adults", I knew it wouldn't work. So I took my revenge another way. This probably isn't making much sense, but there you are."

Ellen still looked dubious. "So you decided to bring down an entire company because your boss tried to harass you? Isn't that a bit extreme, Susie?"

"That's not all of it. I tracked down Tony Stella."

"The guy from R and D we talked about?"

"I should have told you. He confirmed that it's an enzyme. The bottom line is that what DeKripps is doing is wrong. I mean developing an addictive ingredient, hiding it from the FDA, and then deliberately putting it into the food of rich people to make them fat and dependent? What were they thinking?"

"Is that what's happened? The FDA didn't know?"

"And by hitting the luxury market they've bitten off more than they can chew, as it were."

"Yeah, I can see that. Honestly, Susie, you should see Barney and the rest of them. They're all at each other's throats. Are they going to go for Bubba?"

"I expect so. But Stella certainly made it clear that Barney knew all about it."

Susan could see that Ellen had figured out which way the wind was blowing. She pressed her advantage.

"You don't have to make up your mind now, obviously, but this could be a way out for you. Think of your own future." She handed her Mark's card. "He's my legal adviser. I trust him. Talk things over at home and contact him if you're willing to tell them what you know."

"But what do I know? I'm pretty low down the food chain. Most of what I know is second hand at best."

"It doesn't matter, Ellen. It's a question of doing what's right, isn't it? And if someone like you sets an example, others may follow."

A wave of tiredness enveloped her again. "I'd better go. Coffee and painkillers aren't doing my wooziness much good. Best of luck."

She manoeuvered herself out of the leather chair, which was less comfortable than it looked, and left her former colleague pondering the bottom of her coffee cup.

Chapter 29

SHE GLANCED ANXIOUSLY at Mark as they entered the glass cube law offices on Connecticut Avenue. He'd told her that it might be useful to meet the lead counsel of the class action before she left for home.

But when they were ushered into the seventh floor corner office of Aaron Steinfeld, she almost walked straight out again. Seated in front of his desk were two sets of couples, each well-dressed but noticeably overweight. She realised immediately they must be plaintiffs in the suit.

Steinfeld, an elderly, reassuring presence whose creased features resembled so many of the seniors still active in Washington, stood up to make the introductions. He was dressed in a pinstriped suit and shoes as shiny as Barney's.

"Pleased to meet you, Ms Perkins, may I congratulate you on the stand you're taking in the public interest." Susan stretched out her good hand. "Mr and Mrs Stephens have flown in from San Francisco, and wanted to meet you."

The middle aged couple struggled out of their chairs to shake hands. The other couple, introduced as Mr and Mrs Kelley, looked like young executives from DC. None of them was smiling. None of them commented on Susan's appearance, as Mark helped her take off her raincoat.

"First of all, let me say that Bradley, Steinfeld and Moore has a strong record in class action cases," said Steinfeld.

"In the case of DeKripps, the federal authorities are also investigating. But we've obtained record sums on behalf of our clients who have taken collective action. I'm the lead counsel, which is why I was keen to bring you all together today."

He turned to Susan. "Ms Perkins, if you would be so kind as to update us on how you came to be where you are now?"

She looked towards Mark for support. He flashed a brief smile of encouragement, and she proceeded to summarise why she had gone public after realising she'd been duped by the company into marketing a dodgy product.

Steinfeld's quizzical gaze went from one couple to the other. The first to speak was Mrs Kelley, a blonde who looked like a retired air stewardess. "Ms Perkins, we are suing your company because of the damage it has done to our two young children." The woman's voice began to tremble. "May I show you?"

Susan had no choice in the matter, as the woman took out a small photo album. She obviously intended to show them 'before' and 'after' pictures of her children. Mrs Kelley sighed as she turned the pages.

"This is our son, Jason, one year ago. Before you put Guilty Secrets on the market. This is him now, Ms Perkins."

Susan was feeling increasingly uncomfortable. She was starting to fear a lynching. She understood perfectly how these DeKripps customers must feel, but she didn't like the way they were referring to her as though she was the company representative.

She took the proffered album and flicked through it. The change in the little boy in short trousers was there for all to see, the normal sized child had morphed into a blob in the space of a few months.

"He simply couldn't stop eating them. I stopped buying them but found empty wrappers in his room. Hundreds of them under the bed, along with the receipts, thank God. He hid them from his own mother. He was spending all his allowance on Guilty Secrets, and I didn't even know!"

She turned the page. Susan had to stop herself from gasping when she saw Jason's sister, blonde like her mother.

The slim, pretty girl in the first picture was scarcely recognisable in the next.

"And how old is she?" she asked.

"Thirteen."

She could see that the woman was on the brink of tears. She felt terrible. She imagined how she would be behaving if the same thing had happened to Mimi. She also felt responsible. She *was* responsible, there was no getting away from that.

The Scum had put its finger on it in the headline about kids being addicted to 'magic' chocolate. She'd never given it a thought when devising the strategy for rich people.

Of course they'd dreamed up the ad with a woman and her child. DeKripps knew how to sell to families. They'd deliberately targeted the children's market with a product that turned out to be dangerous for people's health. DeKripps and its shareholders had got rich and so had she. But at what cost?

"And now that Guilty Secrets are off the market, is their health improving?"

Mr and Mrs Kelley looked at each other mournfully.

"Slowly," he said. "But fat is a lot harder to lose than it is to gain. And they had less control over that gain than most, right?"

"I'm so sorry," she said. What more could she say? She wanted to get out of that office as soon as possible.

She asked the couple at what point they had realised the link with Guilty Secrets, and whether they'd contacted the company. They looked at each other again before Mrs Kelley said, "Of course we wrote to customer services. On more than one occasion. But we never received a single reply."

What had Barney done with the correspondence?

"And did you keep copies of the letters or emails?"

"We did. And our next step was to contact our lawyer."

Half an hour later, after listening to the Stephens explain how they'd flown in by corporate jet and were determined to "break" DeKripps for what the company had done, she and Mark escaped.

"How do you think that went?" he said. She was waiting for him on the street while he finished up inside.

"It was an ambush. I don't know why I allowed myself to be persuaded to do that. You told me it was strictly voluntary but they were behaving as though it was *me* on trial. Anyone would think I developed the enzyme. I didn't like to mention it in there but DeKripps actually tried to kill me!" she said, raising her sling.

"Well, I did warn you that you'd have to be strong. It's not going to be a walk in the park, you know. In fact, you should also prepared to be called in by the FDA in due course. They're sure to be interviewing all the DeKripps executives."

"But didn't Steinfeld warn you they were going to be there?"

"No, he didn't, actually. I was as surprised as you. But you need to remember that you're on the same side against DeKripps. And I would vouch for Steinfeld. He has more class action experience than probably any lawyer in Washington."

"I guess I'll have to trust you on that. But how old is he? He looks like a Mummy. I hope he can survive until the trial."

"Hey, careful where you're going with this. Don't even think for a moment that a lawyer would support age discrimination."

"But don't people ever retire in this town?"

He laughed. "Maybe their pensions aren't good enough. We're not in Europe, you know. Look Susie, you're leaving tomorrow, right? Let me buy you a goodbye drink before you go."

They strolled down towards the Dupont Circle Metro and

round the corner to a wine bar.

"So what happened in there after I left?" she said as they went down the steps into the lounge.

"Oh, Steinfeld was just telling me that DeKripps wanted to settle."

Chapter 30

SPOTTING A BENCH in a quiet corner, Susan lowered herself hesitantly into it. Mark sat across from her.

She didn't know what to think. Mark had announced the news so casually but this sounded like a big development to her. Had her sacrifice been for nothing?

"Out of court? You mean there won't be a trial?"

"It's to be expected in a case like this. Obviously their reputation is at stake, they'll be praying they can avoid a trial. But Steinfeld says the plaintiffs are adamant because of the public interest."

"Thank God. They were pretty fired up in there."

She was glad they had the space to spread out; they'd arrived before the evening rush.

"So, what's your poison then?"

"Guilty Secrets of course." They smiled at each other. "I'd love a glass of Chardonnay. Don't mind me, though, if I spill it all over my blouse with my wrong hand."

He seemed nervous. He seemed to be turning something over in his mind.

"Susie. I have to tell you this. I'm attracted to you but you're my client. That poses a particular problem for me."

Until that moment she hadn't been sure it wasn't all in her mind.

"To tell you the truth, I'm very much attracted to you too. You know that though, don't you?"

He nodded. "But what I'm saying is that this can't happen. At least not yet."

"What do you mean?"

"It's not ethically correct, having a sexual relationship with your client. As a lawyer, you might lose all sense of objectivity. It's opening a can of worms."

"But you're my legal adviser, not my lawyer."

"It comes down to the same thing. I could be disbarred."

"You could always deny it, like Clinton. I did not have sex with that woman!"

"Funny." He was gravely serious. He called the waitress and ordered their wine, along with a couple of pizza slices. Susan remained silent.

"In fact, we shouldn't even be here. It's socializing. We should be discussing business in my office."

"Oh. But in the great scheme of things, I mean, how bad would it be? It's not like DeKripps poisoning the entire population, is it?"

"No, but that's not the issue. It's a question of decency."

"I have to admire you for saying that. But actually, I could jump into bed with you right now. Except that I've got a broken shoulder," she said.

"Me too, Susie, believe me."

She asked him if he'd been married. He had, after Harvard, but the marriage hadn't lasted or produced children. "In case you're wondering," he added.

"But a clever, attractive guy like you must have had other relationships since then?"

"Yeah, sure. Maybe my heart wasn't in it, or theirs wasn't, because it never worked out. Also I was working pretty hard. Before I came to DC I worked in Indiana. Two sets of bar exams after qualifying. What about you? What did your husband do?"

"He was a scholar and a poet." Why was she trying to impress him with her dead husband's credentials? "He was French, actually. He wrote about Camus, the French writer." She'd pricked his interest.

"*The Stranger*? I read it in my spare time when I was at law school. It made quite an impact on me at the time."

"Is that what they call it here?" she said. "The translation

I read was called *The Outsider*. Actually, I think outsider is better. It expresses the alienation. It doesn't really make sense to call it *The Stranger*. He wasn't a stranger. Or I suppose it could be *The Foreigner*. But outsider is best. Definitely."

She paused. Then she said, "You've brought me here to tell me that we can't ever be together, haven't you? Is that why you called it a goodbye drink?"

"Not never. Just not now. I have to be careful. As a professional person, you understand that."

Unfortunately, she did understand. She made one last desultory attempt. "I won't tell anyone if you won't." But she regretted it immediately. He must think she was desperate. But he grinned and said, "You're pretty badass, aren't you?"

"It's just that I'm not used to a clinical conversation about a relationship that hasn't even started. This is a bit too cerebral for me. In my book, if you fancy someone, and they fancy you, then you jump into bed." Something else she regretted saying.

He held up his hands as though to say, what can I do about it?

"There is an alternative, isn't there?" she said.

"You mean I could recuse myself?"

"Yes."

"Do you want me to do that, Susie?"

"No. Bad idea. I want you to be involved in this case."

"Good. Me too," he said. "And there'll be plenty of time to get to know each other better over the next few months. You really are a very special person, Susan."

"That's so kind of you to say so, Mister Palin," she said, trying to affect a Deep South accent, while adjusting her grubby sling.

He asked her what she planned to do after the trial. She

told him of her plans to study law, joking that he was her model.

He looked surprised. But without missing a beat, he said, "Have you considered studying over here?" She hadn't, but the idea immediately appealed to her.

"Why law though? I'd have thought you might have been put off by your experience here."

"On the contrary. I loved my job, I really did. I'd never been hugely ambitious after university, and of course Mimi came along, so I was grateful for the chance to do as well as I did. But when you're inside a company you only see the inside, you're part of the corporate culture.

"When I think about it now, I can see there was plenty that was ethically questionable. I mean, look what they call 100 percent orange juice these days. It's a joke. And do you know what cellulose is? The stuff they list on the Food Facts? They want you to believe it's fibre but it's sawdust! And don't get me started on Crunchaloosa. Western diets breeding Western diseases. And it comes to you with the FDA's blessing."

"Really?"

"Barney and Frank used to say, not only, 'Let's give the consumer what they want', but 'Let's make some money'. They, we, were thinking about the shareholders. The profit motive. And that's where there are legitimate questions, I think, about company behaviour. I should've seen a huge red flag when Barney said that the compliance and regulations departments weren't to know about Project Candy. But to come back to your question, I want to feel I'm making a difference, helping people. That's what's changed I suppose."

"You mean do something like Mimi?"

"Funnily enough, I never actually thought of her work in that way. But I suppose that now I wouldn't rule it out.

Campaigning for something you believe in, something important. I used to think she was there mainly to annoy people."

They finished their drinks, discussing the next moves in the legal process. Then she slipped on a sleeve of her raincoat, pulling it round her injured shoulder, and he walked with her to a cab. This time there was no goodbye kiss as he opened the car door.

As it closed with a heavy clunk, something landed gently in her lap. It was a little gift-wrapped box. She untied the ribbon and tore open the packaging with one hand and her teeth. It was a flacon of Coco Mademoiselle.

Chapter 31

ALL OF THE Perkinses were waiting for her when she arrived at Heathrow on the redeye flight from Washington.

"Whoa! Morning!" Susan dropped her wheelie as her mother threw her arms round her, causing her to wince in pain. She hugged Mimi as best she could, and then kissed Meadow on the cheek.

"Welcome home, darling. I've been beside myself with worry. Let me look at you, Danger Woman!"

"How are you, Mum?"

"I'm a bit tired. I didn't sleep. But the arm feels like it's starting to heal. I'll get it checked out by the doctor in Hackney."

For the first time in years she walked proudly past the welcoming crowd at Arrivals. Mimi, sporting a short haircut which set off her chiseled features while revealing ears full of piercings, led the way to her car, the first she'd ever bought.

"It's Josh's actually. A friend wanted to get rid of his old Fiesta so we picked it up for 300 quid. It's actually been more useful than I thought."

"And how's Josh?"

"He says Hi. He's fine. He's still at Granta and it's going well. We were talking about paying the rent ourselves on the flat."

That was news to Susan. "You don't have to, you know."

"No, that's fine. You're the unemployed one now, remember." Mimi tossed her head as though signalling the end of the exchange, and unlocked the car where Nellie was barking away.

"Down Nellie, down," her mother murmured as the dog sprang up. Mimi strapped Meadow into her seat in the back, before setting off cautiously towards London in the early morning traffic.

Her first visitor that week was Lily. She took out a celebratory bottle of wine from the fridge and they went to a nearby gastropub for supper. But Lily didn't feel like celebrating. She'd gone to the police about a stalker who'd been tracking her concerts and had discovered her address. She'd found him waiting for her on a couple of occasions when leaving the flat.

"At first I thought he was a fan, after he hung around at the end of one of my shows. Then I thought it was weird that he turned up at concerts all over the country. But when I saw him posted outside my place it was terrifying."

"What does he look like?"

"Normal guy. Jeans, jacket. Nondescript really, apart from the silent staring."

"Did you talk to him? Or whack him with your flute case?"

"No, of course not, I was too frightened. I just ignored him. Then I worried he might become violent. But the worst thing is that the stage fright has come back. With a vengeance. When I get up to play before an audience, I'm paralysed. So I've not performed since last month. It was so embarrassing last time."

"You poor thing. But why didn't you tell me?"

"Because compared with what you were going through my problems seemed unimportant. I've not been on the news, and at least I've still got all my limbs in working order, the last time I checked."

She knew that Lily had suffered from some kind of breakdown before university. As a result, she always kept plenty of medication to hand to deal with the nerves that struck her before a performance.

Once, when Susan had been invited to a recital at Wigmore Hall, Lily told her that only minutes before she came onto the stage she'd been throwing up in the loo.

Of course she'd performed like the virtuoso she was, slender in a long black gown, and played three encores, joking that she was in danger of exhausting her repertoire. She gave up solo playing not long afterwards.

But now Susan wished she'd paid more attention to her friend's mood swings. She'd always attributed the stage fright and self-doubt and sudden collapse of self-confidence to Lily's creativity.

She held out her hand. "Are you going to be okay? Do you need me to come home with you to scare off this guy?"

"He'd be terrified by the sight of you," she replied with a grin. "You could always try singing to him, that'd send him running."

They agreed on an early night. On the pavement outside the pub, Lily asked her about her plans. But Susan was more worried about her. She hailed a cab over Lily's protests, gave the driver the Bermondsey address and said she'd be coming back to Hackney. Then she levered herself into the back seat next to her.

"I'm not having you go home in the dark on your own."

"So what *are* you going to do next?" Lily said as the cab trundled along. She said she intended to apply to study international law at Georgetown University.

"Georgetown? You mean go back to Washington? I *see*!"

Susan ignored the innuendo.

"The deadline is March for next September, so I'd better get my skates on as there's so much paperwork."

"But what about the DeKripps trial?"

Susan said she was waiting to hear from Mark, whom Lily called "the most ethical lawyer in the world".

"Don't you miss him?"

"I do, actually. I think you'd like him."

"Well, I look forward to meeting him."

They reached Lily's street. There was no sign of anyone outside her building. Quickly, she got out of the cab, kissed Susan on both cheeks, and rushed inside.

She ticked off her chores over the months that followed. She finished the redecorating thanks to a team of painters for whom she prepared bacon sandwiches. She completed a successful application to Georgetown and was accepted for the following September.

She brought down from the attic Serge's files crammed with his published writings on Camus, dozens of articles, mostly in French academic journals. He'd managed to do all this as well as full-time teaching and being a father to Mimi.

How well had she known Serge? How well does anyone know anyone, even in a marriage? It was like *L'Etranger* having two titles in English for the same book. She loved one version of Serge, but she presumed Mimi must have seen a completely different side of him. Yet he was the same person: a lover, teacher and scholar wrapped into one.

What discoveries would she make about Mark, as they got to know each other better?

The two of them were in regular contact about the DeKripps investigations, which were being followed closely by the American press whose stories increasingly focused on similarities with the cases against Big Tobacco in the 90s. Congressional hearings were being scheduled, with Barney and Bubba expected to appear.

But Mark also warned her that she might be called by the House or Senate Committees.

He reeled off possible summonses from the House Agriculture Subcommittee on Department Operations, Oversight, Nutrition, and Forestry, the House Agriculture Subcommittee on Management, Research and Specialty Crops, and the Senate Agriculture, Nutrition and Forestry

Committee. The list was endless.

"Are you kidding? So many of them?"

"Susie, this is DC, remember?"

He also confirmed her suspicions that the DeKripps customer service representatives had acknowledged destroying complaints about Guilty Secrets, acting on the express orders of Barney. So that was what he meant when he said he'd dealt with the complaints.

She researched the earlier lawsuit brought by the Department of Justice against the cigarette manufacturers in '99. She was particularly struck by the final opinion of Judge Gladys Kessler at the end of the trial in June 2005.

She'd chastised the industry which "survives and profits from selling a highly addictive product" blamed for causing diseases leading to "a staggering number of deaths per year." The judge also drew attention to the resulting burden on the national health care system.

Reading on, she saw that according to the judge, the tobacco companies "have marketed and sold their lethal products with zeal, with deception, with a single-minded focus on their financial success, and without regard for the human tragedy or social costs that success exacted."

It was chastening. Every word could apply to DeKripps, except that the cigarette manufacturers were accused of conspiring for at least fifty years!

She also dimly remembered the case against Nestlé, the multinational accused of "killing babies" with breast milk substitute in the 1970s and dug into the history on that.

The problem hasn't gone away, she thought. What about DeKripps' sugar and salt-laced foods that she'd marketed? In the 70s it was babies, now everybody's health is threatened by the food giants. By the time the DeKripps case came to trial, if it ever did, they might even have proved a link between sugar and obesity.

In her own work, she'd been painfully aware of the risks of making false claims about food. Dannon had been taken to court in America for claiming one of their yoghurts had 'scientifically' proved benefits for supposedly regulating the digestive tract. She looked up the case, and saw that it a class action had cost the company $45 million.

DeKripps would be risking far more. Judging by the Big Tobacco cases still going through the courts, particularly in states like Florida, the bill could run into billions. Her company hadn't made any false claims—Guilty Secrets had been a lie from start to finish.

Sometimes, in the evening, she would chat on Skype to Mark, who kept her abreast of the multiple investigations, and tried to calm her worries about weaknesses in their case. When she asked about the Project Candy file that she'd stolen from Barney's office not carrying sufficient legal weight because it was anonymous, he reassured her that it was "child's play" to trace the computer it'd been written on.

What about the plaintiffs' dramatic weight gain? Couldn't it be proved that other foods had contributed?

"Look, we've been through this before, we've got the intention, the result *and* the receipts," he said. "And with a bit of luck, we'll have more DeKripps insiders too, ready to testify."

Any news from Ellen? "Not yet. But don't worry, we still have time." How could he be so confident?

With the video on, he gave her a virtual tour of his apartment, except for the bedroom where he said his clothes were strewn everywhere. In any case, it didn't seem appropriate yet. Way too personal.

They exchanged views on the latest episodes of Mad Men, but only if Susan had caught up with the US schedule. They wanted to avoid spoilers at all costs.

"So what do you think about Betty Francis getting fat?"

he asked her.

Susan felt uncomfortable watching the TV character guzzle ice cream on screen. The storyline embarrassed her, reminding her of the couples at the lawyer's in Washington. There but for the grace of God, she thought.

She luxuriated in the bath, a daily ritual she'd missed in America. She'd never understood Americans' horror of the bath, when they complained about the lack of hygiene and the germs in the dirty water.

She spent more time with Mimi, watching Meadow grow. Her granddaughter was now walking, and repeating Mummy, Mummy in a way that sounded like Mimi, Mimi. Occasionally, just occasionally, she was allowed to babysit.

"On a bluff, on a bluff, there lived three billygoats gruff. Little billygoat, middle billygoat, Great Big Billygoat Gruff!" she would sing, lowering her voice and shaking her a little at the climax, triggering squeals of joy. Mimi herself appeared to be mellowing, thanks to her relationship with Josh who no longer needed to mediate between mother and daughter.

Not only was Mimi less prickly with her but she'd also removed some of the real thorns from her body, including the piercings around her ears. Only the surviving nose stud was a reminder of the past. It actually suited her.

One morning, she switched on the radio in bed and heard Mimi being interviewed on the radio. She recognised her voice instantly, although naturally she hadn't been given advance warning.

She was being asked to comment about a report which had concluded that the previous year's earthquakes in Blackpool had been caused by shale gas fracking.

Unlike her rants about DeKripps, she was cool and collected, and made an impressive case against. She was invited onto the programme because USAway had sent some protesters to join "Frack Off" campaigners.

Not for the first time, Susan thought Mimi's hysterical reaction to Big Food, and possibly even her vegan diet, had its roots in the rocky beginnings of their relationship. Now she was so proud of Mimi's radio appearance that she phoned her mother and sent Mark an email about it.

The news from Lymington was that the very last representative of the "flying circus", as her mother called the journalists outside her front door, had vanished. "Do you think I can send them a bill for my ruined rose bushes?"

"You should also send them one for all those cups of tea." She rang off after promising to stay for a few days before leaving for Washington.

Mark's reply wasn't the one she'd expected. It was more like a telegram. It read: "Way to go, Mimi. Saw Ellen today. She's joining us."

Chapter 32

IT WAS HIGH summer. In Hackney that meant scattered showers. Susan was in the back garden watering the flowerbeds, wondering how to prepare for an appearance before a Congressional hearing. Including how she should dress.

Mark had tried to reassure her but she'd watched the one where Mimi had been arrested, and didn't want to be mauled like Tony Hayward.

"Just be your professional self," he said. "They're always very courteous and like the sound of their own voices. Tell the truth, the whole truth, and you'll be fine." But she was still fretting about the introductory remarks she'd have to write.

"Don't worry. Half the time they just put that in the record, so you can forget about it," he said. He'd also ensured that her testimony to any of the Congressional committees would be behind closed doors.

"Barney's the one who should be alarmed, not you."

She heard the doorbell ring from the garden. She wasn't expecting anyone, and she peeked through the front bay window before opening the door.

"My God!" she said, turning to stone. It was Ellen with her family; Jed, her husband and the twins. Ellen was as preppy as ever, an alice band in her hair. The two boys stood between their parents, wide-eyed, looking expectantly at Susan.

But what had happened to Jed? He looked at least two stone heavier. His square jowls had filled out and his neck had all but disappeared. He was wearing an unflattering pair of shorts under a loose cherry polo shirt which failed to conceal his belly. His sunglasses were pushed back over what used to be cheekbones. His ankles, sockless in a pair of moccasins, were quite swollen. He was chewing gum, of course. He looked more like middle-aged Frank than the attractive young man that she'd last seen in Chevy Chase.

She opened the door, putting on a welcoming smile.

"What on earth are you doing here?"

"I didn't know whether you would want to see me, so that's why I didn't call ahead."

"That's amazing, I was just talking about you the other day."

"We had tickets for the Games. But I wanted to apologise to you, you know, for what happened. I've felt terrible about it ever since I last saw you in Washington."

"Don't worry about it. That's all water under the bridge," she said. She didn't really think that, now that the whole planet knew about her hot sex at the Merchant, but she said so anyway. She gave Ellen a hug.

"And thanks," she said, looking her straight in the eye. "Come in, all of you, don't just stand there."

"You remember Darren and David, don't you?"

She approved of the fact that Ellen had resisted the temptation to dress them identically, as it would have been impossible to tell them apart. They looked even more like their mother than when they were younger, with Ellen's snub nose and full lips.

"So what did you see at the Games?"

"We had tickets for the opening ceremony."

"You did?" Nobody she knew had succeeded in getting tickets and she'd watched the ceremony with Larry and Meredith next door, on their large flat screen TV.

"Did you see the Queen jumping out of the helicopter?" She bent down to the children's level.

"Yeah," they said together. "It was awesome."

"And how old are you now, Darren and David?"

"Four."

"My, you're almost grown-ups now."

She ushered the family into the dining room. Jed was obviously under instructions to keep out of sight with the boys who were already casing the joint, looking for toys to play with.

"But how on earth did you find my address?"

"Through Mark. He's been so helpful with this whole thing."

Jed took a mug of tea into the garden where the twins were hunting for spiders and snails. Susan pulled a chair out for Ellen at the dining room table.

"So how are things? What are you doing now?" she asked, pouring them both a cup of Earl Grey into china teacups.

"I've taken a sabbatical. But in actual fact I'll be back in DC in a few weeks' time, as I've been accepted at Georgetown to do law."

"Yeah, I heard. Mark told me," said Ellen.

"I'm going to be the caped crusader. Or the crap crusader, as Mimi says. I'd recommend a change of direction anyway. It's kind of invigorating."

Ellen didn't know what her own next step would be, but she intended to spend more time with the children and said Jed's salary could provide for them all for a while.

"Good for you. I'm sure the right thing will come along. We've just got to get through this with our reputations intact."

She hadn't intended to remind Ellen of how she'd destroyed hers.

She steered the subject back to DeKripps, sipping her tea. "So do you feel OK about testifying against them?"

"I do now. But I wrestled with the decision for quite a while. I didn't tell you when we met last, but Barney offered me your old job. A promotion."

"And?"

"And I didn't take it. That's why I didn't mention it to you."

Susan leaned back. "We were loyal company employees. Too loyal. But you know, the more I think about it, it was obvious that the writing was on the wall. We should have done something about it sooner, as a company, I mean. And senior employees have a duty to the public to do the right thing."

Ellen nodded.

"When you think how long we've been heaping sugar into food, and sticking our heads in the sand about diabetes. And look at obesity in America. Do we seriously think there's no connection?"

"I've been having exactly the same conversations with myself," Ellen said. "I actually handed Barney a New York Scrutineer article on this two years ago. But it was a taboo issue at work. Now there's more and more linking HFCS to obesity and diabetes. What makes me sick though is how DeKripps went after Kramer."

"Me too. Do you remember that meeting in Barney's office?"

Again, Ellen nodded. "I heard Kramer had a heart attack recently. Anyone would after a smear campaign like that."

"Oh dear." Susan could restrain herself no longer. "Do you mind if I ask you something? What's the matter with Jed? He's ballooned since I last saw him."

Ellen looked ruefully at her Earl Grey. "It's Guilty Secrets, of course."

"Oh my God. Really?"

"You were right. Of course it's an addiction, I just couldn't see it. I thought he was keeping some in the glove box of the car, just in case he needed a snack, but then I found them all over the place. You should have seen the bills he was running up – and he wasn't even keeping them in the fridge."

"Poor Jed. Are you going to join the class action?"

"I don't know yet. We've not really talked about it. It's tough for him. The doctor says there's too much stress on his heart now he's put on so much weight." Their eyes turned to the garden where he was dabbing his flushed face with a tissue. He noticed their gaze and waved it at them.

"Jeez, it's hot out here," he said.

"We should be going," Ellen said. "But I did want to apologise to you. I should never have betrayed your confidence."

"Honestly, don't worry about it. Of course I was disappointed and hurt, but really, that's all in the past now. We've got to stick together so that DeKripps doesn't get away with murder. And you'll have to be careful too. You can be sure they'll try to intimidate you after what they did to me."

She set down her tea cup, more heavily than she'd intended.

"Anyway, hopefully, in a few months it'll all be over," she added. "You don't know anyone else who might help, do you?"

"I'm working on it." Ellen got up to leave and embraced her warmly. "You look good, Susie."

"I'm watching what I eat of course. Diabetes."

"What, you've got it?"

"Afraid so. Type 2. The self-inflicted type. Or not self-inflicted at all. Maybe I should sue DeKripps myself."

Susan led the way to the front door. Standing on the doorstep to say goodbye, she called out, "So is Obama going to win the election?"

Jed turned round, still holding the two boys by the hand.

"It looks tight," he said in his Texan twang. "But it's Obama's to lose. Romney just makes one gaffe after another."

"He was just here in London, and he said something stupid about the Olympics. He said the preparations were rubbish. The mayor got his own back though."

Jed turned his cheeks into a taut smile. "But we've still got the conventions to come, and that's when people start to make up their mind."

He probably wasn't an Obama supporter, Susan thought as she closed the door. Physically, he resembled the ruggedly handsome Republican challenger, or at least he used to.

She logged onto her emails and saw a message from Mark, asking her to ring him. He picked up straight away, as though waiting for her call.

"They've nailed Stella."

"I know. We've already discussed that."

"No, I mean, really got him." She waited for the explanation. The police had been going through the bank accounts of his Seattle commune, and they came across a $100,000 transfer to the scientist's account from DeKripps.

"So that means—"

"It means that DeKripps paid him off to gag him," said Mark. "That's why he took the Fifth."

"And guess what?" he added. "The investigators found that the unsigned confidential document about Project Candy was written on his computer."

Chapter 33

THEY HAD THEIR backs to the giant granite cross atop the green swathe of Tennyson Down, and gazed towards France, buffeted by the sea breeze.

"Can we see Brittany from here do you think?" Lily asked.

"No way."

"Even on a clear day like this?"

The wind whipped the white horses at the foot of the cliffs.

"You must miss Serge. I do," said Lily.

"Of course. I think about him every day, even now. He's here," she said, touching her heart. "But it gets easier, or at least less painful. And having Meadow around makes a difference. I think it's given Mimi and me a new focus."

Lily was on form. She seemed more positive. She'd obtained a restriction order against the stalker who'd disappeared from one evening to the next. The police had found him thanks to the credit card he'd used at the box office.

She also confided that she'd sought professional help for stage fright. "Inspired by the new flute, actually."

"I'm so glad," Susan said, wishing she'd persuaded her to consult an expert years ago. Who knew where her musical career might have taken her?

They sat down on the grass in front of the monument. "Want to play Name that Tune?"

"Only if I win." She stretched out her arm for Lily to start tapping.

It was one of their last outings before Susan's departure for Washington. They'd taken the Isle of Wight ferry and raced to catch the open-topped bus to the Needles. She led the way upstairs, and didn't warn Lily about the hairpin bends as the bus rumbled towards its destination. They both screamed like teenagers on a rollercoaster, seemingly on the point of plunging into the turquoise sea with every lurching bend. All it would take would be an unexpected gust of wind. A group of American tourists seated behind them were clinging onto the seats in front, looking queasy.

"More fun than a Segway," she said to Lily. They thanked the driver on the way out. "The brakes work after all," he said, with a grin.

After the long climb to the top of the down, they traipsed back to Yarmouth along a disused railway line. They walked in silence for a while along the footpath framed by wild flowers.

"By the way," said Lily. "Daniel rang me the other day. He wants a divorce."

"Oh no. How do you feel about that now? Has he got someone else?"

"I feel alright, actually. So much time has gone by, and I hadn't even given him any thought in the last few months. That has to be a good thing, right? I think he wants to get married again, but to be honest, I didn't even ask. I heard from one of his friends at the BBC that he's with a jazz singer."

"Well you've had other things on your mind, such as getting rid of a stalker," she said. She caught hold of a tall blade of grass and began sucking it between her teeth.

"Is he still making documentaries?"

"Last thing I heard, he had a commission on whales."

"So what are you going to do?"

"I've told him I'd think about it, but I want to make a clean break. Do you agree?"

"Definitely. But what does your Father Confessor say?"

"Not seen him for years. I suppose you could say I'm a

lapsed Catholic now, like everybody else our age."

"Yes, Serge said the same thing. In fact, I don't think he would have chosen a religious funeral. How anyone can be a practising Catholic these days, in the knowledge of how the church abused its own faithful, is beyond me."

"Don't confuse belief with worship, Susie. Being lapsed doesn't mean that you don't believe in God. You need a values system bigger than yourself. What about your moral compass?"

Lily had hit a nerve. "That's something I thought about at DeKripps. But the sense of doing right didn't come from believing in God. Although obviously we're inculcated with Christian values."

They made their way along the path, negotiating puddles, clinging to overhanging branches. "Being a whistle-blower certainly made me think about good and bad. It was worse because I know I'm telling the truth and I've been maligned by these smears."

They walked on in silence, their eyes on the trail ahead.

Finally Susan took the blade of grass from her lips and said: "It's strange, you might think that when Serge died it would have restored whatever faith I had. But in fact it was the opposite. I could see that when I went to identify the body at the hospital. When I kissed him, he was stone cold. He was dead, and that was it.

"It was the same at the funeral, when the priest was talking about the glory of God and the life everlasting. I knew that it didn't exist. I'm not saying it was any harder or easier to come to terms with, but Serge was the first dead body I'd ever seen. As far as I was concerned, there was a finality I'd never expected. That's also what made it so hard to endure."

"That's what the rituals are for though, aren't they? Even if you don't have faith, they help you get through it by giving you some kind of structure. The priest in Dingy was doing his best."

They reached Yarmouth as the sun was setting. Susan loved the ferry journey back to Lymington on calm summer evenings, the burnt orange sunlight glinting on the Solent, Hurst Castle silhouetted in the distance. It could be Venice, the water was as smooth as glass. How lucky she was that her mother had settled in Lymington, after bouncing around the stockbroker belt with husbands one, two and three.

They arrived in time for dinner in one of the quayside restaurants, where they cracked open a bottle of Chardonnay with their crab salads.

"What are you going to do about the house?" Lily said.

"Why, are you interested?"

"Not me. It's too big for me."

"That's what Mimi said too. She says it's not convenient for work either. Too many memories as well, I expect. So I'm going to rent it out again. But I think that when I come back, I'll probably sell it and downsize."

"When, or if? What if the most ethical lawyer in the world surprises you?"

"I don't see how his scruples would disappear. He was pretty firm the last time I saw him. Anyway, cheers," she said. They raised their glasses and toasted "DeKripps is Krap".

"What about the trial?" Lily said.

"What about it? There's still no date. The various strands are still being investigated. The FDA, the police, they're all on the trail. I don't know whether it's taking longer than it should but sometimes it gives me butterflies in my stomach. And apparently DeKripps have offered another settlement as they don't want it to reach court."

Lily didn't seem surprised. "Remember Big Tobacco. They're risking big bucks."

She accompanied her friend back to the station and headed back to her mother's, where Nellie was being taught to roll over and jump through a hoop. The Yorkie refused to jump for Susan, even for a chocolate biscuit.

Usually in the evenings in Lymington, she had only Nellie and the television for company while her mother was out at bridge. So she tried to focus on her life post-DeKripps and the preparations for law school.

She'd brought some books for her university course, which she attempted to read, until one morning she came downstairs to discover that Nellie had flung soggy pages of *An Introduction to Criminal Law and Procedure* all over the sitting room. She smiled to herself, thinking: The dog actually ate my homework.

She heard voices in the kitchen. Was Mimi here? Then she caught the low burr of a man's voice, followed by her mother's gentle laughter. She cleared her throat, feeling like an intruder. They were sitting at the kitchen table drinking tea and looked up sharply as though they'd been caught in the act.

"Morning darling, I was just telling Malcolm about our experience with the paparazzi, living behind closed curtains for weeks like lab rats," her mother said. "Malcolm, Susan, Susan, Malcolm. Did I mention that he's my bridge partner?"

He stood up, ramrod stiff, to shake her hand. He was tall with a moustache and the rakish look of a retired army captain, cravat tucked neatly into a striped shirt. "Please sit down," she said, before making herself a cup of coffee and escaping upstairs.

She's done it again, Susan thought. Husband number four, coming up.

Chapter 34

IT WAS TIME to leave. Susan was waiting downstairs for Mimi, her two large suitcases side by side at the front door. When she'd left Hackney after Serge's death she'd taken a flight to a place of darkness and uncertainty and gloom. This time, she knew exactly where she was going and what she wanted. She'd survived.

She wandered through the house in the early daylight, checking that everything was off: the lights, the gas, the electricity and water. She had her head stuck round the downstairs loo, checking the stopcock, when Mimi rang the doorbell. She opened the door and spontaneously hugged her. Mimi hugged her back before helping her to the car with her cases. Meadow, in a pair of dungarees, was seated in the back.

"Can we go past the church on the way out?" Susan wanted one last look at St Peter's church in the square where she'd taken Serge to Christmas carols when Mimi was young.

Yellowing leaves were sprinkled at the foot of the tall tower where the clock's gold fingers announced ten past eight. An orange plastic bag, filled with somebody's rubbish, was slung over the railings.

They drove in silence to Heathrow. At one point she'd considered inviting Mimi to join her for the trial in Washington, but that was out of the question because of her immigration violation. Anyway, it would be unfair to expect Josh to take care of Meadow alone.

Mimi had never been one for airport farewells and Susan she was surprised she'd offered to accompany her. She was even more surprised when they reached the terminal for her flight and Mimi announced she was parking the car.

The three of them made their way inside the building, Mimi pushing Meadow in a stroller, and Susan dragging her suitcases into the hall. She turned to Mimi. "Don't worry, I'll be fine. You must go. Don't forget to keep in touch with granny."

Mimi stepped forward. "She'll be alright. She's got company now."

Again, she hugged Susan, and said "I love you, mum."

"I love you too, Mimi. Don't forget to email me that beetroot risotto recipe."

She gave her daughter a last embrace and quickly turned away, the tears springing into in her eyes. When she looked round again from the bag drop queue, they'd already left the terminal.

She'd loaded up her e-reader with plenty of thrillers for the next few months to keep her mind off her own drama. Josh had emailed her links for a "best of" Serge's articles on Camus, which would save her combing through the entire collection. But she couldn't concentrate on reading during the flight and found herself flicking through the online films in search of distraction. Her thoughts were beating ahead of her to Washington.

She'd dressed quickly that morning for the flight, and now regretted not having taken more care with her appearance. As the plane turned over Gander with a few bumps and flew down the eastern seaboard, she felt a mounting anxiety and knew exactly why.

Mark had said he would try to be at Dulles to meet her. But would he? It would mean he would have to take the afternoon off work. By the time the plane banked for its final descent, swinging through the clouds towards Washington, she was clinging to her safety belt and silently praying he would be there at Arrivals.

The plane was full. It seemed to take an age for the

engines to be switched off, and everyone sprang to their feet at the same time. She grabbed her khaki jacket and laptop from the overhead locker. She waited to disembark behind a group of passengers jabbering in a foreign language she couldn't identify but who seemed to be worried about a connecting flight. The mobile lounge was waiting for them. She knew the drill, and tucked herself in at the front in order to be among the first to escape.

"Welcome to Washington," said the elderly driver. He adjusted his glasses and locked the doors before the vehicle began lumbering towards the immigration building.

She switched on her phone as they swayed along. No messages or missed calls. She looked at her watch and noticed it was still on London time, so she put it back five hours. They still hadn't arrived at the docking bay. She looked out of the window impatiently. The sun was shining, the temperature was a pleasant 70 degrees, she heard someone say. Finally, with a bump, they arrived and the passengers were released.

She walked as fast as she could down the escalator to immigration, looking across the vast hall. Her heart sank. The queue for non-US citizens was interminable. There were flights from China, the Gulf, and Mexico ahead of them.

They inched forwards. Why were there so few agents on duty at this time of day when they know that so many flights arrive at once? By the time she reached the front of the queue, she was irritable and overcome with tiredness.

The immigration officer, a woman with a heavy Hispanic accent, looked at Susan with barely concealed disbelief.

"So, Ms Perkins – you're a – student?"

"That's right." Susan stared at her right in the eye.

The agent quizzed her at length about her study plans in the US. She had a brand new F-1 visa in her passport so all was above board. But the woman wanted to know why she kept coming back to the country.

"I had quite a few things to tidy up after leaving my job," she said, leaving her answer vague. It must have been too vague, and the questions kept coming.

"What kind of things?" she demanded.

"I left some clothes with a friend and had to come back to pick them up." It was a white lie but a lie nevertheless. The woman was obviously unconvinced. Did she really suspect her of being an illegal alien?

"You weren't working?" she said, her lip curling.

"Of course not." Susan held her breath, expecting the agent to ask for her contacts in DC. But the question never came. After one last stare with unblinking eyes she stamped her passport and asked her to hold up her hands, and look into the camera, for the final screening.

She had been waiting so long to pass immigration that the luggage from her plane had been left on the floor beside the carousel. She sighed. It took her ages to locate her second suitcase, lying apart from the rest.

Then, she faced another queue to get through customs. She decided to head to the restroom first to freshen up and looked nervously in the mirror. Would she stand up to scrutiny? Her face was flushed, and her hair was a mess. Her freckles stood out like Belisha beacons. She examined her hands as she dried them. On impulse, she slid off her wedding ring, squeezing it gently over her finger joint, and zipped it into a handbag pocket. She fished out some face powder and did the best she could to cover the beads of sweat on her nose. Then she made her way to the customs line, the final obstacle before the exit.

"Have a good one, Ma'am," the agent said as he took the blue card from her.

The doors swung open into Arrivals. He was the first person she caught sight of, and was grinning broadly. He was a head taller than the people next to him and gestured to meet him round the corner.

They flung their arms round each other, and kissed. It was a long, hard kiss on the lips. It was a Hollywood kiss, the sort that has people applauding because it goes on so long. Mark brushed coils of her hair out of the way with one hand.

"Let me look at you."

She nuzzled his cheek, which was soft and warm. They gazed into each other's eyes, smiled, and then kissed again languorously, this time pressing their bodies against each other.

When, at last, they came up for air he said, "Welcome back."

He steered her through the terminal towards the car park. He pulled one of her suitcases and she the other.

"I've got some good news, by the way." She waited. "I've handed over the DeKripps case to the senior partner at the firm."

"What, Smithson?"

"No, Hopkins."

He paused, waiting for her to ask. But she didn't need to. He'd done this so they could be together. She stopped dead. "You mean you've recused yourself? Your scruples got the better of you?"

"Not exactly. The boss called me and told me he was taking the case. It was as simple as that. You know, a high profile case like DeKripps…"

What difference did it make? The result was the same. "It means we can be together."

"That's wonderful! But aren't you disappointed?"

"Of course not. It's actually what I wanted. Although I'm jealous now, of course. Everyone wants a piece of you."

She smiled.

"You mean the 'Widow Whistle-blower'? But why didn't you tell me before?"

"I wanted to surprise you. But that's not the only thing I have to tell you."

"Oh come on, that's not fair. What's happened?"

"Barney was arrested last night."

She let go of her suitcase which slapped onto the floor outside DeKripps' Angeljuice bar.

"What do you mean, arrested? How come I didn't know about this?"

"The time difference. Sorry. Then you were on the plane..."

"Of course. Not your fault. I'm sorry, I'm a bit tense." She was so tired she could scarcely articulate. She reached for his hand and squeezed it. "This is the best news I've had in a long time."

They emerged from the terminal into the clammy afternoon. As soon as they'd left the carpark and were driving in a middle lane along the highway she began to pepper him with questions about Barney.

"What's the hurry?" he said. "If you're not too tired, I've booked to take you out to dinner and I'll give you the skinny tonight."

They crossed the Potomac on the key bridge into Georgetown and stopped at an estate agent off M Street to pick up the keys to her new furnished digs. Then Mark accompanied her to the ground floor apartment in a small compound up the hill off Reservoir Road. She looked at him with slight apprehension as she turned two locks on the door and stepped inside.

"It's a bit dark, isn't it?" she said, switching on the lights and heading through the living room to the kitchen.

Their footsteps clicked on the parquet. While he flicked open the blinds and noticed the bars on the windows, she checked cupboards containing crockery and glasses. Pots and pans were in storage drawers under the counter.

She came through to the living room and sank into a shabby chic armchair which looked in need of new covers, stretching out her legs and yawning.

"Seems fine to me," he said. "But what do I know?"

She went back into the kitchen and filled the kettle. He followed her, taking her hand and pushing her gently against the counter.

"Wait," she said, touching his shoulder, "I'm sorry, I need to freshen up. Could you give me an hour or so?" What was she thinking? How long had she waited for this moment? Then, fleetingly, a shadow: Serge.

He'd already turned and was walking back towards the front door, when she caught him by the hand. "Come with me," she said.

"You sure?"

"We didn't check out the bedroom."

It was only a few blocks to the restaurant. Susan floated on a cushion of air down the redbrick pavement past the clapboard townhouses and university buildings.

"Here we are," he said, holding open the heavy wooden door.

"I know this place – it's one of the best restaurants in town."

"Haven't we got something to celebrate?" he said, turning to grin at her as they followed the maître d' to their corner table on the ground floor. "It's not necessarily what I'd planned when I booked," he added.

She wondered whether she would continue to smile stupidly at everything he said for the rest of the evening.

"So now put me out of my misery and tell me what's going on," she said, picking up a menu.

"First let's order. Then I can tell you about the police investigation into the attack at Metro Center."

"There's progress? So that's it." There she was, smiling blissfully again. She wasn't hungry, but she ordered some fish. She felt his knee under the table, pressing against hers.

He told her that police had isolated the CCTV images showing a bald man in an anorak who had deliberately shoved her in front of the incoming train. But then it had taken time to establish his identity and to connect the attacker with Barney, whom he had telephoned minutes before the crime.

"How did they know it was Barney?" Her brain was still fighting the jetlag.

"Right. He's no fool. Barney had of course bought a new cellphone which he must have thrown away. In any case when the police searched his place they couldn't find it. But he made one mistake. He bought it in a Georgetown phone store with his own credit card."

"And that's how they traced the phone to him?" Mark nodded.

So now her former boss faced potential charges of conspiracy for attempted murder in addition to food crimes.

Chapter 35

SUSAN HEARD MARK padding around in the kitchen, opening and closing the fridge door, as he prepared brunch. The smell of fresh coffee wafted along the corridor. Since moving in with him, only a few weeks after returning to Washington, one of her signal achievements had been to persuade him to ditch his stewed American filter coffee.

His phone sounded. Maybe it was a friend trying to persuade him to go for a run. It was something he did on Sunday mornings while she studied. But he'd promised her that today he would prepare her the most delicious blueberry pancakes this side of the Atlantic.

He came into the bedroom, where she was propped on a pillow consulting her tablet, trying to find a beachside place to rent for a few days when Lily visited with her new boyfriend. He was a doctor Lily had met online and sounded like a perfect match. Mark looked sombre.

"That was Aaron Steinfeld. You know, the class action guy?"

Why was he ringing on a Sunday morning? Mark cleared his throat. "It seems that the CEO of DeKripps has committed suicide."

"Bubba? You're kidding."

"Is that what you call him? Yeah, well his wife found him hanged at home last night."

"Hanged! Where? In Kansas?"

"Yeah, Topeka. Apparently he'd been depressed after the DeKripps share collapse."

She put down her tablet in silence. She'd wanted to punish the corporation, but it had never crossed her mind that anyone would die. Let alone the boss with the friendly manner who'd encouraged her at their video conferences.

She'd actually liked him. But what if he was behind the Guilty Secrets scandal? What if he was the one to have ordered the smears and the attacks against her and her family?

She sank back while she digested the news. How could there be any room for doubt? DeKripps had tried to murder her. If she shut her eyes, she could still hear the screech of the Metro train braking, smell the sparks.

Mark sat on the bed beside her, put his arm round her naked shoulder where a faint red line was all that remained of the scar from her shoulder operation, and kissed her gently.

"It's obviously going to be big news. Aaron must have been among the first to hear. It's possible that journalists will try to contact you, of course."

"I'm certainly not going to dance on Bubba's grave."

"No, you're right. We should keep a low profile."

"But just a second. What does this mean for the trial?"

She sat forward and took his hands. "I mean DeKripps has to be held responsible for what they've done, right?"

"It could certainly mean a delay. Let's face it, this is a big deal. But I know what you're worried about."

She turned towards him. "Do you?"

"Yeah. Barney."

She waited.

"Honey, I can *guarantee* you that Barney is going to jail. It might not be soon, but it will happen. I promise."

She grabbed a robe and went into Mark's den where he had his desk and a television. Dropping into a leather chair, she picked up the remote and turned to a news channel.

"Oh my God, Mark," she leaned forward. "The flying circus is in Topeka."

"Quick work," he said, joining her. A blonde reporter was standing at the bottom of a long drive flanked by tall trees leading to a white mansion with a portico. They caught the end of her report—Bubba's death was "not suspicious" according to the police. But then she handed back to the studio where they were discussing the possible impact of the CEO's death on the forthcoming DeKripps trial. One of the analysts described it as the "trial of the century."

"I've seen enough," she said, handing the remote to Mark who switched to mute.

"The trial of the century. Is that what you ordered, Ma'am?" he said, with a tug on an imaginary forelock.

"I want justice, that's what. Immoral criminal conduct should be punished. And it's pretty obvious that DeKripps must be the tip of the iceberg. Because all the food companies are at it. They've all been pouring harmful sugars into our food and think they can get away with it. The only difference, as far as I know, is that DeKripps crossed the line into crime. So if this doesn't lead to tighter regulation, I don't know what will."

"Well, good luck with that in this town," he said.

She knew he was talking about the lobbyists, the Congressmen in their pockets and the tight relationship between Big Food and the federal regulators.

"It has to be worth a try though, right?" She leaned over to kiss him. She could hear in the distance the tinkle of text messages dropping into her phone.

He grinned. "If you get arrested at a Congressional hearing, you'll know who to call." Did she really sound that much like Mimi?

"You know it's over for DeKripps though, don't you?"

"What do you mean?"

"Think about it. When companies are hit by scandals like this and there's a shareholder stampede, they go belly up before you can say Enron. How many airlines do you know that survive a major crash? TWA, Swiss Air, they're done."

"So you're telling me, as you'd say here, that DeKripps is toast?"

He laughed, straightening up. "Now what about some of those famous blueberry pancakes?"

She watched him disappear down the corridor, calling out, "And hold the sugar."

She turned back to the muted TV where they were recapping the DeKripps story.

The last image she saw was Barney, his head bowed, being led from his Georgetown home by two uniformed police officers.

"See you in court, buster," she said out loud, and switched off.

Acknowledgements

Food Fight is my debut novel and it's dedicated to the memory of Sylvain.

So many old friends and new ones helped me in the writing and rewriting of this book. I thank particularly my first readers, Margaret Crompton, Janne Nolan and Catherine Taconet, for their frank critiques and encouragement. I'm indebted to Mike Gray, my Hampshire guide and sounding board.

Stanley Colvin and David Ferrera in the US gave me precious advice, as did Barry O'Brien, and Pat and Trevor Davies in the UK. Mary Friel, Gerard Spencer and Alan Newman kindly shared their expertise too.

My thanks also to Felicity Baker, Rupert Cornwell, Celia David, Anna Fifield, Becky Metcalfe and Claire Soares. The input from my brother, Graham, and Laure Crampont, helped me over the finish line.

And a big thank you to my agent, Annabel Merullo, for having faith at a critical time.

About the author

Anne Penketh is a British journalist and foreign correspondent who lives in Paris.

11634655R00165

Printed in Great Britain
by Amazon.co.uk, Ltd.,
Marston Gate.